THE EXPENDABLE P. I: SNAKE AMONGST SHADOWS

BY

CHIMAIJEM I. EZECHUKWU

THE EXPENDABLE P. I:
SNAKE AMONGST SHADOWS
BY
CHIMAIJEM I. EZECHUKWU

Editor: Sam Amalemba

Cover Designer: Cindy Soso

Typesetting: Michael Williams

BIS Publishing Services

January 2014

First Printing: 2014
BIS Publishing Services an Imprint of BIS Publications

ISBN 9781903289211

BIS Publications
PO BOX 14918
London N17 8WJ
www.bispublications.com

Tel: 07903791469

Ordering Information:

Special discounts are available on quantity purchases by corporations, associations, educators, and others. For details, contact the publisher at the above listed address.
Trade bookstores and wholesalers:

Please contact BIS Publications Tel: +44(0)7903791469; or email info@bispublications.com

Dedication

I totally dedicate this book to Almighty God and to my ancestral heroes from Umuchu in Aguata Local Government Area in Anambra State in Eastern Nigeria, West Africa.

To my late father, blessed Barrister Arthur Ifeanyi Chinuta Ezechukwu, who was the first son of late Benedict Obiezunna Irogbolu Ezechukwu; we are champions forever. The tradition continues.

Acknowledgements

I would like to thank the people who have contributed immensely to this project because they believed in it.

I thank my Aunt, Mrs. Veronica C. Unozor for always being in my corner, and Mr. Vernon Colman for his continued wise guidance. Thanks also goes to all those that I once shared time and were colleagues with at Northumberland Park Community School; a special thanks to Maureen Krupsky, who saw the potential after reading my manuscript, Anthony Jones for his help with the graphics and to Mr. Peter Molife who offered suggestions, historically.

Thanks also go to my cousins Mr. Ikenna Unozor and Maurice Lotanna Unozor and Chijiofor Ezeuko. My dearest friend Herbert Chijioke Nwanjiaku and Mr. Emmanuel Okparajiaku, an old colleague and friend of mine back in Umuchu.

Finally, a big thank you to my immediate family especially my dearest mother Mrs. Uzoamaka C. Ezechukwu and my siblings for their unwavering support. This project wouldn't have been possible either if my lovely wife Ann and my father-in-law, Barrister Patrick Akunne, had not given me their full support.

Last but not least, I thank the BIS Publications team; Michael Williams (CEO), Cindy Soso (Designer) and Sam M. Amalemba (Editor), for this opportunity to finally see my work in print. Welcome to my family.

Tottenham, 2010

CHAPTER 1
Part I

It had been a warm evening but it was now cool. In an old flat in Tottenham a man climbed a staircase. It seemed as if he was murmuring to himself, because that was what he was doing. He was about six feet tall, well-built and ruggedly handsome. The furrow on his brow suggested that he was quite unsure about something. The furrow seemed to remain there permanently. But despite all this there was something about him. Something nobody could actually point a finger at.

Mac Logan had spent a quiet evening at a Pub called 'Charlie's' and was now going home. He unlocked the door of his flat and stepped in. He was switching on the lights when the telephone rang. Logan went over to his desk and picked it up. 'Jarrett' he whispered. The sound of his voice was strange, it didn't seem part of him, and it was guttural and harsh. 'Where the hell have you been sonny?' A familiar voice asked. It was Derek Hawke. 'Nowhere you wouldn't want me to be, skinny man' Logan whispered smiling, dismissing the question. 'Are you OK Hawke?' 'No, I'm not okay' Hawke replied, uneasily 'Look, I might have a job for you and I think it's a tricky one Mac, and I'm not sure if you can handle it. I'll be around to your place in a few minutes. See you soon'.

The phone went dead, so Logan hung up too. He was puzzled, what kind of assignment was Hawke going to ask him to undertake this time. Logan became a bit nervous; he remembered that whenever he started a new job he always felt apprehensive.

4

Logan knew that when Hawke said 'tricky' it certainly meant that danger was involved. He sighed; relieved to know he was going to expect trouble. He needed some action because it had been quite a while since his last job.

Logan remembered vividly for a moment how he started working for Hawke. He had had a really bad car accident in Wood Green. A deep gash on his throat had meant the loss of most of his voice and so was of no use to the Police anymore because he literally whispered when he spoke. At the Police Station where he had been attached, nobody actually liked him because he was an educated cop, who didn't do things by the book. So nobody asked about his sudden disappearance except Hawke, who had worked with him on occasion.

The two men had got along well with each other but there were always disagreements. Logan was now used to that and a lot more, since his tragic accident. Derek Hawke had resigned from the police force because he wasn't given any chance whatsoever, by his superiors, to expose or bring to justice certain underworld figures in the city. There couldn't have been a better reason to bow out. Fate as it seemed, had other plans for them. Hawke had contacted him in the hospital, and had offered him a new job. He was asked to work under different conditions. Logan had mastered his predicament with time. On record he was now officially missing. In the newspapers his disappearance had run in some of the dailies.

Derek Hawke had certainly seen to it all. He had also pointed out something else in their new working relationship. Logan had to take up a new identity, because he was now expendable. A short time later there was a knock on Logan's front door, he opened it and in walked Hawke. 'So what's this all about then?' Logan asked. He poured a drink and offered it to the man standing near the window. Derek Hawke was a belligerent man in his mid-forties. He was thin and of average height. The freckles on his, not so handsome, face gave him a charm he resented so much. Hawke accepted the drink. 'For what it's worth I'm not quite sure but it might have a lot to do with a man who uses a cane', he said. 'And this man incidentally seems to be linked with my employer'.

Hawke took a peek through the window and he could see a man with a cane looking up at him. Logan went to have a look then moved away from the curtains, he had taken a good look through the window to see whether he spotted anyone outside. There was no one there. He turned around to face the skinny man. 'Are you out of your mind Hawke?' Logan asked seriously. 'There's nobody outside. You must be hallucinating'. Derek Hawke took a good look through the window again then looked at Logan. 'He's gone' he almost shouted in disbelief. 'There was somebody standing outside. I'm not going crazy Logan!'

'You'd better not be' Logan whispered. 'Who is this guy anyway?' 'I don't know who he is Mac' said Hawke frustratingly. 'But I think he's somehow involved in this case, otherwise he wouldn't be following me'. 'It still doesn't add up skinny man', Logan whispered. 'Why should he follow you?' He was puzzled. 'That's something you'll have to find out for me' Hawke said thoughtfully 'Right now, let's get down to this business'. He sipped his drink and sat down in one of the armchairs. 'My employer gave me this problem, but I felt you should handle it because it's right in your backyard'. Hawke was talking about a lawyer who hired him occasionally to investigate unusual crimes for him.

Hawke was now a Private Detective with a license. He had no office but didn't like working in one anyway. Logan knew that Hawke's employer was quite wealthy. He also knew the man retained his friend to investigate intriguing cases.

'What exactly do you mean?' Logan asked. 'I want you to look into a mugging Mac' began the detective 'two nights ago my boss learnt that one of his friends had been attacked on his way home by a gang of thugs who seem to meet quite often in this area'. 'Why can't the police handle it?' Logan asked sitting down in another armchair. 'Oh they are looking into the matter' Hawke said. 'But they've also been investigating a pattern of similar crimes. You see, my boss feels the police are probably wasting time catching and bringing the men to justice'. 'What makes this so special then Hawke?' Logan asked, sighing while getting up from his chair. 'That's what you have to find out sonny' Derek Hawke said. 'The victim was an honest man. I've tried to dig up some dirt on him but found nothing. He's clean and he doesn't have a slate of any kind. He wasn't carrying anything of any importance on him when he was mugged, so why was he attacked in the first place?' 'What's this guy's name?' Logan asked. Hawke replied, 'His name is Paul Lukman but he does know a crook called Tom George'. 'So, what's all this got to do with George?' Logan asked.

'George as it seems' Hawke said. 'Worked for Lukman as an informant but for a price. My boss thinks that George had something to do with all this'. 'But I thought you said the crimes committed before all this happened formed a similar pattern' Logan whispered grimly. 'I know what I said Logan' said Hawke angrily. 'And that's why all of this doesn't really make any sense!' 'Which brings us back to the very same question Hawke' Logan said bluntly 'who has been

6

following you and why?' 'I don't know who was following me tonight Logan'
Hawke said thoughtfully 'but I'd like you to find out why'.

II

Logan was lost in deep thought, he was thinking about the job, Derek
Hawke had left his flat. Logan knew there were many unanswered questions
connected with this job. He kept wondering why. He remembered that Hawke
had told him before he left, that Lukman wasn't going to be of any help to
them. He had been seriously injured and was in a critical state in a hospital.

So where was he going to find the answers he needed and who were these
thugs? He wondered whether any of his contacts would know anything. 'I need
to come up with something' he muttered, suddenly getting up from the chair.
He looked at the time. It was now eleven o'clock. Logan went to his desk and
picked up the phone. He dialed a number, and when he got through he said, 'I
think it's time I arranged a meeting with someone'.

It was midnight at the Fair Blues restaurant in Wood Green. There was
only one man in the place and he was nursing a drink at a table. His name was
Hank Bell. He was unusually tall. He was also big. His face was drawn and his
eyes were pale brown. His demeanor was sober. He looked up as someone
walked through the door. He knew who it was.

'Old Sam said you were coming but you're late' Bell said, directing his gaze
at Logan. Logan said nothing. He was wondering where the barman Sam was.
He had spoken to him on the phone earlier that evening but had never met
him.

After a paradoxical caper which involved Bell, Logan knew that the man
liked spending some of his nights at this restaurant and bar. That is why he
checked to see whether Bell was there that night, he was. 'I'm sorry Hank'
Logan whispered. 'I got here as soon as I could'. He grabbed a seat and sat
across the table from the big man. 'Old Sam's not around as you can see' said
Bell. 'I remember you said he never was. I'm surprised he answered my phone
call' said Logan smiling thinly. 'Anyway, I came round to see if you could tell
me anything about a man called George, who's some sort of crook'.

'You're in trouble again, aren't you?' Bell sniggered. 'But I suppose you've
got good reason to be'. 'Can you tell me anything about George?' 'What do you
want to know?' Bell asked sipping his drink. 'I'm looking into a mugging and
George might have something to do with it'. 'Did you say a mugging, mate?'
Bell asked. 'Yes I did' Logan sighed. 'Look, from what I've heard George is a
tough customer, but I don't think he would get mixed up in such a little thing'.

'Why do you say that?' Logan asked frowning slightly. 'From what I've heard that's something he would never do, his reputation would be at stake', the big man replied 'Besides rumor has it on the streets that a young fellow called Joe could be responsible for that. There's been a couple of other attacks like the one that you've described and some people think he's behind all of them. Anyway, Joe hangs out with his gang around Bethnal Green, and as funny as it may seem he sometimes works for George'. 'Where can I find this fellow?' Logan asked. 'I don't know' said Bell 'But he's usually seen with a few friends at a pub near here called Crow's. You'd better check that out first'. 'Thanks pal' Logan whispered getting up. 'You've been a real help. Now stay out of trouble big man, so long'. Hank nodded his head and sniggered as Logan left the place.

CHAPTER 2
Part I

The following day a cabdriver stopped a few yards from Crow's pub. 'There it is' said the cabbie, he was talking to his passenger. He climbed out and went around the vehicle to open the jammed door for the man. The driver thought that there was something wrong with the man because he could hear him murmuring to himself in the car. He let the man out, then jumped back behind the steering wheel and sped off. He did not bother getting paid. He thought the man was mentally sick and caused him lots of problems.

Logan did not mind a free trip so put his money back into his pocket and made his way towards the pub. The place was quite big and it stank, cigarette smoke filled the air. A few heads turned to look at the newcomer as he came in. There were some couples dancing to the music playing in the room, and there were other couples at tables laughing and chatting. Three young men were playing poker at one table.

Logan went straight to an empty table. He had phoned Derek Hawke that morning and told him what Bell had said. He had also told him about his planned visit to the pub. Although Hawke didn't like the idea at first, he decided to go with it in order to get the information they needed from the thug called Joe.

There's got to be an explanation for all this thought Logan sitting down at a table. Why put Lukman out of commission? Suddenly somebody touched him on the shoulder. It was a waiter. He was a big bloke. 'What would you like to drink, Sir?' he asked politely, smiling thinly. 'Nothing at the moment' Logan

9

whispered looking up at the man 'But you can help me with something else pal. I'm looking for someone called Joe, where can I find him?' 'What's Joe to you Mister?' The waiter asked curiously. 'Nothing much.' Logan replied. 'He's just someone I need to talk too'.

The waiter excused himself and went to the table where the three men were sitting. He spoke to one of them and pointed a finger at Logan. After exchanging a few more words with them the waiter left.

A few minutes passed then the three young men got up from their table and strode over to where Logan was sitting. They all looked dirty and scruffy. One of the men held a bottle. As they reached Logan's table the one with the bottle said 'My name's Joe'. Joe sat in a chair across from Logan. The other two men stood behind him. 'I was in the middle of a winning game you know' said Joe, angrily. 'So what's your problem mister?' 'Jarrett' Logan whispered huskily 'Call me Jarrett'. 'What's this all about?' Joe asked. Logan smiled grimly 'I want to know who paid you to attack Lumen and why?' he asked. 'You're not one of George's men are you?' Joe asked. 'You can call me a bum, pal' Logan whispered 'but who hired you?' Joe looked at his friends and laughed, his friends followed suit. Then suddenly he smashed the bottle on the table. 'Grab him, boys'.

The room was suddenly quiet. People stopped dancing and watched to see what would happen next. Logan knew there would be trouble so he went into action. He got up, pulled the chair from behind him and used it to club one of the two men who were now coming at him. Joe got up but lost his balance and fell on top of the smashed thug. The other one managed to dodge the chair and moved in and smashed Logan down with a stool he had grabbed. Logan fell hard and hit his head on the wall and nearly passed out.

The thug put a hand into his old coat pocket and brought out something wrapped in a dirty cloth. He stepped forward unwrapping it as he moved, a knife appeared in his hand. He raised the gleaming blade about to stab the helpless man on the floor, when suddenly something happened. The thug's knife hand stiffened in the air. And, as if that wasn't enough another arm went around his neck. The last thing the man heard before he drifted off into eternal bliss was the snap of his neck bones; he then crumpled to a heap on the floor.

Derek Hawke took a step towards Logan. Then suddenly turned around and pointed his gun at Joe. He shot twice and Joe went down. The other thug decided it was a good time to leave, so he fled. Derek Hawke picked up a bottle of water from a table. He threw the contents on the dazed man on the floor, and then attended to him while watching the strange faces in the room. Logan got up

10

slowly. He said nothing as he was led out of the Pub by his boss. As Logan left with Hawke he could swear he heard someone ask whether Joe was going to make it.

The landlord of the Pub called 'CROWS' phoned an ambulance service and also called the police. The ambulance service bundled up the corpse and left for a hospital where a Casualty Doctor confirmed that Joe was dead. The Doctor said something to the nurse there and then left the room, while the nurse covered up the body. Then the Casualty Doctor went and informed the young man's so-called relatives of his findings. One of the two men came forward. The Doctor felt uncomfortable all of a sudden, but he broke the news sympathetically to the man and then excused himself to attend to another patient. The two men stood motionless staring at each other. The second one heard footsteps behind him. He turned round to face a well-dressed man. The stranger smiled then said 'You two will have quite a lot to answer for if you don't tell me quickly how this happened to Joe'. 'Who are you?' The second man asked. 'I'm sure the poor fellow must have mentioned my name sometime, boys' the stranger grinned. 'Anyway, if you don't know, my name's Payne, Eddie Payne.

II

'What exactly were you trying to do in there?' Derek Hawke asked. He stopped his car near a park in Broadwater Farm. Logan was sore with the bruises from the fight at Crow's. The two men had left the pub and driven off immediately. 'I should be asking that question' Logan whispered 'you blew it skinny man, have you been following me?' 'Not really' replied Hawke 'But I had one of my men keep an eye on you, and it looks as if it was for a good reason too'. 'You shot a prime suspect in there, Derek' Logan whispered 'how does that help me find the truth now?' 'I know the Police will ask awkward questions, but I will take care of that' Hawke said seriously. 'Something else has come up and it has a certain twist to it that I don't like'. 'What is it?' Logan asked. 'Lukman's wife was kidnapped last night. Her name is Tabby; she also appears to be the daughter of the archaeologist Professor Titus James. It seems the Police have started looking into this, but I need you to find out why she was taken'. 'George might know something', Logan whispered. 'The man you shot stopped working for him a while ago'. 'Then who was the thug working for?' Hawke asked 'I need you to find out Mac. But, I also need you to find out what George knows, and fast'.

11

CHAPTER 3
Part I

Eddie Payne paced the floor of his sitting room back and forth. He was living in a rather palatial flat in Convent Garden. In his hand was a picture of a strikingly beautiful woman. Payne's face was creased in a frown as he sipped a glass of wine. He thought that the smiling figure in the picture looked unhappy. Payne crumpled it up and threw it in the dustbin beside him. He sighed, and stood up from his desk. Payne was a tall, lean man on the wrong side of thirty; he was also undeniably good looking. He sipped more wine, but hesitated a little, as he stared at the bin. He was thinking about the woman in the picture.

Samantha had been reliable until she came in contact with a man named Derek Hawke. That was a silly mistake. Payne remembered vividly that her relationship with this man had caused a lot of problems for his team, and had almost ruined a successful job. He wasn't bothered by all that anymore since Samantha was dead. He remembered that he had asked Joe and his boys to do the dirty deed. All of a sudden Payne wondered whether Hawke knew his ex-wife was dead. No one could tell him what the ex-policeman was up to.

Joe's friends had told him everything they knew about his death. Payne couldn't understand why Jarrett had shown up at Crow's. Also, he couldn't understand why Derek Hawke had turned up there too.

Eddie Payne decided to withhold this news from his boss. He knew a lot was at stake at the moment. But he wanted nothing to go wrong with the new job. It had to be a success. He was going to make sure of that. Eddie Payne stopped pacing. He sipped some of his wine again and looked at the wastepaper basket. Although he regretted losing Samantha, he agreed with the boss this time. Samantha was blackmailing the boss so she could tell everything to the police to get her freedom from the gang. But despite all this, Payne craved to know who arranged Paul Lukman's mugging and why?

II

It was the middle of the night, there was a full moon and the stars were very bright. A tall shadowy figure crouched on a window sill before climbing into a darkened room through its window. He switched on his slim torch. Logan was puzzled; it looked like someone had beaten him there.

The Bethnal Green house he had broken into belonged to Tom George. Logan was in the man's bedroom looking at the bed. All its sheets lay on the floor with pillows. Newspapers and magazines were also scattered all over the place. He picked up one, taking a glimpse at the nude girl on the front page. He dropped the magazine down on the floor again. He walked towards the wardrobe and looked into it, but it was empty. He wondered why George's room was in such a mess. Logan turned his attention to the dressing table, trying to pull out one of the drawers when he heard a faint sound, and it had come from George's sitting room.

Logan switched off his torch and stepped towards the bedroom door, when he heard the sound again. Someone had definitely broken into the house, but who was it? He stood behind the door for a moment but nothing happened. He switched his torch on again and opened the door slowly, it squeaked a bit. Immediately he knew he could have a problem. Logan headed down the stairs towards the sitting room. As he went in there, he was hit by something quite heavy and he collapsed on the floor. The attacker struck him twice again in the lower region of his back. Logan gasped for breath and purposely resisted a fight and pretended to be unconsciousness.

The silent intruder picked up the torch that Logan had dropped on the floor, and then went to switch on the room light. He was coming back when Logan turned on his back and got up slowly rubbing his neck. The man stopped in mid stride when he saw him.

'I'm sure you can do better than that Jarrett' the man said grinning. He was of average height and build. He was also well dressed. He looked disabled because he had a bent back and used a walking stick. His features hid what a tough and athletic individual he was. The walking stick was made of a good

13

wood and designed like a gentleman's cane. But it held a secret because in fact there was a razor sharp sword hidden inside.

'Shut up' Logan whispered sibilantly. He grimaced as he got up slowly. Nothing had been touched in the sitting room. It was just an ordinary looking room. Logan recognized the crippled man facing him and remembered he was dangerous because they had crossed paths in the past. He made sure the man saw the pistol he carried in the shoulder holster concealed by his jacket. But he wondered what had happened to the man, his name was Quentin Baker and he was known as the Rat.

'A lot's happened since we last met Jarrett'. The Rat smiled. He switched off the flashlight and dropped it into his pocket 'But I wonder why you're so glum. I've heard you're still a thorn in the flesh'. 'Shut up Rat' Logan warned. 'Take off your coat and throw it down on one of those settees over there'.

The Rat saw the strapped gun on Logan. He hesitated a bit then said. 'Now what?' he asked.

Logan said nothing. He walked slowly towards the settees and picked up the coat, his eyes still on Baker. He rummaged through the coat finding nothing except a notebook. He ran his fingers through its pages and his eyes spotted something that made him gasp. It was a man's name, someone whom he had met during a deep undercover operation as a cop. This was a few years before the accident that had almost cost him his life. Logan remembered his superiors in those days had asked him to spy on this man and his shady deals. The name in the book was Jason Phelps. He was a multimillionaire businessman.

'Now start talking Rat, where's George?' Logan asked bluntly. 'And who are you trying to impersonate this time?' 'I'm not impersonating anybody if you really must know' the Rat said calmly. 'Now, George, unfortunately he's dead. I found his body in a car parked in the street, with a knife stuck in his throat. Someone killed him, but I had nothing to do with it. You won't believe it, but I broke in here to try and find out why'.

'Tell me the truth Baker', Logan whispered. 'Who are you working for and why have you been following Derek Hawke?' 'That's none of your business Jarrett' said Baker chuckling. 'I'm not going to tell you so you'll have to find that out for yourself. You know nothing about me, and even if you did, you can't do anything about it'. Logan couldn't see where this conversation was leading to, and he didn't like that. 'Now what's your game Rat?' he asked 'You're not making sense'. 'I don't have to'. Baker smirked. 'If you agree to help me find an associate of mine, I will. His name is Eddie Payne and he's got some information I want. You don't have a choice Jarrett'. Logan sighed. 'Don't raise your hopes too high. Anything can happen, and I'd rather not get into any trouble with the police', he said. 'Where do I start looking and how do I contact you?' 'You don't contact me I'll contact you' Baker said going to the settee where his coat was 'Remember Jarrett, no funny games. I'm sure you'll have no trouble in finding Payne, just find him soon'. He picked up his coat and put it on. 'I think you're forgetting something'. Logan whispered. He felt disgusted. The Rat dipped, his hand into his coat pocket coming up with the pencil torch. He tossed it over to Logan. 'You'd better disappear' he said seriously. 'I'll be taking a hike too'.

III

Detective Sergeant Willie Briggs was attached to the Murder Squad in Scotland Yard. He was a tall, lanky fellow. Briggs was quietly dressed in a three-piece suit. The expression on his face seemed bitter and his eyes bore through thick glasses. Briggs climbed into his car and drove off. The vehicle was an old brown Ford. Briggs was in a bad mood. He was fast asleep in his bed when the call came through in the early hours of that morning that there was a car parked somewhere in Bethnal Green with a corpse in it. He had grumbled when he recognized the anonymous caller's voice.

Briggs knew it was the mystery man called Jarrett. So he had hurriedly put some clothes on and then phoned his office. He had asked his boss to send some men to the scene of the crime. Briggs had wondered what the man had got himself into now. Briggs wished it had something to do with the new case he was investigating. He said something stupid to himself and sighed, shaking his head as he raced towards the crime scene.

IV

Eddie Payne hung up the phone and stepped out of a phone booth in Enfield town. He looked up into the sky and smiled thinly. It was now almost daybreak. He climbed back into his car. 'That's been settled now, Doctor Ellis'. He said. 'The Professor won't upset you anymore, because I've made sure he won't contact the police again'. 'I'm not over-reacting here, Mister Payne, I just want to get this job done successfully' Doctor Eric Ellis said nervously. He was sitting in the front seat of Payne's car. It was a posh blue ford Cortina. Payne shrugged his shoulders.

He had been informed by a snitch that George was found dead in his car. Someone had made sure that the crook's death was a cruel one. Payne had wondered who had done this. He couldn't come up with any answers. Payne thought about the two men that had been seen at Crow's. He felt it was now important to find out what he could about Hawke and his friend. Although strange things had happened since Samantha's death, Payne knew it would still be unwise to tell his boss about all this. Payne also realized Ellis could be unpredictably dangerous, which was why he had responded to the man's phone call. He wished he could do more to dissuade the Doctor's colleague.

Professor Titus James had been a hard nut to crack. Payne decided that both men would be eliminated. His boss had made sure the Professor's daughter was kidnapped. Payne grinned at Ellis as he started the car. He wondered if it was still necessary to arrange Paul Lukman's death.

CHAPTER 4
Part I

The elderly man walked quickly along the street, there were only a few other pedestrians. He was aware that there was no one following him, but he still looked scared. He was about seventy and his clothes had seen better days. Professor Titus James glimpsed at his watch and saw that it was now ten in the morning. He had left his flat early that morning and had gone for a walk. He kept walking but turned around to see whether anyone was following him. Nobody was, so he hurried on again. He was in such a hurry that he stumbled and almost fell down, but he regained his balance. The Professor stopped walking, took a deep breath and wiped the cold sweat off his forehead.

Professor James was frightened. Someone had threatened him over the phone that morning. He didn't know who was doing this; all he knew was that it was a man. The man had said that he would make life miserable for him if he didn't stay away from the police, or didn't comply with him. That threat was already beginning to happen. His son-in-law lay in hospital seriously ill, and his daughter Tabby had been kidnapped by some men. The Professor was sure about one thing though. He knew that the men who had kidnapped his daughter were working with the anonymous phone caller, who was obviously hell bent on trading her for a secret the Professor was keeping. That secret was now one the Professor was beginning to dread, because of the ties it had with an Inca archaeological site in Paleque, Mexico.

The Professor had been asked to run things there. He was aware that some of his colleagues disapproved of that because they felt he was not the right person for the job. Two of them had already resigned. They had wanted the

17

position just as much as he did, but that had brought his memories flooding back.

One of the men was his daughter's ex-boyfriend. The Professor didn't know where Doctor Eric Ellis was now or what he was doing since he quit the job and left the site. The Professor wondered if he had anything to do with all this. He had not got on very well with Ellis when they worked together at the site. This was before Ellis suddenly disappeared, leaving no word of where he was going. The Professor only knew that the men behind this plot were desperate enough to kill because of the information he had.

The Professor wished he hadn't accepted Paul's proposition to help fund the dig during the year. Although he knew his son-in-law was comfortably well off, he couldn't understand why he had suddenly become a victim. It was all very puzzling.

The Professor continued to walk down the street, he didn't know where to go, or who to contact at this point. He felt helpless. As he thought about his daughter, one very disturbing question sprang to mind, who on earth was trying to find out the location of the burial site in Mexico?

II

'This is outrageous' Derek Hawke spluttered. 'I don't believe this is happening. What makes you think you can pull this off Mac?' The detective sat at a table in Charlie's Pub. Logan was sitting across from him. 'It's our only chance of finding out what this guy Payne really does' he said.

Logan had contacted Derek Hawke that afternoon. He had spoken to him about his findings the other night, but had not told him anything about the Rat. Logan couldn't tell Hawke about the Rat. He realized that his boss would panic. When Hawke asked him about Eddie Payne, he told him that he had found out about him when he found a note, which was presumably written by George's killer and was in George's shirt pocket. But that didn't explain why George was murdered, and who did it? Logan was mildly surprised when Hawke told him that Eddie Payne was associated with a number of construction sites, and owned a couple of woodworking firms in town.

When Hawke decided to meet him at the pub Hawke told him that one of his operatives was a foreman at one of those woodworking firms in Edmonton. Hawke had phoned his operative, but the man couldn't tell him anything about Payne mainly because he rarely saw him and knew very little about him. So where was he and what was he really up to, and why was Rat involved in all this? Logan could not believe that he had come up against another dead end. So far it seemed he hadn't had much luck with this job. Two people were already dead and he intended to find out why. Hawke's man had agreed to fix him up with a temporary job at one of the woodworking companies; he knew he had to start looking for clues somewhere out there. Hawke didn't like the idea, but had no choice but to go along with it. But something else bothered Logan. He was wondering what all this had to do with Jason Phelps. 'I still don't like this'. Hawke said. 'But we don't have a choice, do we?' 'You know we don't'. Logan finally said. 'I've got a phone call to make'. He got up from his seat. 'We've got to do something about this sonny. This is a bad job and that's why I'm asking my man there to watch your back'. Logan said nothing. He just nodded his head.

III

Detective Sergeant Willie Briggs got up from his desk. He went to the window. Briggs took a cigarette from the packet in his breast pocket and lit it. He could see his car parked outside, but knew that was not the problem. Something else was. It was the new murder case assigned to him at the office. Briggs couldn't believe he had stumbled onto something that was closely connected with another case he had been working on. Briggs strongly believed that his findings were definitely linked with Samantha Hasting's death. I've got to find some more clues, he thought but where do I begin?

Briggs went back to his desk. He switched on the reading lamp, and stubbed out the remains of his cigarette in an ashtray. He ran his eyes over the forensic report of Samantha Hastings which was on the desk, then said, 'Damn'. He wished he knew what this particular fiasco was really all about. He knew at the moment, his findings didn't make any sense. Two people brutally killed and one of them mugged first, but why?

The police were still investigating a few unsolved cases surrounded by sinister reports about similar assaults on the streets. Briggs agreed the two victims had suffered the same fate. Briggs wondered whether somebody had decided it was time these people were written off. Eddie Payne had been involved with one victim. If it was Payne then what was he up too? Why would he kill his lover, that's if he did, and was he associated with George? Briggs had already put out word on the streets about Payne. His informant had promised him that evening that he would come up with something. Briggs had also wondered whether the man called Jarrett knew something about this case. Cold shivers ran down Briggs' spine. He had come to terms with one fact. This new case was quite a handful. He remembered his boss had asked to see him, the following morning. He wanted some more light shed on the matter. Briggs paced the room but then after a while went back to his desk again and closed the report. 'I know I'm missing something here' he muttered. 'The question is what is it?' Briggs felt it was time to go home. It had been a long day and he realized he could do with some sleep. He left the forensic report on his desk and as he quietly walked out of his office another question lingered on his mind. Were the two victims linked with a notorious drug cartel based in London? Briggs knew the police had been trying to smash this organization for months.

Next day Briggs parked his car in the parking lot and ran into his office building with his briefcase. He was late for his meeting. This was because his informant had contacted him that morning. Briggs was intrigued by what he had learnt from the man. He hadn't time to go over all the details with him. But, Briggs felt he should pass this information onto his boss. Running up the staircase, he headed straight towards the Superintendent's office. Willie Briggs rapped on the door twice and without waiting for an answer he barged in. 'What's wrong Sergeant?' Chief Superintendent Noah Thomson asked. He was sitting behind his desk. The man was stocky in build and in his mid-fifties; he looked well fed and had a receding hairline. The Chief Superintendent was smartly dressed in a black suit. 'What time do you call this Sergeant Briggs?'

'I'm sorry Sir'. Briggs said. 'Something important got in the way, something I just couldn't ignore'. 'And what exactly could that be Sergeant?' Thomson asked getting up from his seat, he wasn't looking pleased. 'We scheduled this meeting for ten o'clock this morning, it's almost noon! Well, come in then. Don't just stand there, have a chair. And for heaven's sake shut the door, we've got a lot to discuss'. 'Yes Sir'. Briggs shut the door and sat down in an armchair that had seen better days. He remembered that he had been debriefed here on several occasions in this office. 'Well, what are you waiting for?' Thomson asked. 'What have you come up with?' Briggs was about to pick up his briefcase but on second thought left it where it lay' 'It's about Eddie Payne Sir' he said nervously. 'I think I've found some dirt on the bloke'. 'Get on with it Sergeant'. 'Well, it's like this Sir'. Briggs began carefully. 'I had one of my informants track one of his men down. This guy spilled the beans on Payne. Eddie Payne is an entrepreneur. He uses false names when it suits him and he's a bit of a criminal genius in his own right. Payne's a shady one all right. He goes out with loads of different women. One of his many lovers was actually the dead girl, Samantha Hastings. Before her death this woman worked for an outfit. This outfit was a spy network and Payne was the chief of operations. Stanley, my informant thinks this outfit is still in business, but he's not sure'.

'There's a catch to all this, Sergeant'. Thomson said impatiently. 'So what is it and cut to the chase?'

'I think Payne's the culprit Sir, I think he really is a suspect in all this'. Briggs said carefully. 'But you don't have any proof of that, do you Sergeant? You're grasping at straws'. Superintendent Thomson picked up a file from his desk. The desk was cluttered with paper work on it. He flipped the file open and glimpsed through the documents in it. He suddenly closed it, and raised an eyebrow in response to the answer he was still waiting for. Briggs shrugged his shoulders in defeat. 'I guess you're right there, Sir'. 'I hope you know what you're doing Sergeant'. Thomson said sternly putting the file down again on the desk. 'Because there's been a new development'.

Briggs took in deep breath and leaned forward to hear what his boss had to say. 'What's happened?' he asked. 'The local police down at Bethnal Green phoned me today'. Thomson began seriously. 'In fact, just a few minutes before you stormed in here. They think they've got a lead on the gang that's been causing all this trouble. But they haven't nabbed them yet. For some reason they believe that these yobs were in a fight with two men at a pub called Crow's. The police are only relying on vague descriptions they were given, it appears that one of those two men could be one of our former colleagues. What's his name now? Oh yes, it's ex-Police Inspector Derek Hawke. The profile the local boys were given at the pub matches his description but they didn't get much on the other fellow. I also understand the dead girl Samantha Hastings was once Hawke's wife. I can't figure out what he was doing there, but I've also been wondering whether he was investigating a case. The bad news in all this is that the head of that gang is dead. He got shot during the fight, so far the local boys have only found out that his Cristian name was Joe. His friends seem to have made a run for it because nobody knows where they are now. The cops are putting a lid on this one for the time being because they don't have enough details yet'. 'What about the man whom you think could be Hawke and the bloke with him?' Briggs asked. 'The police sergeant in charge of the case didn't disclose that to me'. Thomson said grumpily. 'I assume they've got them under surveillance. In the meantime let me tell you about something else'.

Briggs nodded his head but his mind was in a whirlwind at that moment. Was Derek Hawke really involved with this case? And was the man he called Jarrett part of this too? Briggs believed that the man could be working on the same case he was investigating. He listened attentively as his boss rambled on about a drug bust the Vice squad had recently made. It seemed his boss wanted him to follow that example by showing some results.

IV

Detective Sergeant Willie Briggs smiled faintly as he stubbed out his cigarette butt in the ashtray on the coffee table. He was sitting comfortably on a settee in a very nice living room. 'Thanks again for the tip last night'. He said calmly. 'Now what can I do for you Mister Jarrett?'

Briggs felt it was a good question to ask. The beautiful woman sitting down with him owned the place. Her name was Ruth Ryan. She was the mystery man's girlfriend. Briggs knew she lived in the posh flat in Bounds Green. 'Tell us what's bothering you Willie' Logan said. He had arranged this meeting with Briggs on the phone at Ruth's insistence. Briggs suddenly stood up. He took another cigarette from his pocket and as he lit it up he said, 'You're right. Something is wrong. You see, before driving up here I was told by my Superintendent that I might be handling the investigation into George's death. At the moment, I've been looking into another murder, as funny as it may seem, I think that both of these murders are linked together somehow' 'What do you mean?' Logan asked, taking a peek through the curtains. 'Well'. Briggs said sighing. 'A young woman was murdered a few weeks ago. Surprisingly enough she was mugged first. I read the autopsy report and saw her corpse. Nobody's been able to identify her yet, but I think, and have reason to believe, that she used to be Hawke's wife. 'What are you talking about Briggs?' Logan asked, turning round to face the Sergeant. 'Are you crazy?' 'I'm not crazy Mister Jarrett' Briggs said hesitating. 'Your boss, when he was still in the police force, used to be married to a girl he loved very much. Her name was Samantha Hastings. Unfortunately, she was cheating on him. It was rumored that she was seeing someone else, a local businessman called Fred Watson who we recently found out was Eddie Payne. When Hawke found out about Watson they split up and went their separate ways. Some of my men think that there's a lot more to this story than I've just told you. I'm not sure because I've never really asked Hawke what went on'. Logan was bewildered; he said nothing and looked at Ruth.

'So how are the two cases linked with each other Willie?'
The girl asked suddenly. 'Good question Miss Ryan'. Briggs said. 'It's quite complicated. You see, last night the Superintendent got a phone call from someone who would not give his name. The man claimed that he knew that Payne had something to do with the girl's death. I was going to ask if you knew

anything about this since you decided to call me tonight'. 'What time did this bloke ring your boss?' Logan asked. 'He said the man rang him about two, this morning'. Briggs said. Damn it! Thought Logan, Baker must have made that phone call when I left him. 'I don't know anything about that Willie, but that isn't why I called you here tonight' he said finally 'I'm also investigating a mugging. But I'm not sure if it has anything to do with the message your boss got last night'. Logan said. 'But I can tell you one thing for sure, the job has certainly something to do with Eddie Payne, and I want to find out why'. Two hours later Willie Briggs left the flat. Logan had asked Briggs to find out more about Payne. Logan couldn't believe his boss had once been married. He thought about the dead woman and what she had to do with this, and if Hawke knew anything at all about the death of his ex-wife. Briggs wasn't sure if Hawke did know, but Logan didn't know what to think any more since he had learnt about this. 'It seems you've got your work cut out for you, Mac'. Ruth said, smiling at him. Logan nodded his head. 'Remember Quentin Baker is exactly what he calls himself, a Rat', he whispered.

V

Three days later, Logan started work as a delivery man at the Pinocchio Centre in Edmonton. Hawke's operative had managed to fix him up with a job there, despite difficulties to convince his assistant. Logan discovered why the man wasn't happy; his men hadn't been paid for the past two weeks. The man whose name was Marks just couldn't understand why his foreman had recruited someone for him when his men weren't paid. The most annoying thing was that no one seemed to know where the owner of the firm could be found. Marks wanted to tell all this to him, but Logan had already decided to stick around the firm no matter what. He knew it was the only way he was going to find out about Eddie Payne. On his first day at Pinocchio there was no sign of Payne. Hawke had told him after work that the man called Joe didn't make it; Hawke also said that Payne was probably looking into the shooting. The two men with Joe had suddenly disappeared. Nothing about this job surprised him anymore. He couldn't help but wonder if Hawke knew something he didn't, and if he did know, why was he keeping it from him? Other questions loomed in his mind. What was Jason Phelps' role in all this? How was he really connected with Rat? Logan didn't have the answers to these questions. The following morning some very angry workers met Marks on the site, and complained bitterly about their situation, and what they would do if nothing was to happen. Marks tried to reassure them that nothing could be done until the owner of the company sorted out his problems.

Later, at lunchtime, four hefty men in the group decided to meet Marks. They had decided to get some real answers from him. They cornered him in one of the buildings on the site where his office was. Marks was sacking a man when he saw them. One of the four men brought him down with a flying tackle. The leader of this group also appeared to be the leader for all the workers; he urged them to kick Marks who was now on the ground. The laborer who had been sacked ran off looking for help. Nobody was around as most of the workers had left the site. He almost ran into the new delivery man, a man he knew as Jarrett. Logan had finished his rounds for the day with the truck, and had come back to the site to park the truck and return the keys.

'What's wrong?' Logan asked 'You're shaking all over'. The man pointed towards the office. 'There's a fight going on over there, and some of the men are beating up the boss'. Logan ran towards the fight. The men were yelling and shouting at Marks as they beat him up. Logan stepped forward with caution. The leader of the group saw him first. 'What are you doing here?' Logan asked, but was told 'Stay out of this man'. The other men turned round suddenly, leaving the man they were hitting on the ground. Marks tried to get up but he couldn't and Logan could see the man was badly hurt and in pain. 'Why don't you scum bags' take on someone your own size?' he said slowly, trying to start a fight with them. One of them rushed forward, his arms reaching out to grab Logan. Logan sidestepped, and then hit the big fellow with a blow. The punk nearly fell over but was held firmly in an iron grip. Logan then smashed his elbow into the yob's face. In that spilt second another man jumped in. Mac was ready for him, but something happened. The punk was shot, he dropped to the ground like a sack, his knee shattered and crying in pain. Logan spun round, the laborer he had talked to stood a few yards away and with him was a man holding a gun. The gun was pointed at the shot man on the ground.

'I think that's enough, gentlemen'. The man snapped. He gestured to the man beside him to help the shot man. . 'Who are you?' Logan asked. Eddie Payne smiled. 'I should be asking you that question. I'm the owner of this place'. Logan smiled thinly as he was now face to face with the enemy.

CHAPTER 5
Part I

Doctor Eric Ellis paced the floor restlessly and looked at his watch for the hundredth time. It was now one o'clock. Payne's boss had phoned him at home and had instructed him to wait in a hotel room at the Legacy Hotel near Victoria tube station. Doctor Eric Ellis guessed that something had happened. He wasn't told what. It had come to him as a big surprise. He remembered he had spoken to the man once before, and that was on the phone. What had gone wrong now? Were the police on to something or was Payne's boss trying to change his plans again? Ellis didn't know why, in fact he wasn't confident about this job. If only Payne's boss could pull it off, he would simply disappear with his share of the loot. Ellis couldn't care less for anything else. He had already sent in a resignation letter stating that he wasn't with the university anymore. But that was by the way, what was Payne's boss going to tell him when he came in and why wasn't Payne handling this? Ellis tried to think whether this had something to do with Professor James again. He was proving a real nuisance.

He peeped through the window but suddenly there was a knock on the door. Doctor Ellis quickly opened the door and stepped back frantically, when he saw the snub-nosed pistol pointed at him. There was a thud as the man holding the pistol shot twice and Doctor Ellis crashed to the floor. The man with the pistol made sure the Doctor was dead and then closed the room door gently behind him. His name was Carl.

II

Logan couldn't believe his luck. He was in the office with Payne. The man wanted to have a chat with him, but Logan wondered if Payne was the crook he was really looking for, or was there someone else hiding behind him? There just had to be an explanation, otherwise why would Payne be avoiding everyone he knew, even the people who worked for him. What exactly was he playing at and who else apart from the Rat was involved with all this? Payne had made a few phone calls and had sent for a Doctor to attend to the wounded man. He explained to some of his laborers who had just come back from lunch that he had been out of town for a while. He told them that his foreman would make sure they all got paid in full, and a bonus payment would be added for the trouble that had been caused by him not giving the right orders to his staff.

Logan had introduced himself as the new delivery man. He suspected that Payne might know something about him. Payne wanted to know why his foreman had hired someone when he had no need to. But he didn't pursue this any further when he realized that the man in front of him was the man that was seen with the ex-policeman Hawke. What did he say his name was again? Jarrett. But what was he really doing in this place? Or was it a coincidence that he had taken up a job at the company. Payne felt it wasn't but decided to play along with whatever the chap told him. Payne intended to find out because he wanted to know more about Hawke. 'I can see you're in good shape Jarrett, do you work out?' he asked 'I do'. Logan whispered. Payne nodded. 'You could make some good money as a bodyguard Jarrett. I'm actually looking for one. If you're interested'. The phone suddenly rang; he picked it up and said 'Hello'.

'Listen, carefully Payne', a man's voice said. 'Ellis is dead. I think it would be wise to change your plans as I suggested, it will be very appropriate as of this time. Meet me at the house. We have business to talk about'. The phone went dead. Payne looked puzzled as he hung up, then he smiled as he saw Logan watching him 'That was a friend of mine, he phoned to tell me that another friend was involved in a terrible accident. It's quite tragic how some people can meet an untimely death'. Payne seemed lost in thought for a while then asked 'What were we talking about Jarrett?' 'You were offering me a job Mister Payne'. 'We'll talk about that later'. Payne said. 'I think you should call in one of the men to help close this office, I've got a meeting to go to that I have to attend'. Ten minutes later Logan flagged a taxi and told the driver to follow the car that swerved out of the company yard.

26

III

Jason Phelps was in his sitting room. He was a small man on the wrong side of forty. He was powerfully built and wasn't particularly handsome, Phelps was dark in complexion and was bald. Only one thing seemed to have brought him some importance. His squinted right eye had contorted his features and left them without emotion. Phelps sighed and put the phone back on the desk, then stood quietly and decided to think. Although he had passed on his message to Payne, he expected trouble from him. Phelps didn't really like Payne. He knew the man would object to what Carl did at the Legacy Hotel. But there wasn't any time to argue about that now, at least not since he had something in mind. He felt this new idea was going to work. It only had to be put into action, that's exactly what Payne was going to do after he briefed him. The plan was perfect. He hoped that there would be no flaws in carrying it out. Doctor Ellis would have spoilt the whole plan if he was still alive, but unfortunately he had to go. The man might have been a brilliant scholar but he was certainly a real pain in the neck. Phelps looked at the door that led to the hallway and wondered what the Lukman girl was doing in her room today. She wouldn't talk to him or anyone in the house which he had been renting for the last six weeks. That woman was as stubborn as her husband, he thought. Her father was going to tell him everything. If he didn't, he would see to his son-in-law's death. Phelps had a feeling that Payne would have liked to have seen to that immediately. Jason Phelps felt excited all of a sudden. He cast his mind back to his last journey to Mexico. That had been three years ago. Phelps wondered whether it had been wise not to have read up on the strange legend of the small village that guarded the burial site and the treasure that it hid, which he wanted to lay his hands on before anybody else did.

Paul Lukman was already trying to set up an expedition to see whether the hidden treasure could be retrieved from the burial site. Phelps thought only the villagers knew about this location that was until he found out from Doctor Ellis that Professor Titus James knew where the burial site was. Phelps only wanted to find the location of the burial site. And that was why he had to kidnap the Professor. Although the treasure was confined to a hidden chamber in the burial site, it was worth millions of Pounds and consisted of everything you could think of, from jewelry to cups and plates to ornaments, figurines and shrines. Phelps had become intrigued when he learnt that it was an un-plundered Inca burial site. He was still thinking about this when the girl barged in. His hand pressed a silent alarm bell hidden underneath his desk. 'I don't know what you want!' The girl screamed. A thickset man then came into the

27

room. 'Take her away Carl'. Phelps said. The man pounced on the woman, grabbing her by the arms. She shrieked as the man forcibly pushed her out of the room. 'The fun has only just begun my dear girl'. Phelps said slowly, sitting back comfortably in his chair, smiling but thinking about the next few days.

IV

Eddie Payne climbed out of his car, slamming the door hard. He walked up to the front door in Palmers Green and knocked on it. Logan watched him from a few yards in the taxi. Logan knew he had stumbled onto something, but he didn't know what yet. Jason Phelps smiled when he saw Payne walk through the hall into the sitting room. 'Make yourself comfortable Eddie'. Phelps said, beckoning Payne to sit down. 'We've got business to discuss'. 'I heard what you said over the phone Jason'. Payne said seriously 'what are you playing at?' 'Nothing!' Phelps said. 'I'm only trying to tell you that the plan has changed a little. Doctor Ellis is out of the picture now. Eddie, I know that you'll enjoy this when you hear what I have to say'. Payne said nothing. He sighed. Phelps sat up in his chair. He wondered what was going through Payne's mind, Phelps had worked far too long with the man, and he knew he could have something up his sleeve. From past experience Phelps knew the man didn't like surprises.

'Start talking Jason. I'm getting impatient, I was called away from personal business for this'. 'I presume you don't take me seriously then'. Said Phelps angrily. 'I'm all ears, fire away' Payne grinned. He could not fathom out why Phelps had taken matters into his own hands all of a sudden, and he wanted to find out why. Payne was actually amused by all of this. What had his boss come up with now?

'I asked my man to get rid of Ellis at the Legacy Hotel'. Phelps began very slowly. 'I had to do that, so that Professor James won't ask too many awkward questions when he meets me. He mustn't know anything about his dead colleague's involvement in this. It could spoil things'. 'Are you in a hurry Jason?' Payne asked. 'Why, have you got a problem with that Eddie?' 'No' said Payne 'But, you've still not made your point'. 'I will' Phelps said. He slipped his hand underneath the desk. He was beginning to feel uncomfortable all of a sudden. 'I want you to kidnap the Professor tomorrow night' 'I won't have a problem, doing that Jason'. Eddie Payne said. He stood up. 'But what good will that do, since the pretty lady hasn't talked yet?' 'Not much I'm afraid'. Phelps Said calmly. 'But I've got my reasons for doing all this, and I'm sure it will work. Besides I don't think the girl knows anything'. 'Don't say that Jason. It makes

28

me feel sick'. Payne said disgustingly. 'She might be adamant, but you never know with women'. 'I'm sure you would like to beat the truth out of her Eddie'. Phelps said slowly. 'But you're not going to do that until you get her father. Threatening to beat her up would obviously make the Professor tell us what he knows about the burial site'. Payne chuckled. 'That's one of the best things I've heard in days' he said 'What do you mean?' Phelps asked. 'It's got nothing to do with this'. Payne said. 'I've been thinking of recruiting someone else. We've lost two of our best operatives already, but we can forget all that and start afresh'. 'You can do all that after this Eddie. Do you have anyone in mind?' 'Yes' said Payne. He hesitated a bit. 'You're going to have to give me sometime Jason. I need to find out something about this man first. You see, he only started working at one of my firms a few days ago'. 'What's his name?' Phelps asked. Payne said, 'Jarrett'. Jason Phelps was startled for a moment. He then got up slowly from his chair. 'You look as white as a ghost'. Payne said, 'Do you know this fellow, Jason?' Phelps went slowly to the window, and then suddenly turned around whipping out his gun as he did so. He pointed it directly at Payne. 'I'm not sure I do Eddie' he said coldly. 'But you know what? You made a mistake'. 'What's that?' 'You lowered your guard and took certain decisions into your own hands when you shouldn't have Eddie'. Phelps said. He shot the man twice. Payne fell down, but amazingly tried to get up. Phelps shot him again, to make sure he stayed down this time, Payne was dead. Phelps darted towards the desk and pressed the silent alarm. Moments later the thug called Carl walked into the room. 'Get rid of him Carl'. Phelps said. 'Take charge of this job. I need you to kidnap Professor James tonight'.

V

'This is incredible Mac'. Derek Hawke said suddenly. 'Where's all this leading too?' 'I don't know' Logan whispered. 'But I'd like to find out skinny man'. The two men were in Hawke's car. It was parked in the same road Payne had driven into that afternoon. Logan had contacted Hawke at Charlie's bar and had told him what he had learnt so far about Payne. Hawke suggested they put the house under surveillance that night. 'So this fellow Doctor Ellis was linked with archaeologist Professor James?' Logan asked. 'Yes'. Hawke replied tersely. 'And according to my source at the university campus, he wasn't really getting on well with the Professor'. 'That certainly won't help us find out what he was really up to'. 'No' said Hawke 'but it buys us enough time to find out why he suddenly disappeared'. 'Which brings us to the same question Derek? Who are we really up against, and why are we finding it so hard to know what they're up to?' 'You can say that again Mac'. Hawke said. 'Payne is someone's stooge all right'.

Logan pointed a finger at the figure coming out of the house they were watching, and making his way to a car parked on the road. 'Follow that car Derek'. He whispered gruffly. 'I think this is our chance to get to the bottom of all of this'. Derek Hawke sighed starting the car. 'For once I think we agree about something'. He tailed the red Daewoo as it swerved and turned into different side streets. He glanced at Logan and knew something was bugging him. He didn't know what. Logan found it hard to believe that Hawke did not know that his ex-wife was involved with this mess. Logan was annoyed with himself because the only lead he had was of Payne's hideout.

Logan remembered the phone call in Payne's office. He wished he knew what the conversation was really all about. He had a gut feeling that everything about this job had a lot to do with Professor Titus James. Logan wished that Briggs and Ruth could provide him with some answers to solve this mystery. The red Daewoo suddenly stopped in a side street. The driver hopped out and walked towards an apartment building, he was carrying a torch in his hand. 'What happens now?' Hawke asked. He parked the car carefully on the same street. Logan was almost out of the car.

'Stay here skinny man. If I'm not back in ten minutes, you know what to do'. 'What do I do?' Hawke asked angrily. 'Search me!' Logan whispered. 'I'm running late'.

He ran across the road after the man who had gone into the block of flats which were three Storey's high and old-fashioned. Logan kept running as he saw the man heading for a front door on the second floor.

Meanwhile Professor James was about to go to bed when he heard a knock on the door, he immediately became afraid. He heard the knock again, and wondered if the police had come up with something connected with the kidnapping of his daughter. He dropped that thought immediately and wondered whether the men who had kidnapped his daughter had come to visit him. The Professor went straight to the front door and opened it without checking first. The door slammed back in his face and the Professor staggered back, he almost fell down. Carl came in like a flash, waving his stiletto knife. 'Get up old man, and get dressed. You're coming with me' he said. The Professor tried to steady himself, but was still shaken. Almost immediately Logan crashed in. Carl turned around and faced Logan. 'Who the hell is this?' he asked, surprised. Logan smiled grimly. 'I'm here to find out why you're here'. 'I'm going to wipe that smile off your face'. Carl said darting forward. He swung the knife at Logan's face. Logan dodged the lunge and grabbed the killer's arm. He kicked Carl very hard in the crutch and then pushed him hard to the floor, the knife clattered down with him. Carl reached out to grab the knife but Logan lashed out again with his foot, catching Carl in the face, the thug sunk into oblivion.

'Who are you?' The Professor said. He sat down in a chair, feeling very dizzy. 'My name's Jarrett'. Logan stammered. 'I'm sorry this happened'. 'So am I' Derek Hawke said. He walked into the flat. 'You'd better tie that guy up Mister Jarrett, we've got business to talk about with the old man, that's Professor Titus James'.

CHAPTER 6
Part I

Professor James talked about the hidden treasure, its location and its links with the archaeological burial site. It was all adding up, but there was something that still didn't make sense. Logan couldn't pinpoint what it was, and still couldn't figure out why Hawke's ex-wife was killed. It seemed weird to think the woman had anything to do with all this. Logan wondered if the Rat had known her. He had also wondered whether the crook had something to do with the kidnapping of the Professor's daughter. Logan hoped that Ruth would come up with a lead of some sort. He could see why a man in Phelps' position would kill to have all that treasure. He wondered if Hawke's boss was involved with any of this as well. I guess you can't trust most rich men, he thought.

Professor James phoned Jason Phelps. He told him that a thug had been caught breaking into his home. The millionaire businessman believed that his man Carl was caught by the police. The Professor wanted to see him that night to discuss their problems. Logan remembered his last brush with Phelps. He knew that Phelps was capable of doing anything. Logan planned to save the Professor's daughter. Hawke believed it was risky. After Carl confessed he had been assigned by Phelps to kidnap the Professor, Hawke dragged him off too somewhere secret.

Later on Logan phoned Briggs and left a message on his answering machine at home. He didn't want Briggs to tell Hawke about his ex-wife just yet. The Professor didn't like Logan's crazy idea to rescue his daughter. But he didn't have a choice in the matter. He only wished his daughter would be safe. Logan was making sure that nothing would happen to the Professor or his daughter. On the way to see Phelps, Logan wondered if Hawke had called the local cops.

Professor Titus James shuddered as he stopped his car in the empty street. He looked uneasily at the gun stuck in his gut and then at Logan. 'I don't think this is necessary Mister Jarrett'. 'I'm only being cautious' Logan stammered. 'Now get out of the car and remember, do everything exactly as I say. Phelps is an extremely dangerous man'. The two men reached their destination. The meeting place was in a deserted area in Tottenham Hale. There were warehouses up for sale in the vicinity but nobody wanted them. Jason Phelps had picked the meeting point, and had chosen well. Logan wondered if he would catch the crook considering the circumstances. He also hoped Hawke would arrive at the place on time as they had planned.

Professor James coughed as if he was about to talk, but Logan's left hand covered his mouth. The professor could feel on his throat, the coldness of blue steel of the gun Logan held. Then all of a sudden car headlights flashed directly at them from the distance, and in a few seconds everywhere in the street seemed alive. The Professor was frightened but stood his ground in the glare of the light as more car headlights were turned on. Logan said nothing. He could see there were three cars parked in a slight curve. From behind the wheel of one of them there was a murmur of some sort then someone shouted. 'You're late, we said twelve o'clock and it's now three minutes past twelve'. The voice belonged to someone in Phelps' Team. It wasn't Phelps. Logan and the Professor ended up standing a few yards from the cars. Nothing happened for a full minute then the Professor shouted with great difficulty. 'It's not my fault Mister Phelps'. 'Whose is it then?' The voice in the dark asked.

'Mister Jarrett's'. The Professor replied. 'And he's not talking to me. He wants to see you, Mister Phelps'. Silence followed, nobody said a word. After a long while the voice said, 'Tell Mister Phelps what he needs to know' 'Damn it!' The Professor said. He was still in Logan's iron grip. 'Talk!' 'All right!' The voice said angrily. 'What does he really want?' 'How do I know?' Professor James said. 'Please let him see you, Mister Phelps'. The murmuring started again, shortly after this, another voice shouted from a different direction. 'I must say I'm quite surprised to see you Mister Jarrett. Can you tell me why you're really interested in the Prof's daughter? You're already spoiling the fun I was about to have with him'.

There was certainly no trace of emotion in the voice. It was cold and chilling. Logan knew it belonged to none other than Jason Phelps. Logan whispered something into the Professor's ear, and then the archaeologist said, 'For heaven's sake. The man is going to use his gun on you or me, if you or your men try anything stupid Mister Phelps'. 'Why should he?' Phelps asked angrily. 'He's in no position to, besides Jarrett still hasn't said what his intentions are yet'. 'Mister Jarrett wants to make a deal Mister Phelps'. Professor James said. 'He says it will be in your best interest if you listen to what he has to tell you. He tells me you've met before'. Jason Phelps was stunned. He said, 'Is this some kind of a sick joke? If it is, for the life of me I can't imagine which sort. You're full of surprises Mister Jarrett. I wonder if you are whom you claim to be. Who are you really?' There was no response to this question so another voice asked seconds later, 'Do we have a choice boss?' 'I don't think we do Samson. Bring the girl here'. Phelps replied harshly.

Minutes passed and nothing happened, suddenly a young woman loomed out of the dark running towards the two men. She breathed heavily and called out to them, 'Dad, it's a trap!' In that instant all hell broke loose. Machine gun fire stitched the ground with bullets. It came from Phelps' car and hit the girl. She fell down shrieking in pain. More bullets blasted the ground where she lay. Logan bit his lower lip cursing himself silently. He knew this was coming. He had tried to gain some time until Hawke came with the troops. Damn it! Where were they? Everything had gone the way he had planned it until now. Flinging the Professor down on the ground, he returned the fire with his pistol.

Headlights shattered and a man screamed. Just then Hawke arrived on the scene with some thirty policemen. A fleeting shadow ran off into an alley. Logan knew it was Phelps. He was about to chase after him, but before he did he said to Hawke. 'Get the Prof and call an ambulance, the girl's been hit'. He then took off.

During the commotion Phelps's men ran off in different directions. The policemen scrambled out of their cars and gave a chase. Derek Hawke ran towards the girl and sighed heavily as he helped her. 'I wonder why I break the rules with you Mac' he muttered. 'I just hope you stay out of sight'.

34

II

It was bright, sunny and just after midday the next day. A tall, lanky fellow made his way towards a table. Ruth Ryan sat there. She was wearing dark sunglasses and was strikingly beautiful in her dress. Ruth heaved a huge sigh of relief when she saw Nick Slater. Ruth had wondered if the man had cancelled the meeting, he'd agreed to have with her, that afternoon at the café near the park. She had asked the man not to come late. Nick Slater was late and was doing nothing to hide that fact.

'What took you so long Nick?' Ruth asked, knowing she would not get a straight answer. The man had reached her table and was trying to make himself comfortable in a chair. When he did, he ignored the question and smiled.

Nick Slater noticed that there were a few couple's eating sandwiches and drinking beer in the café he had stepped into. The place was just a few yards away from the hustle and bustle of Bounds Green station, which overlooked the big park in the area. 'Come now, Miss Ryan' he said. 'I thought we had an agreement here. Never mind. I was busy taking care of your little problem'. Nick Slater was in his early fifties. Although he had a craggy looking face, he seemed like a fairly intelligent bloke. He was wearing a fedora which was slanted slightly. Even though the suit he wore was well pressed, it was not expensive. The girl had hired the man to keep an eye on the Rat, and had used his services before in the past.

'I'd almost given up on you'. Ruth said. 'Let's get down to business'. She looked around to see whether they were both being watched, but there was no indication of that happening. She could not afford to be compromised. Ruth knew Logan needed information and fast. There were already enough complications linked with this caper. 'I'm impressed'. Nick Slater said. 'But I must say that your fascination for the bizarre still intrigues me. I shouldn't really find all that hard to comprehend, since both of us appear to be in the same line of work'. 'What have you got for me?' Ruth said. 'I'm looking the other way after this job lady. There was definitely something not right about it to begin with'. Slater said. 'What you decide to do is entirely up to you. But from what I've learnt your boyfriend might be way over his head in trouble if he isn't careful. The man you seek is very dangerous. In fact the word out on the street is that you don't mess with him'. 'Keep talking'. The girl said. She knew she could rely totally on Slater's remarkable talent for collecting information. 'Rat is employed by a lawyer called Meyers under the name Louis Kidman'. Slater sighed. 'His real name is Quentin Baker. He's also been hanging out with some

35

fellow high up in the Police, whom I understand has had a run in with some Colombians'.

The girl fidgeted a bit in her seat for a while then said, 'Tell me more'. 'There's nothing more to tell'. Nick said sighing again. 'By the way, nobody knows how he got crippled. Do you have any ideas?' Ruth shook her head. She was still thinking about what Nick had said. She eventually said, 'Get digging into his medical history'. Nick Slater looked at her with something akin to contempt. 'When will you ever learn to say please?' He asked. 'When you learn to become a real gentleman' Ruth said. 'When haven't I?' Nick asked, taken aback. 'I'd have to think about that one'. Ruth said thoughtfully' Meanwhile, I'd like to think you'll still keep doing the good work'. 'What do you think I've been doing for the past two days?' Nick said distastefully. He sensed the change in her demeanor and the familiar banter in her voice. It was friendly again. The man was almost sure Ruth was excited about something. He only wondered what it was. He said nothing.

'Do me a favor Nick'. Ruth said. 'Find more dirt on Baker. His current employer might be associated with the policeman in some way'. She got up from her chair. Nick Slater looked at her seriously and said, 'This will cost you, lady'. 'I know'. Ruth said 'That's why I'm counting on you to make it worth my while. One thing's for sure Nick. Mr. Jarrett will definitely appreciate this'. 'I'm not sure about that Miss Ryan'. Slater said. 'But I'll do the job nonetheless'. He got up from his seat and strolled off. There was a puzzled look on Ruth's face. For a moment she thought about the Cop. Who was he and who were the Colombians?

III

Ruth Ryan had a puzzled expression on her face as she watched Logan pace back and forth in his flat. 'What are you going to do now Mac?' She asked. 'I've no idea Sweets' Logan whispered. 'This isn't over yet. Something's definitely not right especially with Phelps now on the run'. He turned round to face his girlfriend. Three days had gone since the fight in the slums. Logan had told Ruth all about the shootout. He also told her that Professor James and his daughter were now being taken care of, in the same hospital Lukman had been admitted in.

Logan couldn't find Phelps. The crook, as it seemed, had disappeared without a trace. There were now rumors on the streets that he had fled the country. Logan had phoned Hawke that morning and had told him about his findings. Derek Hawke had contacted the police about Phelps' disappearance.

Phelps' men had been rounded up by the police, and were being held for further questioning. Logan was relieved to know he had destroyed Phelps's plans. But he was uneasy when he had learnt what Briggs and Ruth had come up with. Briggs had found out that Payne and Hawke's ex-wife had once worked together as a team, which was part of Phelps' spy Network. Briggs couldn't tell if anyone else was on the team. Logan believed Rat could be connected with the spy ring. Briggs also discovered Payne had something to do with Samantha Hasting's death. It seemed the girl wanted out of the organization, but she was murdered to keep everything very quiet and not tell anyone what she knew. Logan confirmed most of his suspicions when he had read the file Briggs had been working on, which he had then copied and given to Ruth.

It seemed Rat had wriggled his way into a lawyer's life, and that lawyer turned out to be Derek Hawke's boss. Logan wanted to find out why. Logan suddenly went to his desk and picked up the telephone and dialed the number Ruth had given him. The phone at the other end rang and after a while someone picked it up. He said, 'Your game's up Rat! I know your secret, just like you know mine'. Logan dropped the phone. It rang again. Ruth looked at Logan. Logan picked the receiver. He said, 'Jarrett'. 'Who gave you my phone number Jarrett?' Rat asked. He was in a posh office in Central London. The office belonged to Adrian Meyers. 'You've been following me, haven't you?' 'I won't answer that question Baker, or is it Kidman now?' Logan asked. 'Tell me something Rat, you knew all about the dead woman didn't you?' 'How did you figure that out?' Rat asked tersely. 'Both of you were associates of Eddie Payne. Both of you incidentally worked for Jason Phelps' Logan replied. 'You're deeply involved in something and you're not talking about it, something that had to do with the accident you had'. 'Cut it out Jarrett' the Rat snapped. 'I've always admired that inquisitive mind of yours, but none of that is any of your business'. 'Payne's dead'. Logan said. 'He was found in a rented flat in town. The police think that someone killed him. Phelps was renting the place Payne was found murdered in, and because of that it's all over the newspapers'. 'You might still be the best sleuth in the business Jarrett'. Rat said dryly. 'But you'll never put the pieces of this puzzle together'.

The line went dead so Logan hung up the phone and looked at Ruth. The girl went straight towards him and hugged him. 'Thanks Sweets', Logan whispered 'You can see this job is far from over'. 'I can see that' Ruth said smiling. 'But what are you going to do about it?' 'Now that's a good question'. Logan whispered. 'I think I've got an answer'. 'What exactly do you mean?' 'I don't think Phelps has flown the country yet'. Logan whispered. 'I might be able to catch him. The Rat might contact him' an hour later Ruth went home. Logan kept thinking. What was the Rat really up to, and did it have anything to do with Phelps' plans? There were so many unanswered questions. Logan hoped to find something that linked Rat with Professor James. There had to be something that did, he thought. He was bent on finding out what it was.

Unfortunately, Ruth's informant couldn't find anything that linked Quentin Baker with Phelps spoilt intentions, so Logan pondered on whether Rat's involvement in all this had anything to do with a particular job. Phelps and his cohorts probably had no idea that the Rat was still alive. Logan had read in Briggs report that the gang had taken an interest in Paul Lukman. Reasons for this were still unknown. But the police had established that Lukman was a well-known collector of anything ancient, Phelps had demanded something from him. The Police didn't say what Phelps wanted from the collector. Logan knew Rat was being secretive about something. If Quentin Baker was interested in finding what Phelps had demanded from Lukman he would certainly go undercover using an alias, which would help him get around. It would also allow him to work for someone like Derek Hawke's boss, a man who knew Lukman quite well. Logan shivered as he thought of something else. He still wondered if Hawke's boss knew more than he had let on, or was he conniving secretly with the Rat. Logan couldn't shake off that thought then he remembered something. The Rat tried to contact George for some reason. It seemed very obvious now that Baker was not only carrying a huge chip on his shoulder about something, but was hiding under a false identity. Why? 'I might just get down to the bottom of this if I knew what happened to the Rat' Logan muttered to himself. He went to the desk again and picked up the phone. He dialed a number as he knew it was time to get in touch with his boss.

CHAPTER 7
Part I

It was almost lunch time, the speedboat bobbed slowly towards the house boat in Chelsea harbor. The young fellow gave last minute instructions to the man driving the boat, then caught hold of the rope ladder and hoisted himself on board the house boat. The man was smartly dressed. His name was Brandon Richards.

Richards was a pimp and a well-known fence. There was no one on deck but he could hear music blaring somewhere, it appeared to come from one of the cabins. He was puzzled, anyway, but he thought at least Johnny's expecting me. Richards went towards the cabins but then waited a while. Still no one came, so then he picked and entered a compartment without hesitation. There on a bed lay a girl reading a magazine. She almost screamed when she saw the man. 'Where's Brown?' he asked 'Johnny's in his cabin' the girl said 'He's listening to Classical music. He sent the boys off on an errand'. 'You don't need to get up darling' Richards grinned. 'I'll make my way to his cabin. Johnny's expecting me'.

He shut the door behind him and went to the cabin where he'd heard music coming from. Richards rapped on the door twice, the music was turned down and the occupant came out. His name was Johnny Brown, he was a fat man with bushy eyebrows and he was one of Richards' dodgy men. The fat man looked at his watch and groaned when he saw his visitor, 'I've been waiting for you Richards. What time do you call this?' 'Sorry I'm late Johnny but something cropped up'. 'Then you'd better come in'. Brown said. 'I thought we settled everything last night. Now what's wrong?' Richards ignored the question and followed the fat man into the room and said, 'You've got good taste in women' he smiled. 'Who's the damsel in distress?'

'Enough of that Richards' Brown snapped. 'You know I'm a busy man. Has something happened?' 'You could say that it has Brown'. The cabin was neat and tidy so Richards sat down on a chair. 'I'm not sure, maybe, that's why I came to see you'. 'What do you mean?' Brown asked. He turned off the stereo in his room and sat on the bed. Richards sighed. 'I got a phone call from a guy called Louis Kidman this morning, have you ever heard of him?' he asked. 'No. I haven't' replied Brown 'Why should I? 'You seem worried about something?' 'I think I've a right to be Johnny' Brandon Richards said slowly. 'This guy whoever he is, offered me a bribe to stall Phelps from leaving town'. 'What does that mean, and how much is this guy offering to pay you?' Brown asked. The fat man was beginning to feel uncomfortable. He didn't like this news at all, and he had good reason not to. At first Brown didn't want to get involved with Richards' plan to help Jason Phelps. He knew all this was very risky for him. He had read about the man's escape in all the daily newspapers and knew the police were looking for him. Brown only decided to help when Richards paid him a visit the other night. The fence told him that Phelps was hiding in his house. It seemed Phelps had run to the fence and had managed to convince him to do something about the trouble he was in. The fat man had learnt that Phelps would do just about anything to get out of the country, and he was ready to pay lots of money if someone like Brown would take on the job. Brown had accepted the job on one condition that he would be paid the money up front. Brown knew Richards had done business in the past with Phelps so he didn't concern himself with the thought of whether the man would pay back Richards or not. The only thing that had crossed his mind then, was whether he would pull off this job. He had been paid quite a large sum of money, twenty-five thousand Pounds in all. The fat man had decided Phelps would be better off leaving by sea. He felt nobody would suspect a man traveling under a false name by ship.

Brown had sent off his men to go in search of a man named Douglas. Douglas was an expert forger and could handle Phelps Passport, if he was paid the right amount of money. Brown was aware that Phelps had bank accounts all over the world so he wasn't surprised when Richards told him that the man wanted to escape to Mexico. But Brown still wished secretly that he hadn't anything to do with helping Jason Phelps to leave the country. 'It simply means that this guy Kidman definitely knows something about the mess Phelps has got himself into'. Richards said angrily. 'He offered me twenty five-thousand pounds and a whole lot more if I kept quiet about the whole affair'. 'How much money are we talking about?' Brown asked seriously. 'A lot more - but that's none of your business Johnny'. 'Then what is Richards?' Brown asked. 'How the hell did this man find out about you, since you don't know him?' The fence suddenly got up from his chair. 'Contacts' he said. 'You know, it surprises me to say this Johnny, but I think I gave the game away when he saw I was interested in the cash he had to offer. But of course I had other reasons for giving in. I'm a good business man, and I'd like to meet this guy in the flesh'.

'What else did he tell you? I'd like to know what I'm dealing with here Richards'. Brandon Richards nodded his head. 'Yes, you've got a point there' he said. 'But there's also a little problem, Louis Kidman didn't say when he'll call me again, but I'm sure he will. I just wanted you to know about this because it seems that somehow we'll have to delay this job for a while. At least until I see this other thing through. You see, I think Kidman could be involved with something else I've been trying to look into. Some fellow called Jarrett'.

'Does Phelps know anything about this Richards?' Brown asked. 'He doesn't, and he won't. That's why I came to see you. I want you to come up with some kind of excuse if he starts getting worried'. 'You've got a lot of nerve to come on board to tell me all this Richards'. Brown said disgusted. 'But I'll do it, what's in it for me anyway?' 'Money!' Richards said smiling. 'I'll start paying once I get in touch with our new associate. But I'd really like to know why he wants to meet Phelps'. 'Well'. The fat man said. 'That's your problem'. 'You'll be hearing from me soon'. Richards said. He walked to the door. He looked at his watch and saw it was now one o'clock 'I'll see myself out. My boat will be here shortly. 'You're the boss Richards'. Brown sighed. 'Do what you feel is best. But, leave my girl alone'.

II

'Are you out of your mind Hawke?' Logan asked angrily. 'What were you trying to prove when you let that monster escape? 'No, I'm not out of my mind. I deliberately let him escape. Remember, I said I would put one of my best men on him'. Derek Hawke shut the door gently behind him and made his way to a settee. He sat down and looked up at Logan. Derek Hawke had come round to the flat to explain a few things. Logan had learnt that his boss had let Phelps' man escape. Hawke had told him over the phone that the thug might know where Phelps was hiding and could lead them to the place.

41

CHIMAIJEM I. EZECHUKWU

'I presume you let him grab the newspapers somehow didn't you?' Logan asked dryly. 'Yes' Hawke said nervously 'but that's not the point. This is. We've got to find Jason Phelps'. 'Point taken, skinny man' Logan whispered. 'But that stooge could have gone anywhere. Are you positive your man won't end up dead somewhere if the man finds out he's being followed?' 'Give me some credit damn it'. Hawke snapped. 'Nothing, like that's going to happen because the word's gone out on the streets that this man's gone missing'. 'I see' Logan whispered. He wasn't happy with this revelation. 'So when does this fellow get back to you?' 'Soon' Hawke said. 'In fact he might call here. But that won't stop me asking you about the man with the walking stick?' 'What did you just say?' Logan asked startled. 'You heard me, Mac? Hawke said sternly. 'Are you hiding something from me?' Logan shook his head. 'No' he whispered. 'I just didn't realize you were going to ask that question'.

Logan realized again that Hawke still had no idea that his dead wife had something to do with this case, and to tell him about the Rat would be letting the cat out of the bag. 'Come on, Mac'. Hawke urged 'What aren't you telling me?' This is insane thought Logan, I've got to divert Hawke's attention before he finds out I'm avoiding the question. Suddenly the phone rang. He picked up the phone. 'Who's this?' he asked. 'I want to speak to the skinny man'. The husky voice said on the other end of the line. Logan raised a hand and his boss got up from the settee. Hawke took the receiver from Logan. 'JB?' he asked. 'Phelps's man was seen heading towards the Silver Bar restaurant. I think he's planning to meet someone there. That restaurant was one of Phelps favorite places'. 'Stay on it'. Hawke said. 'I've got other things to take care of'. He dropped the phone and looked at Logan. 'What do you think Mac?' 'I don't know what to say' Logan replied. 'It's a long shot. This man could be meeting anybody'. 'Well, that still doesn't explain why you've been avoiding my question' 'I haven't'. Logan whispered. 'I was just thinking. You see Derek, I'm quite sure your boss knows more about this, than he's letting on to you'. Hawke was surprised. 'Sit down, Mac' he said. 'I think you need to tell me something'. Logan shook his head. 'You don't get it do you. Your boss might have employed that spy to keep his eye on you'. 'Why?' Hawke asked baffled. 'He's never done such a thing before. And that would be utterly absurd anyway. Look, I know the old man has his strange habits. But he wouldn't do that, he trusts me'. 'I know he does Derek'. Logan whispered. 'But at the back of my mind I have a very funny feeling that he's the one, not telling you something.'

'Where's all this leading to, and what the hell are you talking about?' Hawke asked. 'I asked my girlfriend to make some enquires about the creep following you'. Logan whispered. 'Did she come up with anything?' Hawke asked impatiently. 'Yes, she did'. Logan whispered. 'Well, come on, then'. Hawke said. 'Who is he?' Logan sighed. 'He calls himself Louis Kidman' he eventually whispered. 'But I don't think that's his real name'. 'What makes you say that?' 'Ruth found out the man is a crook'. 'What happened to the man?' Hawke asked. 'You know that's the strange bit'. Logan whispered. 'Nobody knows for sure what really happened to him. But it's my guess he might have taken a fall during a job'. 'Well that still doesn't explain why you think my boss knows something we don't'. 'I wouldn't be so sure about that skinny man'. Logan whispered. 'This guy has been seen hanging out with your boss for quite a while now. From what I've learnt, they've been spotted together at some of the best places in town. That counts for something which state's a lot'. Hawke wanted more answers. 'Damn it!' he exclaimed. I wish this wasn't happening. You still haven't convinced me yet'. 'I intend to'. Logan whispered.

III

Jason Phelps suddenly woke up from a deep sleep. He was wearing pajamas and was in a bedroom. Phelps was sweating and he felt numb, he had another nightmare. It was late and getting dark, but he could still see in the room. Where was Richards? Thought Phelps. The fence had told him he was going out to do business with someone. Phelps slowly tried to get up from the bed he was laying on, but he couldn't. He was very weak so he lay down again with many things going through his mind at that moment. He had been through hell these last few days. Phelps still couldn't understand why things had turned out the way they had. He should have known that someone else would be in on this deal. After all, the mystery man called Jarrett had found out about his idea to steal the hidden gold in Mexico in the first place. He must have learnt something from Payne. Damn it, this shouldn't be happening Phelps thought. Phelps knew he had screwed up the whole job but he still held the mystery man responsible for all that. Thanks to him he was now a fugitive. Phelps remembered vividly how he had stumbled and fell while running away from the cops. He had managed to lose them but he had almost suffered a heart attack. Phelps had never run so much in his Life. He remembered getting in touch with Brandon Richards using a petrol station phone. Phelps had been in a state of shock when Brandon Richards found him by the petrol station after everything had quietened down. Brandon Richards had offered to take Phelps back to his place, and the fence had promised to help him escape out of the country, but Phelps was frightened. He had good reason to be. He had seen the mystery man in his dream. Phelps was sure he would hunt him down soon if something wasn't done quickly. Phelps asked Richards to try and find out who the man really was.

The mystery man had ruined everything. Phelps hadn't come out of the bedroom much except when he really had to, and he had most of his meals in there. Phelps had to admit that Richards home was beautiful, well-guarded and the security systems were fantastic. Richards had made sure Phelps was comfortable and well fed, but Phelps doubted very much whether Richards' man could pull this job off. There were so many risks involved. Phelps didn't really want to rely on Richards or anyone else at this point, but he had no choice. Suddenly the phone rang. It was on the table beside the bed. Phelps hesitated, and then picked up the phone; he felt it could be Richards. 'Who's speaking?' he asked softly, his voice quivering. 'Brandon'. Said Richards on the other end, there was Jazz music in the background 'How are you?'

'I'm managing'. Phelps said weakly, recognizing Richards's voice. 'Where are you?' 'I'm at our favorite meeting place, The Silver Bar'. Richards said chuckling 'I've got some good news for you. I've also got a few surprises. 'What do you mean?' 'Carl's here' Richards said seriously. 'You're not kidding me, are you?' Phelps asked. He was suddenly alert and he tried to sit up in bed. 'Why should I, do you want me to waste him?' 'No' Phelps said' 'Is he really with you?' 'Yes. He is'. Richards said sighing. 'I better bring him home then, I haven't learnt much from him though'. 'What do you mean?' Phelps asked. 'It's hard to explain' Richards said puzzled. But I think he's shaken up about something. It's to do with your mystery man. You should see him, he's scared stiff'. 'Bring him with you'. Phelps said. 'We might learn something. What's your man doing? I'm beginning to get bored'. 'I can't imagine what you're going through. Brown's still on the job, but there's been a complication. He might want, or need more money. We'll talk about that when I get back. Sit tight'. The phone went dead. Jason Phelps put back the phone on the table. He didn't know what to think now, and he was at a loss for words. What could be going wrong now? Phelps thought. The mystery man was lurking in the dark somewhere out there, but he just didn't know where.

CHAPTER 8
Part I

Brandon Richards dropped the phone and looked at his watch. It was just after seven. He sighed. Richards was in the manager's small office in the Silver Bar restaurant on Old Street. He had contacted Jason Phelps using the phone there. The manager suddenly entered the room. He was tall and lean and immaculately dressed in a dark suit. He had to be because of his job. 'I take it that it's been quite an evening Mr. Richards' he said 'Do you want anything to eat or drink?' 'No thanks Saul' Richards said slowly 'I'm afraid I'll be taking my friend home very soon, is he still in the bar?' 'Yes, the man is anxiously waiting for you'. Richards nodded his head. 'I'll be out soon, you had better tell him Saul, and I'll be right behind you'. He said. The manager smiled warmly and left the office. Richards paced the floor. He sighed again. It had been quite an evening all right. He was worried about something. An anonymous phone caller had made contact with him. Richards knew it was the stranger who had offered him a bribe to slow down Phelps leaving the country. Richards was puzzled. What was this guy actually up to, and why was he so desperate to meet Phelps?

The man didn't say much when he was asked, but he made it clear to him that he was meeting him that night with the money to pay him. That meeting was set for ten o'clock. Richards felt a cold shiver run down his spine. What on earth was he going to do now? He felt uncomfortable with the whole idea, he knew something wasn't right, but he didn't know what. Richards wondered if this stranger knew that Phelps was hiding at his place. Richards didn't think he did, and he wondered where the man called Jarrett fit into all this. There was

45

something else. Phelps's man had walked into the restaurant looking for help. It seemed the man had been there for a long time. Phelps' man had told him that the mystery man was with another man. It was Hawke. The man had also told him he had been held a prisoner at some dump that was used as a hideout, but he had managed to escape from there.

Richards was lucky he found Phelps's man when he did. He had just come into the restaurant to have a drink and to meet some old friends. Richards recalled Saul had asked a few nosey questions about Phelps, and then told him about the man who wanted to see him. Richards eventually decided he was going to find out what Kidman was up to, even if it meant jeopardizing Phelps's plans. He made for the door then suddenly stopped. He wondered whether he should contact Johnny Brown, he felt he could use him again. Meanwhile in the bar, the manager watched Carl closely, and then cast his eye at the smartly dressed newcomer who had walked in. The newcomer was a young man and he seemed loaded with cash. His name was Jed Booker.

II

Logan quietly slipped into the hotel suite. He closed the door behind him and switched on the lights. So far so good he thought but not good enough, I'm running late and it's now eight o'clock. He sighed. I just wish I knew what you were really up to Rat he thought. Logan knew he couldn't let anybody find him here. He had come smartly dressed to the Dorchester Hotel, in Central London. It was one of the best hotels in town. He had asked the pretty receptionist at the desk the name of the man staying in the suite. Logan knew the man's name but simply wanted it confirmed, and did. At his flat earlier, Hawke had let the name of the chap working for him slip and so had told Logan where he could be reached. Logan decided to pay the man a visit, after Hawke had left his apartment.

Logan knew Hawke still had fiercely loyal friends who worked for him as operatives but he didn't know there was someone who was a rich playboy on the list. Logan wondered where the man was. He noticed the rooms were big; they were also neat and tidy. Logan was heading towards the window when he heard footsteps in the corridor. He switched off the lights and darted back into a corner, hiding behind the door. Someone was opening the door, although he wasn't sure who it was, he was willing to take the chance to find out who was coming into the suite. He wished it was the informant. Logan sprang into action as the figure walked in, and switched on the light, it was a man. Logan came down on him in a flying tackle and both of them went down in a heap on the floor. Logan grabbed the man's wrists and pinned them right behind his back.

'Who are you?' The man asked. He was struggling to break free from Logan's grip. 'Shut up' Logan whispered. 'You don't need to know that. I'll ask the questions here'. 'What do you want from me then?' Logan was mildly surprised but he ignored the question. For a moment he wondered if he was talking to the right man. 'Where's Phelps's man being taken or do you want me to beat it out of you?' 'What makes you think I know that?' Jed Booker asked. 'Look' Logan whispered 'I don't have time to argue with you, but I know you're working for a guy named Hawke'. 'All right' Jed Booker said angrily. He was still struggling, 'But you'll regret this if I find out who you are'. 'Don't count on it'. Logan whispered. He was holding Jed Booker down in a firm grip. 'Just tell me where the thug is'. 'He went off with someone, a fence called Richards took him back to his place, I followed them. The fence lives in the very posh area of East Finchley, he's got a big house there, in fact it's a mansion and it's well guarded. The address is 247 Bishop Avenue. You'll find it'. Logan nodded and said to himself, I'd better had because if I don't I'll never find Jason Phelps. In that split second he hit out hard with his left hand with a karate chop that knocked the man, unconscious.

Logan got up slowly from where the man lay. 'I'm sorry, pal' he whispered. 'There was no other way'. Logan opened the door and shut it behind him, he knew his troubles had just begun.

He left the building. Fortunately there was no one around to ask him awkward questions, not even the really nice girl at the receptionist's desk, Logan wondered where she had gone. He dismissed this thought from his mind and stopped a taxi that took him back to his flat. After changing his clothes he made a phone call. He got in touch with an old contact and made enquires about Brandon Richards. What Logan learnt about the fence wasn't good. And he was more than a bit nervous when he realized what he was about to face. His contact told him about the security guards and the dogs that guarded Richards place. He also disclosed how to get into the grounds of the house that night.

Logan hung up after he talked to his contact. He smiled grimly. 'I just wish you could help me on this one skinny man' he muttered. 'But you can't, so this won't be fun and games' Logan shook his head slowly. It was time to face the ungodly again.

III

Brandon Richards refilled his drink of Champagne and then raised his glass in the air. 'I think you should relax Phelps. Give the man a break, at least. He's avoided the cops for God's sakes. Remember they're still swarming all over the place'. Jason Phelps couldn't help but wonder what that really meant. He now wore clothes that he'd borrowed from his host's closet but he also had his pistol, which was hidden away. Phelps stood still in the middle of the lounge and stared at Richards for a while then turned his gaze on Carl. The man was sitting down in a corner. He was afraid. Phelps had decided not to respond to the comment. He had enough troubles on his plate as it was, and he didn't want to fall out with the fence. Phelps had wondered whether Richards knew something else that he didn't. Phelps didn't trust the fence one bit. Phelps had learnt all he needed to know from his own man, but wasn't impressed. He had kept in mind that part of Carl's story could be a concocted tale forced on him by Richards. Phelps wondered then if Richards had any other tricks up his sleeve after the two men had come back late.

'And what is that supposed to mean if I may ask?' Phelps suddenly asked, facing Brandon Richards. 'Leave the man alone damn it!' Richards said seriously 'You can blame him later. We've got enough problems as it is. We have to think of a way to eliminate this new threat'. 'You can say that again Richards'. Phelps said furiously. 'Jarrett has cost me everything. He must pay' 'I'm glad you see it that way Phelps'. Richards said. 'But right now your man could do with a bath. He could do something for us to eat afterwards. I'm feeling hungry'. 'You said you had a surprise for me Richards'. Phelps said. 'You're not hiding anything from me are you, and I hope this has nothing to do with the current plan?' Brandon Richards sipped his drink. He was mildly surprised by the question. 'All will be revealed later'. He said. 'And when will that be?' Jason Phelps asked suspiciously. Richards looked at his watch. 'In the next hour or so' he said. 'I'm expecting someone here, someone I'm sure you would like to meet. His name is Kidman and he's got a business deal to make'. 'Does he know I'm here?' Phelps said alarmed. 'No' said Richards 'But that's why I want you to meet him'. 'This is ridiculous'. Phelps said. 'I should have known!' 'Oh shut up Phelps'. Richards said. 'Don't jump to conclusions yet, this has got nothing to do with double crossing you'. 'What has it got to do with then?' Phelps asked still shocked. 'I don't know this fool you want to introduce to me'. Richards was about to say something when one of his security guards came in. 'what is it Josh?' Richards asked sternly. 'I think we have a little

48

problem Sir. Someone has broken into the grounds'. 'What's going on Richards?' Phelps asked, frantically now looking at the security guard. 'I don't know Phelps'. Richards said. He put his glass on the table. 'But whatever it is, my men had better find out'.

IV

Logan had climbed over the wall in a matter of seconds. The rope he brought with him had come in handy. He hid the rope then moved swiftly through the brush in the dark. Logan wasn't sure, but he thought he had touched something like a thin wire in the bushes just after climbing the wall. He had triggered off an alarm circuit linked with the guard house. The two guards on duty that night had informed their chief and untied their dogs. They had then gone in search of the intruder. Meanwhile Logan kept moving, but stopped at a tree to check his directions. Logan knew he was near the barbed wired fence that he had to break through to get into Richards compound. Everything was intact so he checked his pistol. He didn't get round to finish that because he suddenly heard the dogs bark. They were almost onto him; Logan knew he was in trouble. He stuffed the extra bullets into a trouser pocket and quickly put back the pistol in the holster and decided to run. After a while he took his pistol out again as he ran because he could hear voices. Then something happened as he had almost reached the fence. He stumbled and fell, and then suddenly out from nowhere a guard dog attacked him. Logan tried to shoot it but couldn't and lost his hold on the pistol. The gun fell in the dirt somewhere. The dog was all over him. As Logan struggled to get away from the animal the guards arrived, one of the guards came and shone his torch at the struggling figure on the ground. They whipped out their gun's and pointed them at Logan, while one of the guards put a leash on the dog pulling it back as it struggled to attack Logan again. 'I think you better tell us what you're doing?' One guard with a rifle said, letting the other guard pull the dog away. 'Otherwise I'll have to let good old Tim eat you alive'. Logan looked up wiping his mouth with the back of his hand; he was bruised and badly bitten. Logan had blood all over his shirt and he knew it was time to die.

V

Brandon Richards' chief security guard pushed the mystery man down on the floor in front of the other men in the sitting room. He then tossed the man's pistol on a couch. The man turned to the other security men and said, 'I'll take it from here boys, you had better get back to our hut, and you've done well'. The two men nodded their heads in agreement and left. The chief guard looked at his boss. 'What now, sir?' 'Nothing' Richards smiled evilly. 'But you'd better stay here this is going to be fun'. Suddenly Carl got up and without warning threw himself on Logan. He rained blows at the man then got up and then kicked him until the security guard jumped on him trying to pull him away from the wounded man.

'Beat the living daylights out of him Carl, that's Jarrett, Richards'. Phelps said. Richards chuckled. 'At last we finally get to meet the elusive Mister Jarrett'. He gestured at the security guard and the man quietly moved away. 'It's all right Josh' Brandon Richards continued. 'You see Jarrett here has caused Mister Phelps nothing but a lot of grief lately. Mister Phelps only thinks it's time he started to pay up, that's all'. Carl ran back towards Logan and kicked him some more. Logan rolled over on the floor clutching his stomach in pain. 'Enough' Richards said. He snapped his fingers and Carl looked at Phelps. 'I think we're going to have a leadership problem here Phelps. Call off your man or I'll have Josh shoot him down'. The thug stepped back and Richards moved towards him. Richards took a good look at the man. He smiled and then suddenly lashed out at Carl. The man fell to the floor. 'You've forgotten your manners I presume'. Richards said. 'You'll do what I say in here Carl, and you must never forget that, Ever! Carl nodded his head while on the floor and got up gritting his teeth. Richards looked at Phelps. The fugitive crook said nothing so Richards turned his gaze to Logan, who was still on the floor grunting in pain. 'What brings you to my house Mister Jarrett? I believe we haven't been formally introduced yet. My name is Brandon Richards. 'I think Phelps owes you an explanation Richards'. Logan whispered with difficulty 'I wanted to cut him in on a deal'. 'What's he talking about? Phelps asked shocked. 'Kill him'. Richards smiled evilly. 'I want to hear this, what deal are you talking about Jarrett?' 'The Prof told me where the treasure was hidden in Mexico, Phelps!' Logan said. 'You screwed up!'

'Kill him Richards'. Phelps shouted 'Kill him, if you can't I will'. 'Shut up Phelps'. Richards said harshly. 'I've got this under control'. He turned around again and stared at Logan. The mystery man called Jarrett was trying his best to get up from the floor. 'I think you should tell us more Jarrett. I must say I'm really intrigued' Richards said. 'Did all those people have to die Phelps' Logan stammered. 'What exactly were you thinking when you got Samantha Hastings killed and mugged on the street? And don't tell me you've never heard of Quentin Baker'. 'No!' Phelps exclaimed. He went straight to Logan and tried to pull him up grabbing his shirt collar. The telephone on the table rang. Phelps became alarmed. He pushed Logan back onto the floor and looked at Richards. Who is Quentin Baker for god's sake? Richards thought. The fence sighed and went to the table and picked up the phone.

'Richards' he said. 'What is it?' After a few seconds he hung up the phone. 'Who was that?' Phelps asked. He stared at Richards. 'That was one of the boys, Phelps. I've got a visitor. Kidman's coming in, so get your act together'. 'I'll get my act together when you do' Phelps said. 'Leave Jarrett to me Phelps, he's in safe hands. Jarrett's more than welcome to meet my new associate'. 'And this associate happens to be good at something you're not willing to reveal just yet'. Phelps said with disgust. 'What is wrong with you and who's this goddamned fellow you now want everyone to see?' 'You'll see'. Richards said. He picked up his glass of champagne from the table and sipped it. A few minutes later there was a knock at the door. 'Open the door Josh and be ready for anything. There's certainly going to be more fun and games tonight'. Richards put down his drink and looked at the time, it was now ten o'clock.

The security man went to the door and opened it. Rat walked in. He was carrying a small briefcase. He stopped in mid stride when he saw Phelps, and he was even more hesitant when he saw Logan on the floor. 'I think you had better make yourself comfortable Mister Kidman'. Richards said. 'It's a pleasure meeting you at last. My name is Richards. Please ignore my guests if you don't mind'. 'You sniveling sod'. Phelps said 'You've been dining with the devil. I knew you would betray me Richards. Now you have to pay'. Jason Phelps moved away quickly from Logan and brought out his pistol, which he'd hidden. He pointed it at Richards and shot him right in the face. Brandon Richards fell down and was dead in seconds. The security man was surprised by this, he slammed the door shut and began to get his revolver out of its holster but was unsuccessful because Phelps shot him in the kneecap. The man fell to the floor yelling in pain. Phelps then finished him off with a shot to the head. Jason Phelps aimed his pistol at Rat. 'Put the briefcase slowly on the floor Baker and move away from it'. He said. 'Don't try anything you might regret. You might have nine lives like a cat but you certainly have a lot of explaining to do because I thought you were dead. Get the briefcase Carl and check it'. The Rat put the case down and moved away from it. Carl then went forward and took it. He knelt down and tried to open it. 'You set me up at Lukman's place didn't you?' The Rat asked. 'I'm sure your thug Payne didn't know about that. I suspect you shot the poor sod too. You wouldn't have wanted him to find out you were going to use Tom George to run the American's operation'. 'Shut up' Phelps said. 'You're a dead man walking. You were working secretly for Payne all along and I didn't know it. I knew he was up to something and you were spying for him all the time. Now I can see why the Hastings girl decided to leave me'.

'It was a diversion right from the start'. Rat said angrily. 'You not only wanted us to steal from Lukman. You also wanted us out of the picture for good. You cost me a lot of money and a leg Phelps'. 'I have no scores to settle with you'. Phelps said laughing. 'You got what was coming to you, and you should have known better than to come looking for me. It's a shame Richards is dead for a very silly mistake, and because of that you're going to die tonight Baker'. Phelps instructed his man to open the briefcase. 'What's in there, Carl?' 'Money' Carl said grinning. 'Plenty of it, about 20,000 pounds in all' 'Bring it here'. Carl closed the case. Suddenly he crumpled in a heap on the floor. Jason Phelps shot him in the back. Carl was dead. Logan was stunned. He still lay on the floor but he managed to inch away from where he was. So many things went through his mind. He kept wondering if Phelps had forgotten that he was still on the floor.

Logan was horrified by what he had seen. He knew he could be the next target if he didn't do something immediately. He decided to do something when he saw Phelps move towards the dead Carl. Logan had a good idea of what the fugitive was going to do next. Phelps picked up the briefcase and pointed his pistol at Rat.

Logan picked himself up using every ounce of strength he had left and took a dive, smashed through a window. Phelps shot at the hurtling figure of Logan when he saw him make an escape. He missed so furiously he turned back on Quentin Baker and with one shot, shot the Rat right in the heart.

Phelps automatically thought he had killed Rat with that shot. He never checked, otherwise he would have found the Rat was only unconscious because the bullet proof vest he had worn as a precaution, had done its job and kept him alive.

CHAPTER 9
Part I

Derek Hawke rented an old flat near a slum in Turnpike Lane. He liked to call the place a dump. He felt it was one. He used this place as a safe-house. Hawke was there right now. He was pacing the floor of the small sitting room. The detective believed he had a very strange case on his hands. He was annoyed, and had good reason to be. He was infuriated with the mess Logan had presently got himself in. Detective Sergeant Willie Briggs felt differently about all that, he had seen the extent of Logan's injuries. Briggs thought the mystery man would die.

Briggs had risked his neck to hide the mystery man's body from other policemen. He had found the unconscious Logan in the grounds when the police were called in to investigate the killings at Richards place. Briggs had hid the half-dead man in the boot of his car. It was big enough. The Sergeant phoned Hawke. The detective came and carried off his friend. Hawke had brought Logan back to the apartment. He tried to nurse him back to health but with great difficulty. So he called in a doctor friend that same night to tend to Logan's wounds. The doctor had sedated Logan and had left. He promised to look in if Hawke needed his services again. Hawke felt he wouldn't but offered to monitor his friend's progress. He knew he couldn't take Logan to a hospital. He believed someone would start asking questions about him. Hawke recalled that even under a different name trouble seemed to follow his friend around.

Hawke knew that recent developments in the case still didn't make any sense. He was missing something which didn't correspond with Briggs information. He just couldn't put a finger on what it was. Hawke knew that

53

Briggs had been very nervous about something when they had met up at Brandon Richards place. He also wondered whether Logan had something to do with that too. Hawke was horrified to learn that his friend was found half dead at Brandon Richards place. Hawke knew it all had to do with Jason Phelps. It seemed the crook had got away again, leaving a number of dead bodies behind him. Hawke was mildly surprised when he found out the thug Carl was dead. It didn't add up and nothing made any sense here anymore. Why would Phelps kill his own man? Hawke thought, shaking his head. He still thought that Logan was crazy to undertake such a job without his consent. But the detective knew that Logan would do anything to see that Phelps was put behind bars and he had wanted to do this for a long time now. But Hawke still felt it was the wrong thing to do, especially when he hadn't been told about this move.

'You're lucky to escape death again, sonny. But this time you've really screwed up'. Hawke murmured, gritting his teeth. Everything about this case now seemed even more baffling. Hawke considered his friend's narrow escape from death a miracle, but he admitted to himself that Logan had got in and out of scrapes of this sort before. Hawke knew Logan could be a real nuisance sometimes. He had got used to it. 'You should thank your star's Mac'. Hawke said grumbling. 'You had better get well, because you've got a lot of explaining to do. You've been unconscious for four days now. Damn it, we've got to find Phelps. Thank your lucky stars that Briggs told me when he did. But you blew it sonny, and you nearly killed JB as well for God's sake'. Hawke stopped pacing the floor. He had found out from his boss that Paul Lukman had died a night ago. Hawke was becoming suspicious of his employer's interest in all this. It wouldn't have anything to do with the treasure, or could it? He suddenly thought. He remembered his boss had told him that he would let him in on a secret, but he hadn't. The detective had wondered what this secret could be. He hadn't a clue but something told him it was linked with the case.

Hawke sighed shaking his head. 'This beats me' he said moving towards the door. 'But that's no reason to stop this case now. We need to find Jason Phelps'. Hawke sighed, and then he became puzzled again. It was something he had heard one of the guards say before he died. It seemed Brandon Richards had set up a meeting with a man with a walking stick. In the same untidy apartment Hawke was in, Logan opened his eyes slowly in a darkened room. He was sweating, and lay in a bed. Everything was fuzzy to him. He wondered how he had got there but he couldn't remember. The last thing he remembered doing was smashing through the windows of Brandon Richards place. He was trying to escape being killed by Jason Phelps who was preoccupied with the Rat. Logan wondered whether the Rat was alive. He couldn't be, thought Logan. Phelps must have killed him. The man almost had me in his sights too. Logan tried to move but couldn't because he felt an enormous stab of pain in his left side. Although Logan was covered with a blanket, he could see that he wasn't wearing any clothes. There was a lamp on a table and because it was on, Logan discovered he had bandages on him. Everywhere seemed quiet. Where am I? Logan thought. He suddenly gave up and slipped back into unconsciousness.

II

Johnny Brown sighed heavily as he poured himself a glass of water in the suite. Although the fat man was quite impressed with the hotel suite in the Forte Hotel in Mexico, his stomach churned whenever he remembered he was dealing directly with his newest business venture. Brown didn't like that. He didn't deal directly with any of his business associates, especially when he knew they were involved in a particularly bad crime that he could be connected with. Brown didn't want them near him when he was doing any work for any of them. The fat man had always asked his men to take care of them. Brown didn't like the new job he had taken on for Phelps. He didn't want to have anything to do with him because the job was very risky. The fat man sighed heavily again. He admitted quietly to himself that Jason Phelps was doing his best to remain calm under the pressure they had both faced in the last few days. Brown knew the trouble this man had almost got them into while escaping from England was far from over. Brown didn't like the last six days. He had spent them with Phelps avoiding the coastal authorities in Britain, the USA and Mexico. It had all been extremely exhilarating, but he was weary of it all and wanted his quiet life back again.

The fat man knew that Phelps hadn't told him everything that had happened at Richards place. He still couldn't believe that Kidman had shot the fence dead. Brown still knew something was definitely wrong with Phelps story. But he couldn't put a finger on what it really was. Before embarking on the journey to Mexico with Phelps, Brown had learnt from his sources in London that the police were looking all over for Phelps, and that the coastguard had now joined the search. Brown suddenly remembered the things the coastguard over there had put them through, when the boat had been searched and they had been asked for their paperwork. The fat man could now see why Phelps had insisted that he supervise this job. The US Coast Guard was extremely thorough, but not thorough enough to see through Phelps' fake passport.

CHIMAIJEM I. EZECHUKWU

Brown still regretted helping Phelps escape from Britain. Johnny Brown had carried out the operation with precision, and had successfully smuggled the fugitive into Mexico using a container ship.

The fat man couldn't wait to get hold of the ten grand the man had promised to pay him. Brown felt he had done more than enough. He wanted to leave Mexico immediately and really did not want the police to catch him there. Only one thing seemed to hinder him from doing that. Brown wanted the rest of his payment, and the bonus for successfully completing the job. He had been thinking of hiding the money in a new bank account in London when Phelps Visitor came in. Heck! Brown thought. I wonder what's going through Phelps head right now. We've been here for almost a week, and he doesn't seem to be getting anywhere with this guy he wants to meet so badly. When is the old fool going to give me the cash? I've demanded it, but I've got nowhere, I'll have to threaten him with the police. Brown sipped his drink then turned round to face the two men who were with him in the room. Jason Phelps stood with his hands crossed behind him and his face was expressionless. But he watched with candid interest as the other man lit his cigarette. The man was a Mexican. 'So you see Mister Phelps'. Garcia Abrego said. 'Mister Hubbard would like you to hang in there for a while till he gets these things sorted out' 'I want to meet the man, damn it, I'm ready to meet his demands if he has any'. Phelps said trying to control his temper. 'I don't believe I came all this way for nothing'. 'You haven't, but under the present circumstances you can't see my boss just yet'. Abrego said smiling warmly. 'As I said before Mister Hubbard has promised to contact you, and he will. You see he's busy because the local police are trying to link him with some jobs that have been recently done in the area'. Jason Phelps couldn't believe everything was blowing up in his face again. So far he had managed to escape from Britain with Brown's help.

But he now wondered what was going to become of him, if he didn't meet the American he had come to see. After Phelps had checked into the hotel with Brown, he had made a number of phone calls that had eventually put him in touch with the man. The American had told him on the phone that he would send his right-hand man, but he had not said when he would do this. Phelps had hoped the American would help him find the treasure. He also wanted the man to provide him with a place to stay until things cooled down. He really didn't like staying at the hotel. It was too conspicuous. But it seemed all that wasn't going to happen since the police were onto Hubbard. Hubbard's always

56

involved with something, but what has he done this time? Phelps thought. Jason Phelps gritted his teeth as he suddenly remembered the two dead sentries that had tried to stop him before he left Richards place. Phelps could see himself again leaving Brandon Richards place in a hurry using the Rat's car. He had gone in search of Brown and had found him. He had lied to the fat man about the things that had happened at Richards House.

'What would you like me to tell him?' Abrego asked. He crossed the room and stubbed out the remains of his cigarette in an ashtray. Phelps pointed a finger at the man 'I'm ready to pay Rex Hubbard good money as long as he can do what I want and give me protection'. He said. I just want some cooperation from the man. Call him now'.

The telephone on the table suddenly rang. Phelps looked at it as it kept on ringing. He made a gesture for Brown to pick it up and answer it. The fat man picked up the phone. 'Hello'. He said. After a while he held the phone up. 'It's for you Mister Phelps, your Mr. Hubbard wants to talk to you'. Phelps raised his eyebrows as he took the phone from Brown. 'Hubbard'. He asked angrily, 'Is that you?'

A short while later, he dropped the phone and looked at Brown. 'Go and pack your bags Johnny'. He said. 'It seems we're going to meet Rex Hubbard after all, and he wants Abrego to bring us back with him'.

III

Derek Hawke let himself into the place he called a dump. He carried a bag of groceries. Hawke held his breath when he saw the shadowy form of his partner in the neglected sitting room. 'What are you doing sonny?' He asked. He almost shouted. 'What do you think I'm doing?' Logan whispered ignoring the question. He was standing up and wearing a stained shirt which he had not buttoned up. He had just come out of the bedroom he had slept in for almost a week now. Hawke walked right into the room.

'What's got into you Mac?' Hawke asked angrily. 'Are you out of your mind, where do you think you're going?' 'Never mind that skinny man'. Logan whispered. 'Where am I?' 'You know'. Hawke began disgusted. 'For a guy who's been half dead for a few days, you do have a funny way of showing gratitude'. Hawke supported his friend and walked him to a chair. Logan sat down grunting in pain. 'Thanks pal'. 'What's got into you, Mac?' Hawke asked again. 'You nearly got killed at Brandon Richards place. Why can't you do a single thing I tell you? Stay out of sight! Thanks to Willie Briggs the cops didn't find you on those grounds when he did. You screwed up again sonny'. 'I'm

57

sorry, skinny man'. Logan whispered. 'I didn't mean to get you involved in any of this'.

'Whether you like it or not, I'm involved in this, for God's sake!' Hawke snapped. 'Lukman is dead. He gave up the ghost in the hospital a few days ago. So we practically don't have a case anymore, unless we find Jason Phelps or come up with something'. 'What do you mean?' Logan asked. 'It seems like Phelps has skipped town Mac'. Hawke sighed. 'The police can't find him anywhere in this country. My guess is that he organized something after he left you and those men he wasted at Richard's house'. . 'How do you know about that?' Logan asked surprised. Hawke shook his head. 'There was a security team on the premises the night you got yourself into trouble. A man was off duty but had come to see one of his mates who were on duty. The guard who was off duty discovered the dead bodies and got in touch with the police. I think Phelps had a gun fight with the other men on duty that night, because all the bullets fired were shot from the same gun, a .38 Smith and Wesson. Briggs and his men couldn't find the weapon on the grounds, so they think that Phelps must have taken it with him. It was also confirmed that he took a car that belonged to another visitor the police can't seem to get hold of. The dying guard who had given Briggs the information said the visitor's name was Kidman' 'So?' Logan asked. 'From what I was told, Kidman visited Brandon Richards that night. But his body wasn't found amongst the dead. In other words he may have left the house when the shooting began. Anyway, the police found a car parked near a shoe factory. All this sounds intriguing to know because this Kidman fellows head pops up in places where you least expect'. Logan suddenly remembered everything that had happened to him. Damn it Rat, Logan thought. You had a bullet proof vest on. 'I told you' Logan rasped. 'Kidman was dangerous, I don't know what he's got with Richards but I think he's involved with Phelps. How do we find Phelps?' 'That's a good question Mac' Hawke said. 'You're not telling me something though? 'What do you mean?' Logan asked. 'Well, you've been working very closely with Sergeant Briggs on this case. He was acting a bit strange and was very nervous when I talked to him at Brandon Richards' House; it was almost as if he was trying to hide something from me'. 'What could he be hiding from you?' Logan whispered. He shrugged his shoulders. 'Besides you should know him better than that by now'. 'The hell I do!' Hawke said. 'But forget that for now, we've got to find Jason Phelps'. The detective looked at his watch. He couldn't see much so he went towards the old curtains and drew them open, he saw it was now 5pm.'Any ideas?' Logan asked.

He covered his eyes from the light that came flooding into the room. Hawke said one word, 'Mexico'.

'Why, Mexico?' The detective sighed. 'You never cease to amaze me, Mac. My boss thinks Phelps probably escaped to Mexico' 'Why has your boss decided to take particular interest in someone he might be in cahoots with? It doesn't make sense if we look at what we've learnt so far about this case'. 'I must admit that was what I thought, until the old man came clean with me'. Hawke said tiredly. Logan was puzzled. 'What do you mean?' he asked. 'Meyers contacted me yesterday and explained a few things when I went to see him at his office'. Hawke said candidly. 'He's been working hand in hand with someone in the Vice squad. They've been making a series of enquires for the Mexican police for more than two months now. The Mexican police have been having problems with an American character living there. This guy is involved with organized crime and has been suspected for some time now, of smuggling heroin from America into this country. Jason Phelps has been his link and the police here knew that'. 'Where does Lukman fit into all this?' Logan asked curiously. 'He was in on this right from the start I guess'. 'But that was because my boss may have confided in him'. Hawke said. 'Don't forget the man shared an interest with Phelps. They're both crazy about ancient artifacts. They may have even done business together in the past, but we don't know that for sure. But what I would like to know is, how all this is linked with Kidman. Anyway, my boss wants me to go to Mexico. He wants me to find out anything about this American character. He also wants me to find Phelps'. 'I'm coming with you' Logan whispered. 'I don't think there'll be time to debate that Mac'. Hawke said. 'But you sure as hell better get well before I take you along with me. My boss wants me to travel in a few days' time. In fact, I had better tell him your coming with me'. Logan said nothing, he was thinking about what his boss had said. Kidman's head pops up in places where you don't expect him to be. I'm sure you're right about that Derek, Logan thought. He knew he had to find the Rat.

CHAPTER 10
Part I

Detective Sergeant Willie Briggs stood beside an old lamppost in an empty street and looked at his watch for the third time. It was now eight in the evening. It was misty and getting cold. Briggs was tired and he knew he needed to sleep, but that didn't matter right now. Something else did. He wanted to see the mystery man. Briggs had thought that the mystery man was going to die at Brandon Richards place. He still didn't know exactly what that fiasco was all about, but he didn't regret what he had done to keep him alive and out of sight on the grounds that night.

At first Briggs thought that someone could have noticed something. But it seemed nobody had, and Briggs had ever since then thanked his lucky stars. Where is he? Briggs thought. He's late. Briggs believed that Logan was involved somehow with the murder case he was still investigating. He knew he had worked extremely hard on this one case during the last few weeks, but it seemed as if he wasn't getting anywhere with it until now. He wondered if the man would throw some light on this, especially since something else had been discovered. Briggs had a feeling that he would, and Briggs was now totally convinced that there was more to this particular case than met the eye. Briggs was anxious to meet Logan since he had got in touch with him. Briggs was aware that the area he was in was dangerous territory. Logan had told him that young thugs had been known to hang around the place. Briggs hadn't seen anybody yet. He just wondered why the mystery man had decided to set up a meeting near Turnpike Lane tube station.

SNAKE AMONGST SHADOWS

Briggs decided to light a cigarette while he waited, so he put a hand into his breast pocket and took the last cigarette in the packet. Briggs threw the empty packet into a dustbin that was a few yards away from the lamppost. He returned back to the lamppost then cupped the cigarette in his hands and lit it.

Suddenly he heard footsteps. Logan was right behind him. Briggs sighed. He turned round. 'You're late Mister Jarrett'. He said. 'I'm sorry Willie'. Logan whispered. He stood in the shadows. Briggs could hardly see him. Logan was wearing clean clothes and was clean-shaven. 'You called me here to ask me something I presume' Briggs asked plainly. 'I guess I owe you one Willie'. Logan whispered. 'You don't owe me anything Mister Jarrett. I just did what I thought was right'. Briggs said. 'Thanks all the same'. Logan whispered. 'But I'm not buying that, why did you do it?' 'You never cease to amaze me, Mister Jarrett'. Briggs remarked. 'But I can see why your boss holds you in such high esteem. I would only like to know a bit more about your case'. 'What do you want to know?' Logan asked. He came forward. 'Anything connected with the murder I'm working on'. Briggs said, stamping out the remains of his cigarette on the ground. 'The boys at the station have uncovered something linked with your job'. He turned round to see if anybody was coming, nobody was so he continued to talk. 'The boys found out yesterday that Hawke's ex-wife was seen with the dead man named Tom George. My boss's think that George had something to do with her death. I've suspected this for some time now but I didn't know whether you did, can you tell me about that?' 'Your case and mine might be connected but there's really little I can tell you at this point, because I didn't know the girl was meeting the crook'. 'Are you telling me the truth Mister Jarrett?' Briggs sighed. 'Yes' Logan replied grimly. 'I am. I'm sorry I can't help you Briggs'. 'You're still suffering from the effects of that beating you took. I hope you get better soon'. Briggs said. 'Thanks'. Logan whispered. 'I was wondering if you could tell me something. That's why I called you here'. 'What's that?' 'Do you know anybody by the name of Baker?' Logan asked. Briggs shook his head. He said, 'But word has it that Quentin Baker is a thief. Why do you ask?' 'He might have something to do with all this' Logan whispered. 'But I'm not sure yet'. He frowned. 'Now, that you mention it'. Briggs began suddenly. 'I remember one of my men said sometimes he works for someone in Scotland Yard, a high ranking police officer. I never liked this man'. 'Whom are you talking about?' 'Ken Farrell' Briggs said. 'He's as slick as they come, but I think he's a dirty cop. He's in charge of the vice squad. Nobody's been able to prove that man's a cheat yet'. Hawke said his boss was working with someone in the vice squad thought Logan. I think I've stumbled onto something here. Logan coughed then asked. 'Where can I get hold of this Farrell character? 'He's got a place near the office'. Briggs said. 'He likes to stay there. Is he involved with this business?' Logan shook his head. 'I didn't say that Willie' he whispered. 'He might just know where I can get hold of Baker'. 'Yeah he could'. Briggs said. 'But be very careful, I'm told he's dangerous'. 'Thanks'. Logan whispered. 'I'm sorry I can't help with your case'. 'You've said that before'. Briggs smiled thinly. 'Anyway, I'd better run along'. 'Thanks again'. Logan whispered.

II

Derek Hawke looked up from where he sat and saw his boss walk into the office. Adrian Meyers closed the door behind him gently and went straight towards the chair at his desk and sat down. There was a frown on his face. Hawke could see Meyers had something on his mind. Hawke wondered if this had anything to do with the trip he was about to undertake very soon. He had already told his boss that he was taking his man with him on this trip. The old man had agreed to that, he had left the office to retrieve a message from his answering machine. So what could be the matter? Hawke decided to ask. 'What's wrong Sir?' he asked suddenly. 'I'm afraid you will have to alter your plans a little bit Derek'. Meyers said. He spoke arrogantly, but with eloquence.

Sometimes Hawke couldn't believe that he worked for Adrian Meyers. The old man was a brilliant lawyer and he was also a very influential man. He liked to think he was an eccentric. But he actually wasn't, he was just strange. Hawke knew for a fact that the old man loved pretending to be a fool. Hawke had often wondered why he liked playing the idiot. He eventually discovered that the old man hid his true nature to seek out the truth and bring all those unsuspecting criminals to justice. 'I just received a message that confirms that Phelps is in Mexico'. Meyers said. 'Derek, you will be going there as we planned and Professor James will be going along with you'.

'I don't have any objections with that'. Hawke said mildly surprised. 'But why should, we get Prof involved in this again, don't you think it's a bit risky. His daughter needs him here; the poor thing would probably need someone to comfort her till her husband's funeral is over'. 'She will have to do without him' the old man said coldly. 'Jason Phelps is on the run in Mexico and I want him caught. I have a feeling that he won't stop looking for the treasure he wants. That's why I want you and your friend to take the Professor with you. The Professor will lead you to the burial site'. 'Have you spoken to the Prof, Sir?' 'Yes'. Meyers said. 'I spoke on the phone with him yesterday. He's still pretty shaken up by what has happened recently, but he's thinking about it and I'm sure he'll come round'. Meyers pulled the desk draw open and took something out. It was a cigarette holder which he placed on the desk, then got something else out as well, a gold cigarette case. 'Do you have something else to ask me Derek?' he asked. 'Yes I do'. Hawke said. 'Am I supposed to see anyone in particular when I reach Mexico, or do I go it alone?' 'I was coming to that'. Meyers said. He opened the cigarette case and took one out; closing the case he slid the cigarette into the holder. 'You're going to meet a police sergeant out there by the name of Jose Lopez. He's one of my contacts in Mexico City. He's on the case I told you about, I also spoke to him on the phone just before you dropped by. He's sure that Phelps is in Mexico because he sent the message I just got. Anyway, he knows you're coming'. 'It seems you've taken care of everything'. 'I have'. Meyers said. 'You'll be staying at a hotel called The Unicorn, and the Sergeant will meet you there. You've got nothing to worry about. I intend to take care of the Professor's daughter until he comes back. I'm also going to be at the husband's funeral, when that is arranged. Just bring yourself and that friend of yours back here in one piece, and remember, protect the Professor'. 'I'll do my best Sir' Hawke said. 'You'll have to do much more than that' Meyers said. 'All the same, good luck'. Hawke got up from his seat and looked at his watch, it was nearly nine. 'I'm ready to go' he said 'But can I ask you another question?' 'Of course you can, what is it?' Meyers asked 'I wanted to ask you about Kidman' He lit his cigarette. Hawke asked, 'What exactly does he do for you?' The mention of the name made Meyers flinch. But he cleverly covered his dismay with laughter. 'You might not want to know Derek. Just take it that the young man works here as a personal assistant'. Meyers suddenly laughed again. 'You don't have a problem with that, do you?' He asked. Hawke hesitated but then said, 'I don't. I was just curious'. 'I think you have more important matters to attend to' Meyers smiled wolfishly. 'I'll give you the thumbs up to leave London when I've talked to the Professor again. Good evening Derek'. Derek Hawke nodded his head leaving the office. The detective knew instinctively that his employer was covering up for Kidman, but why? Hawke was still wondering why on his way to his car.

III

Logan approached the house on the quiet lane. It was near the offices of Scotland Yard. The bungalow was beautiful. Logan felt someone was in because he could see light coming from a room, probably the living room. For a moment he wondered what his boss might think if he found out that he was trespassing again. Logan knew Hawke wouldn't be happy. Logan decided to follow up on the new lead he had been given by Briggs. You simply give me no choice skinny man thought Logan. He smiled grimly. He still felt sore from the beating he had taken in the last few days. He vowed to get back at Phelps for what he had put him through. Logan knew he was definitely going to settle that score when he went to Mexico. He remembered he had stared death in the face before, and escaped it again.

He crossed the road, but suddenly the lights in the house were switched off. A few moments later someone opened the front door. Logan hid behind a car parked in the lane. But he could see that two men had come out. One of them was the Rat. What exactly is that scoundrel up to now? Logan thought. Hell that must be Farrell with him, but I can't see the man clearly from here.

The two men walked down the pathway till they reached the lane. They were now only yards away from where Logan hid. 'You heard what I said Baker', the second man scoffed. 'Payne is dead and you screwed up again. You almost wound up dead too and to think that your car was used as a runaway vehicle'. The man's name was Ken Farrell. Logan could hardly see his face, but he could make out the distinct features of his companion. The other man was using a walking stick. 'You're obviously upset Farrell'. Rat said smugly. 'But never mind this won't interfere with the new operation'. 'What do you mean?' Farrell asked. 'I'm going to make Phelps pay for this' the Rat said angrily. 'I'm going to ask Meyers for some time off. I'm going to Mexico to find Jason Phelps'. 'I'm letting you go because you're no good to me here. I have my own agenda, Baker. You can go wherever you like but Meyers shouldn't find out about your schemes. You've already jeopardized the whole plan you fool'. 'Face the fact's Farrell'. The Rat said. 'You only want blackmail money from Phelps'. Jesus Christ! Farrell's been involved in this all along, but why? Logan thought. He was still huddled behind the parked car. 'I'm warning you, Baker' Farrell said bursting out in rage. 'Shut up'. 'No!' Rat almost shouted. 'Shut up Commander, I lost a lot of money and I might just get that back if I go after that fiend. Besides I've got to find that masquerade I told you about. My contacts don't seem to know where they can find him. And that's strange because they've looked everywhere for him.

Anyway, I'm not surprised. That son of a bitch might well be on his way to Mexico by now. I always knew he would think about a move like that since he escaped from the house. If I find the man, he could lead me to Phelps'. 'Going to Mexico to do all that would be crazy, but do what you want'. Farrell said patiently 'I'll just tell the old man you left town for a while, but whatever you do, don't come back here sulking'. 'I'll drop you off somewhere on the way to the office. I need to do some work there'. The two men walked past the Volkswagen and climbed into a sleek car parked at the far end of the lane. It was a BMW. As the car shot off Logan wondered what to do next.

IV

Johnny Brown cursed silently as he sat back in the arm chair. He knew it was unwise of him to be in the same room as Jason Phelps and the American named Rex Hubbard. Brown fidgeted in his seat as he still thought about leaving Mexico. He couldn't imagine being held up by the police with these two men in the room. Brown knew he would be killed instantly if the authorities found out about his involvement here. But he had no choice now, whether he liked it or not he was stuck with Jason Phelps. The fat man looked around the sitting room to see whether he could spot Abrego. He suddenly remembered the Mexican had been sent out on an errand. The fat man had found out that the American had a beautiful home in the middle of Mexico City.

The American's house was massive and well-guarded. Brown had felt uneasy when he was searched for weapons. He hadn't expected that to happen to him. Brown felt that anybody would feel the same way if they were on a crime lord's turf. The fat man hadn't carried any weapons on him on this trip, nor had Phelps. The two men had agreed on that before travelling. The fat man had thought of that idea. It was part of his plan to get Phelps out of England. Jason Phelps still couldn't believe that he had come all this way for nothing. He took a long hard look at the man sitting across the room and got up from the settee. 'I don't believe that you can't help me Hubbard' he said. 'I came all the way from England because you said that you could'. 'I never said that I wouldn't help you Jason' Hubbard said smoothly. He was a tall, lanky and smartly dressed American. 'I only meant that I really can't do that right away. I've got a few things I need to sort out first'. 'You're not telling me something'. Phelps said angrily. 'Relax Jason'. Hubbard said sighing. 'You're getting all worked up for no reason. My man must have mentioned that we've been having some problems with the local police. They think I've been responsible for some jobs in the area, well I haven't. My men and I are only trying to clear the air on that'. 'I'm going to pay you a lot of money to protect me, and of course my interests in Mexico'. Phelps said. 'I'm going to do that'. Hubbard said smiling. 'And that's why I want you to stay here for some time'.

'What!' Phelps exclaimed. 'I seem to have found the root of my problems and that's all I'm trying to say Jason'. Hubbard said getting up from his seat. 'I discovered not so long ago from one of my men, that a certain policeman called Jose Lopez is actually responsible for this mess. As I understand it, this man is very efficient and has clout. I also found out something else, he's been onto me for quite a while working with the British Police to stop a new operation which you know all about'. 'Impossible'. Phelps shouted. 'I won't hear any of this, are you accusing me of something I've not done. The Sergeant might be quite a nuisance, but Scotland Yard and the entire Police Force know nothing about the new operation I was handling, I made sure of that'. 'I know you're telling a fib Phelps and you've got a lot of explaining to do' Hubbard said. 'Someone was onto you. Someone you used to know. A man named Ken Farrell, a Police Commander with Scotland Yard. I have proof of this because I have a man working with him'. Hubbard shook his head and laughed 'You are going to have to postpone a lot of things, my friend. But I will seriously consider your proposition, I am disappointed Phelps and I must admit you've come to the right place. I will take care of all your problems. But I'm afraid you have no right to make any complaints whatsoever. It's my pleasure having you at my place but remember one thing Phelps. I now call the shots'.

Brown got up from his chair, but sat down again. He knew they were now being held against their will. Jason Phelps felt sick, he was back where he had begun, but only this time it was worse. He was now being held a prisoner by Rex Hubbard. Rex Hubbard left the room to see to unfinished business with his henchman. He had jokingly asked his guests to do some thinking. Johnny Brown paced the floor. He was nervous. The fat man suddenly stopped pacing and looked at Phelps. 'What are you going to do?' he asked. Phelps shrugged. He stood near a window, and he was watching his companion. 'I haven't the faintest idea but I wonder what Hubbard has in store for us next' he said. 'I knew I shouldn't have listened to you'. Brown said. 'We can't escape from this place. What do we do?' 'We must be patient'. Phelps said. 'I'm going to have to talk with Hubbard again'. 'What are you talking about?' Brown asked. 'For a man on the run, I think you haven't told me the whole truth' 'You don't need to worry about that'. Phelps said. 'I told you everything I could. Leave Hubbard to me. I'll fix it'. 'I'm starting to get tired of all this, Mister Phelps'. Brown said. 'Why won't you tell me why were really here? If you don't, I might have to take sides with the American. The man seems to know a lot about something you don't. Now tell me what this is all about'. 'Enough of that' Phelps said. He pointed at the fat man. 'I'm going to tell you everything. I don't have much of a choice anyway. But I won't tell you right now' he said. 'Fair enough Mister Phelps'. Brown said, 'But remember, you've been warned'. 'I'm aware of that'. Phelps said tiredly, 'Now will you excuse me for a while, I've got some serious thinking to do'. Phelps turned away and sat on a settee. Phelps suddenly became puzzled. He knew that he hadn't handled things well when he set up the new drug ring in England. There had been a lot of complications. Phelps hadn't admitted that to Hubbard and wasn't going to now. But how did Farrell find out? He had made sure that his former friend would not find out about this new business of smuggling drugs into Britain. It then dawned on him that Lukman may have had nothing to do with this trouble that had been caused. You couldn't have had anything to do with this Payne, or could you? Phelps asked himself silently. He then remembered something else. Phelps went to the dining table and slammed his fists hard on it. Brown jumped up from where he sat immediately. 'What's got into you?' he asked.

'Silence!' Phelps said looking at him, 'Richards must have told you about Kidman didn't he?' The fat man nodded his head. 'Well' Phelps said furiously. 'He's dead. But it appears that before his death he decided to make a fool out of me'. Phelps believed for a moment that Quentin Baker could have worked closely with Farrell. Phelps was convinced about this thought. He felt relieved to know he had taken out the man by himself. But something else bothered him. Where was the man called Jarrett?

V

Logan strode into the alley near Hawke's safe house. He was still feeling weak. Damn you Phelps! He thought, I might be down but I'm not out. He went down the alley looking carefully around him for any sign of life. Everywhere was dead quiet. Logan thought about his encounter that night. He had gleaned a lot from Briggs, and his recent discovery that evening had made one thing clear. It was now imperative that he travelled with his boss to Mexico. But only one thing seemed to bother him about all that. He couldn't let Hawke in on the things he had learnt so far in the case. Logan believed that the detective might eventually find out the truth about Quentin Baker. Logan knew he had to find out what Rat and Farrell had been up to, and why it had so much to do with Phelps. He wished he could tell his boss everything he knew. Logan decided he was going to ask Hawke about Farrell. You might just know something about this guy he thought, I hope you do. Logan finally reached his destination. He looked through the window of the small apartment. The light in the sitting room was switched on. Someone was in. Logan looked at his watch. It was nearly eleven o'clock. I hope you don't scream the house down Hawke he thought, but I've got a funny feeling you will.

Logan knocked on the door. Hawke opened it. 'Come in Mac' he said quietly. 'Where have you been?' Logan said nothing. He was mildly surprised to see that his boss wasn't on the warpath already, Logan wondered why. 'I decided to take a long walk skinny man' he said at last, almost lost in thought. 'So did I' Hawke said dryly. 'But you know something, that didn't help matters much'. 'What does that mean?' Logan asked. He followed Hawke in, closing the door behind him. 'I think the old man is using Kidman for a stint, but I'm not sure why'. Hawke said.

He sat down on a couch in the living room. 'What's wrong with that?' Logan asked a bit surprised. 'Don't you trust him?' 'Something's not right Mac and I can feel it'. 'What do we do then?' asked Logan 'We're going to have to play this one by ear' Hawke said thoughtfully 'we're going to Mexico, but I don't know when yet. I assume the old man's going to give me the word very soon. He wants the Prof to come along too'. 'Professor James is certainly going to be a burden Hawke'. Logan whispered. 'Don't you think I know that? Hawke asked. 'But we don't seem to have a choice in this case anymore. Meyers wants Professor James to show me where the treasure is buried'. 'What about his daughter?' 'The old man told me he was going to take care of the kid'. 'So where does that leave us now?' Logan asked. He went and sat down on an armchair. The place was still in a mess. 'We sit here and wait'. Hawke said bitterly. 'What do you know about Police Commander Ken Farrell?' 'Not much I'm afraid'. Hawke said, 'Why?' 'I think he's involved in all this somehow'. 'Tell me you haven't done something stupid Mac'. Hawke asked. He suddenly sat up in the couch. He pointed a finger at Logan. 'I want an explanation from you. What were you doing tonight?' The telephone suddenly jangled. 'That must be your boss'. Logan whispered. 'Or does everybody know we're here'. 'Nobody knows about this place except the old man'. Hawke said. The phone kept ringing. 'I'll answer it, but you're not off the hook yet'. He went and picked up the phone. 'Hello' he said, then listened. After a while he dropped the phone. The detective looked at Logan. 'Who was it?' Logan asked. Hawke sighed. 'That was my boss'. He said. 'He wants us to travel in a few days. He's got word from a contact out there that Phelps was seen somewhere with two men in Mexico City. I can only guess whom he was going to see Mac. I've been asked to get the Professor. So let's move it, we've got some packing to do'. Logan smiled grimly. 'Aren't you forgetting something?' he asked. Hawke shook his head. 'I haven't'. He said. 'We'll talk about Farrell later'.

CHAPTER 11
Part I

The BA plane touched down safely at the International airport in Mexico City. Logan looked at his watch and saw it was now eleven o'clock. He looked out through the window and it was bright and sunny. He could also see a number of people clustered around waiting patiently for their loved ones to descend from the plane. There were also others in the building waiting for the next flight which was due for take-off in a few minutes. Logan heaved a huge sigh of relief when the pilot announced their arrival. He hadn't travelled overseas in a long time and he felt very nervous all through the flight from London. He remembered the plane had to stop briefly in Miami for refueling, and he had wondered then whether the plane was finally going to reach its destination. Logan looked round and saw his two companions getting ready with the other passengers on board, to leave the plane.

They now had their travelling bags with them but were still sitting down. Professor Titus James was huddled in a seat with Derek Hawke close beside him. Logan suddenly remembered that Hawke had started making arrangements for this trip the moment he had been given the nod by his employer. That had been almost two days ago. They had left London for Mexico on a night flight so that they wouldn't attract too much attention at Heathrow Airport. Hawke had his reasons. He didn't want the authorities to ask Logan too many questions. Logan checked his hand luggage, and then remembered he wasn't carrying a gun with him. He felt naked without one. It had made him fidget a lot during the flight. His boss had told him not to carry any weapons with him because everything they needed would be provided by a contact over there. That man was also going to help them find Jason Phelps. Despite that, Logan recalled his boss hadn't given much away about the Mexican trip. His boss had been thinking. But he was also trying to make the Professor as comfortable as possible. The elderly fellow was feeling uneasy and he believed his daughter could still be in danger. The Professor was simply there with them to point out the location of the burial site that Phelps aimed to find. Logan wondered for a moment if the Rat had already flown into Mexico. He had to find out what the crook was really getting up to with Farrell.

Logan ignored the stares thrown at him as he queued up with some passengers to get off the plane. He was deep in thought and the furrow on his forehead was even more noticeable. He thought briefly about the next few days. He knew there would be more surprises. He only wished his boss wasn't so secretive about the operation they were about to embark upon in Mexico. His companions stood up and queued with the rest of the passengers. Logan got up and followed suit.

An hour later when the passengers were leaving the airport Hawke flagged a taxi. The car was an old blue Chevy and the driver was a dark, heavyset Mexican. 'Where are we going skinny man?' Logan asked frowning. He looked around to see if anyone had followed them. It seemed no one had, but he wasn't sure. 'Didn't you say we were going to wait for someone at the airport Mister Hawke?' The Professor asked hesitating. He didn't know whether to climb into the taxi or not. 'I did Professor, but he's late'. Hawke said puzzled. He looked at Logan. 'Get into the car, Mr. Jarrett. Ask the questions later, right now we've got to get to the Unicorn Hotel. It seems Meyer's contact didn't arrive here as planned'. Hawke helped the Professor into the vehicle and then asked the driver to take them all to the Unicorn Hotel. The driver nodded his head waiting for Logan to climb in. Logan sat beside Hawke. He then shut the door and told the man to drive the car. As the taxi sped off another car followed closely in pursuit. 'Senors!' the taxi driver said, he cast his eye at the rear view mirror. The Mexican had a strong accent. 'It seems someone is following us'. Hawke turned around to see the brown car following closely. There were three men in it. Hawke was surprised. Logan and the Professor saw the car chasing them too. Logan looked at his boss, but could tell he had no idea who was tailing them.

'What's going on Hawke?' Logan asked stridently. 'I haven't the faintest idea sonny'. Hawke said. 'But I can see we've got a problem on our hands'. He shook the driver's shoulder. 'Shake him off our tail'. 'I will try Senors' the driver said. 'But remember you haven't paid me yet'. 'Step on it pal' Logan snapped. 'He's certainly going to take care of that'. Hawke said. He couldn't believe this was happening. Professor James was beginning to get frantic and Logan tried to calm him down. 'I'm sorry you got caught up in this again Professor' he whispered. Professor James smiled nervously. Suddenly he spotted something. 'There' he said, pointing at the brown car still following them. Logan and Hawke looked at what the Professor was showing them. A man was seen in the pursing vehicle trying to take aim with his gun at the speeding taxi. The gunman was sticking his head and his body out of the car, aimed, shot and missed. The bullet whizzed crazily past the taxi. He tried again, and missed that one too. The gunman stuck his head back in the car. Someone in the busy street saw him and shouted and the pedestrians all over the place suddenly ran for cover. All hell broke loose, it was pandemonium. Unfortunately there were no police men around the area. 'Karumba!' The taxi driver exclaimed 'What's this?' 'We're being shot at, that's what it is' Logan stammered. He looked at the taxi driver. He felt helpless.

'Move it, pal'. The Mexican successfully turned his car into a bend with screeching tires. He did it with difficulty, trying his best to avoid hitting a group of people crossing the road. While the Professor tried to hide for dear life in the taxi Hawke fumbled in his pockets and came up with some Pesos he'd just got at the airport. 'Look, take this' he said to the driver dropping the Pesos in the man's lap. 'You'll get some more if you can get us out of this situation'. The taxi driver seemed puzzled. He looked at the money that had fallen into his lap and then focused his gaze on the rear view mirror. He stuffed the money into his shirt pocket as he drove. The driver could still see the brown car on his tail. In fact the car was only a couple of meters away now but was also having difficulty maneuvering itself away from another unexpected group of pedestrians who seemed to turn up at every corner of each street the two cars were heading towards.

'No problem senor' the driver said,' 'but remember these people could be the Police. Are you three men involved in some sort of trouble?' 'I don't think that's any of your business' Hawke said angrily, 'Just drive'. The driver swung his car into another bend. The brown Ford was still in hot pursuit. I hope to God you know what you're doing Hawke, thought Logan. This obviously isn't the Mexican Police. Suddenly out of nowhere a Mustang screeched to a halt in front of them. There were two men in the car. The taxi driver had no choice and screeched to a stop. He looked shocked. 'What is it?' Hawke asked uneasily.

71

CHIMAIJEM I. EZECHUKWU

The Mexican said nothing. He looked behind him to see that the other car had stopped also, but was now reversing out from the street it had followed the taxi into. This isn't looking good, what the hell is going on? Logan thought. He tried to grab the driver's shirt but just then the man slipped away from his grasp and opened the door. He ran away as he saw one of the men climb out of the Mustang.

'God, I think that's my contact Sergeant Jose Lopez'. Hawke said almost shouting. He pointed at the bald man who was shouting at the running driver. The man held a gun in his hand, and then aimed to shoot the driver. 'How do you know that?' Logan asked. He was confused. 'Meyers gave me a good description of the man' Hawke said. He looked around to see whether the car chasing them was still anywhere in the street, it wasn't. The car had now gone. The detective wondered why it had left in such a hurry. Hawke figured it out in a second and knew there was something definitely wrong when he saw the driver of the taxi shot down in the street. The other man in the Mustang left the vehicle. He ran towards the fallen body. The man carried a gun as he ran towards the spot. Hawke decided to go into action. 'Stay in the car Professor'. He said. 'Come with me Mister Jarrett I think Sergeant Lopez has got some explaining to do'. 'If this guy is really whom you say he is Derek' Logan whispered. 'There must surely be a good reason for shooting the taxi driver'. Logan stepped out of the car and the bald man aimed his gun at him.

'Freeze!' he said. 'Police! Don't move!' The bald man flashed his police badge. 'Who are you?' he asked Logan. 'Call me Jarrett'. Logan said slowly. 'But why don't you ask the skinny man?' 'What is that supposed to mean?' The bald man asked. He spoke good English. 'I'm Sergeant Jose Lopez and my colleague over there is Sergeant Miguel. I'm in charge of the Vice squad in Mexico. I'm sorry about all this but I can explain what is happening here. You see, the taxi was stolen by that thug I shot. The man is one of Garcia Abrego's men. Abrego is one of the three men who followed you in the car. They work for an American crime boss named Hubbard. Abrego is the man's right arm in this country. But why tell you all this since you haven't introduced yourself properly to me?' 'That's what I was going to ask you my dear Sergeant'. Hawke said sarcastically. He got out of the car. 'My name is Derek Hawke and these are my associates. We were expecting a more pleasant welcome in your country. We didn't foresee any of this'. 'Nor did I Mr. Hawke' Sergeant Lopez said seriously. 'Until I got word from one of my sources on the street that Abrego and his men were going to try to kidnap someone very important at the airport today. I still don't know how he got hold of the information that this person was

72

coming to Mexico. This incident certainly confirms that Hubbard has someone working for him in my unit, and obviously with the police force in your country too. Anyway, thanks again to my source, Miguel and I were able to track down Abrego's man. The driver's name is Albert Ferro and we learnt he is a professional driver. He is usually used for jobs like this. It seems he won't be doing any more jobs. But thank God the night pigeon is finally here'.

Just then Sergeant Miguel waved his hand. 'It seems we've got a corpse here Sergeant'. He shouted. 'We'll get homicide to take care of the mess, and we'll also notify them about the stolen taxi so that they can contact the owner'. Sergeant Lopez nodded his head. He turned back to face the tourists. 'Now where were we gentlemen?' Derek Hawke shook his head then sighed. 'Relax Mister Jarrett I think Sergeant Lopez is all right. He just said the code-word I was expecting him to use when he made contact' he added very carefully. 'Meyers gave him the code-word'. 'What are we waiting for?' Logan asked. 'It's time to kick some butt'. 'I assure you we will Mister Jarrett'. Sergeant Lopez grinned. 'But right now I think all of you should get some rest. I've got everything you'll need for your assignment Mister Hawke. All the equipment is in the boot of my car. We will also have a lot to discuss at the hotel where you're staying. Welcome to Mexico gentlemen'.

II

The grandfather clock in the small study struck two o'clock as Rex Hubbard hung up the telephone. Hubbard was sitting behind an old oak desk. He smiled thinly. Hubbard waited for the chimes of the clock to die down before he said anything. 'I don't believe I'm still in luck' he said eventually shaking his head. 'What do you mean Senor Hubbard?' Garcia Abrego asked. He was also in the room. Abrego had told his boss all about the car chase and how the police had prevented him and his men from carrying out their plan to apprehend the foreigners that morning. 'You and your men' Hubbard began dryly 'Have been outwitted again by Lopez. I've now got a chance to even the score. That was Farrell on the line. He's put off the heat on the cartel operations we have in London. Something definitely went wrong in England all right, but I don't know what it could be. Phelps has a lot to answer for all this, and so does that Lopez. The heat might be off in England but I'm not finished with those two just yet!' he paused then said angrily. 'Rat is coming to Mexico. I understand he has an agenda, and he's got a bone or two to pick with Phelps too. He's coming here to cause trouble and we don't need that right now do we? I'm going to take care of him. I'm also going to keep an eye on things here while

73

you, my dear friend with your men of course, will embark on a job with Phelps. I will explain everything to you in detail later. But in the meantime get your men ready to welcome Rat'. Garcia Abrego was furious with himself. He wanted to get his own back on Sergeant Jose Lopez. The police man had thwarted his plans before, and had outwitted him again. He said, 'I will do all that you say Senor Hubbard'. 'Oh, you'd better had' Hubbard said decisively. 'Otherwise you've had it with me!'

III

Two hours later Logan stood beside the glass window in the hotel room. He was thinking. He took no notice of the three men with him. Hawke was talking to Sergeant Jose Lopez and Professor James. Sergeant Lopez and his man made sure the homicide squad cleared up the mess in the area. Lopez then drove the men to their hotel and helped them check into their rooms. Afterwards the men met up in the Professor's room. Hawke wanted to get down to business immediately.

'My associates and I appreciate everything you've done so far Sergeant' he said decisively. 'But I think it's time we talked more about this problem. What do you know about Jason Phelps?' Sergeant Lopez was sitting down on the bed with Professor James. 'Not much I'm afraid', he said. 'But I'm certain that this character is definitely with Hubbard'. 'You seem nervous when you say that'. 'Not in the least Senor Hawke'. Lopez said sighing. 'But I'm annoyed that I haven't caught Hubbard red handed at anything yet'. The man is the boss of a band of crooks for Christ sakes'. Hawke said sarcastically 'What did you expect?' 'I can see you've got a weird sense of humor Senor Hawke'. Sergeant Lopez said. 'I disagree with you there. I do believe I'll catch him one day. That's why I agreed to help you on this job. This American has caused more harm than you can imagine with his schemes. This drug operation he has started in your country is one of a few new deals he has set up with various crooks, like your Phelps. We've got to stop them, Senor'. 'We will'. Hawke said 'This might be your chance to do it. What do you think Mr. Jarrett?'

The detective could see Logan was deep in thought. He pointed a finger at him. 'I would like to ask Lopez something'. Logan whispered. 'Go ahead'. Hawke said puzzled. Logan nodded his head. 'Why didn't you tell us you had a tracking device on the taxi? I noticed that Miguel took something away from the car before the homicide team came. You know Lopez you're going to have to be honest with us if we're going to work together'. 'I didn't know you had seen so much'. Sergeant Lopez said slowly. 'You're a very clever man'. 'And so are you'.

Hawke interjected. 'What are you playing at Lopez? We can't take chances with anybody especially with the Professor here'. 'Come, gentlemen'. Professor James said 'We don't have the luxury of time on our side. If we continue to argue with each other, we won't achieve anything. You mustn't forget I left my daughter in England to be here'. He unfurled a big map which he had bought along with him. 'We see your point Professor'. Hawke said patiently. 'But Lopez should have told us he was keeping tabs on the dead taxi driver with some sort of device. Telling us what we really need to know would make this goddamned job easy'. He paused for a second. Then he continued.

'Anyway, it seems you've figured out something with that old map of yours. What have you got?' 'I did some research on the origin of the burial site Mister Hawke'. Professor James began candidly. Professor James placed the map on the bed. He stabbed his finger at a word. It read Tikal. 'This is one of Guatemala's modern day cities' he said. 'The treasure trove is hidden near a small temple there. Tikal is situated in the heart of the Peten rainforest and its origins have been known to lie between 700 and 500BC. It is also well known for being a colony of one of the greatest pre-classic Maya cities called El Mirado. It lies some forty or fifty miles to the north of Tikal'.

'Will it take us long to get to Tikal?' Logan asked. The Professor looked up at Logan. 'My former colleague Eric Ellis was an authority on subjects like this. It's a shame. He's now dead' he said sadly. 'We can get there in a day or two if we have a fast vehicle. So when can I have some rest before we leave for the destination? 'We need to relax a bit too' Derek Hawke said dryly. 'Get some rest Prof. We'll knock on your door, when it's time to go. Lock it when we go out and don't let anyone in, even the bell boy. Your role in this mission is now very important as you can see. This little meeting will have to carry on somewhere else if you don't mind'. The three men left the room quietly. And the Professor locked the door. Lopez glanced at his wristwatch. He felt it was time to go. He left the hotel.

'When are you going to show me the weapons?' Logan asked. He followed Hawke back to his hotel room. 'You'll get to see that'. Hawke said tersely. 'But not until you tell me what's on your mind. Tell me something Mac, for the hundredth time how does that fellow Kidman really fit into all this, and where does your strange theory about Ken Farrell come into the picture?' Logan stopped abruptly and looked at his boss. 'I wish I had answers but I don't' he whispered. 'It will be easy to find all that out if we start our search for Phelps'. 'We will' Hawke sighed. 'Just be patient Mac, I know how you feel. You'll get your chance to even up the score with Phelps when it comes. But right now we must stay focused. I just hope to God Meyers didn't send us here on a wild goose chase. I smell a rat somewhere'. The two men stopped at Hawke's door. Hawke unlocked it with his key. Logan's mind raced fast. I wonder what Rat's been really playing at, He thought, but I can't help feeling it's got to do with some sort of deal that Phelps struck with someone. I thought I had you fooled Hawke. Anyway, who am I kidding here? I've got to find out what this is really all about. Derek Hawke looked at Logan. 'Are you coming in or what?' he asked. 'Get your act together Mac. We've still got some things to talk about'. Logan nodded his head and followed his boss in.

IV

'There you are' Rex Hubbard said walking into the big lounge, Abrego was beside him. The Mexican's face was expressionless. 'What's it now Hubbard?' Jason Phelps said angrily. He got up from the settee. 'You can't do this to me you know'. 'Who said I can't?' Hubbard grinned. 'You are in no position to argue with me Phelps. Remember you've cost me a lot already. I asked you to take care of a business deal that would have got us both a lot of money. But what do you do? You blow it. Anyway, I've got something to tell you and I've also got a proposition to make'. 'I don't see how I'm involved in all this Mister Hubbard'. Brown said suddenly. He looked frantic where he sat. The fat man had been thinking of escaping from the American's home, and he was planning to take the money Phelps had promised to pay him before he made his move. The problem with that plan was that he hadn't even discussed it yet with Phelps. And when he had intended to, that's when the owner of the house walked in on them. Brown knew if he didn't do anything about the situation he was in now, he could wind up dead. As the fat man watched his host nervously, he wondered if that assumption would really come true. 'I can assure you, Mr. Brown'. Hubbard said distastefully. 'You are involved with this'.

The American looked at his colleague. Abrego nodded his head. 'I intend to do this with pleasure Senor Hubbard' the Mexican muttered. Garcia Abrego whipped out a snub-nosed pistol from his jacket and shot the fat man point blank in the face, two thuds and Brown slumped down on the floor. His blood dripped on the carpet. 'Make sure you get the boys to clean this mess up Abrego'. Hubbard said. 'It looks like we could do with a new carpet. Now let's get down to business. In other words, Phelps, let's talk'. 'What the bloody hell do you think you're doing?' Phelps asked totally surprised. He almost got up from his seat. Hubbard smiled mirthlessly 'You pretend as if you care, Phelps. Well I know you well enough and I know you don't care whether that guy was dead or alive' he said. 'I'm only making life easy for you. You don't need hoodlums like your late friend there. I'm actually doing you a favor'. 'You're not, Hubbard'. Phelps said angrily. 'But do your worst. You're going to kill me anyway'. Rex Hubbard laughed. He sat down opposite Phelps.

Abrego still stood where he was. He had now put his gun away in a holster that was hidden by his jacket. 'You have a lousy way of showing your gratitude'. Hubbard said. 'But I will pardon that since we have more important business at hand'. 'What do you mean? 'What do you know about the Rat, Phelps?' Hubbard said seriously. 'What's wrong?' Jason Phelps said. 'He's a dead man. He was a nuisance so I killed him. I thought he was spying for my network but it appeared he was working for someone else. I never got to find out whom. I'm happy I got rid of that scum'. 'You're a stupid fool'. Hubbard said. 'The man you thought you killed is not dead. He's still alive and if I'm correct, word has it that he's coming to Mexico to pick a bone or two with you. I'm going to take care of your little problem only if you agree to accompany me on a little trip to a hidden burial site that you know all about'. 'I have enough problems as it is now'. Jason Phelps said astonished. 'You have the four aces, Hubbard. I'm ready to comply with whatever plans you have for me'. How the hell did you know about that Hubbard? Phelps thought. Baker could have been working for you for all I know!

Jason Phelps knew he couldn't do anything about the present situation. But he was relieved to find out about the American's plans. He would have loved to take care of the Rat himself but he now had something else to deal with. I'll go ahead with your plan for now pigs! Phelps thought. But you're going to help me bring back all that treasure, whether you like it or not and then ...' Phelps sighed then said, 'So what do you want to know?' Rex Hubbard smiled warmly. 'Tell me again about the hidden treasure of Tikal'.

CHAPTER 12
Part I

The next day in Professor James' hotel room Sergeant Jose Lopez said, 'I've already made plans for a vehicle to take us wherever you want us to go'. 'What kind of vehicle would this be?' Hawke asked anxiously. 'A jeep' Lopez said. 'That will do nicely' Logan whispered. 'But when do we leave Mexico City? I have a funny feeling Phelps is on his way there and with his so-called friends too. Remember he won't stop at anything till he gets hold of that treasure!' 'I want you to get hold of that jeep. We'll need it; in fact we'll need it tonight. I'd like us to leave for Tikal in a few hours' time'. 'As you wish, Senor Hawke' Lopez said. He almost left the room, then came back. He looked at Logan. 'I noted a hint of hostility yesterday, when you asked me that question Senor Jarrett, but I have my methods too. I hope we are not going to be enemies?' 'As long as we're honest with each other we won't fall out Sergeant'. Logan whispered. 'We won't'. Lopez grinned. He bowed his head leaving the room.

II

Ken Farrell had a thin smile on his placid face. He was thinking about his evil ways. He got up from the desk in his office and turned round to look at the clock that hung on the wall, the time was now almost four o'clock. Farrell wondered what time it was in Mexico City. After a few moments he made a rough guess of what the time could be over there.

Farrell had made a long distance phone call abroad. He couldn't avoid Hubbard forever since he was on his payroll. Farrell had a long chat with the

SNAKE AMONGST SHADOWS

man. I Hope you haven't told anybody about our working relationship Hubbard, Farrell thought for a second. It won't be good for business. Eddie Payne never knew. So Jason Phelps mustn't know either. Otherwise I won't be able to get back at him for the trouble he caused me six years ago. Farrell undid his tie and went towards the drinks cabinet and poured himself a drink. He was concerned about what he had learnt from the long distance phone call that afternoon. The American had asked him to close down the entire operation if he could. But Farrell didn't do that. He felt he could save the project. He had invested a lot of his time and money in the whole deal. He temporarily closed down the cartel.

He had come up with the brilliant fool proof plan that showed the American's operation had been found out and smashed by the Vice Squad. But something else now required his immediate attention. Farrell worried that someone had squealed to the Columbian tourists in town. Farrell had thought long and hard about this. He kept wondering whether the Rat had struck a deal with them. Farrell was aware that Quentin Baker was capable of doing anything. The Rat could have told the Colombians something but he had no proof of that. Farrell had learnt that they were representing a notorious gang lord who had found out somehow about Hubbard's business deal. Farrell later discovered to his amazement that the gang lord was one of the American's rivals. Farrell sipped his drink. He kept thinking. Damn you Baker! He thought. What are you really up to? I want to believe you've got nothing to do with those goons. But I guess you can't be in two places at the same time. Hell! Why did I let you go after Jason Phelps and some mystery man from your past? I must be out of my mind or something. And now it's costing me a great deal! I think it's time someone put you in your place. I hope Hubbard has arranged something for you in Mexico. He'd better had. Otherwise, I'll have to get rid of you somehow. I think you've served your purpose.

Farrell felt the Rat had bitten off more than he could chew when he took matters into his own hands and flew to Mexico. Farrell would have preferred to have known that his associate was a dead man. Even though he had warned Hubbard that the Rat was on his way to deal with Phelps, he was now not happy that he had told Rex Hubbard about this. He would have liked to handle things himself. He was going to tell Adrian Meyers that Baker was really up too no good. The lawyer didn't know that Rat was only feeding off of him. Farrell sat down behind his desk again. The phone rang. Farrell hoped it wasn't the Rat. The phone kept ringing until he picked it up. Farrell remembered immediately that Adrian Meyers had arranged to meet him somewhere at a social gathering

79

that evening. The lawyer had wanted to discuss a case. The Mexican authorities had asked both of them to look into it. 'Hello' he said quickly. 'Who's this?' An eloquent voice said, 'Adrian Meyers'. 'What can I do for you Sir?' Farrell asked. He actually wished the lawyer hadn't called him. 'I certainly haven't forgotten about our meeting tonight'. He continued. 'You shouldn't'. The old man said. 'We've got a lot to discuss. Unfortunately something has come up and it requires my attention. I'm sorry about that. We might have to reschedule our meeting. This will probably be in a couple of days. Please accept my apologies'. 'That's all right Sir'. Farrell said. 'Has this predicament got anything to do with the case?' 'I'm not sure'. Meyers said dryly. 'But it could. I've just found out that Jason Phelps is involved'. Farrell gulped suddenly. What had happened and what was the old man, talking about?

III

Jason Phelps cast his eye down on the terrain below him. He was flying in a helicopter. The weather was quite windy but the sky gave no sign that there would be a storm. The stocky pilot steered the aircraft expertly. Phelps and the four men with him were all wearing warm clothes. Rex Hubbard was one of those men. The other three men worked for the American and they were all Mexican. Phelps had to admit the American was a genius. He gave him credit for hiring the helicopter from the Mexican Army. From all indications the American was anxious to get his hands on the treasure trove. The thought pained Jason Phelps. Hubbard's face was expressionless. His eyes took in the bushy region. Phelps wondered what was going through the man's head. He was tempted to ask him. He was sitting next to the man. The American had surprisingly asked Phelps to take him to the burial site and had left his right-hand man at home to hold the fort. Phelps was almost sure he hadn't seen these three men at Hubbard's place. He believed that they were the hired help. Phelps had told the American everything he knew. He wasn't sure about some of the things he said, but then it didn't matter anymore. He had lost everything. And he still could not believe that Johnny Brown was dead. He knew that it was a great loss. While at the house, Phelps discovered that Hubbard had instructed his men to search his bags and take away his passport. Jason Phelps shook his head slowly. He kept his eyes fixed on the huge landscape. He simply had no choice but to do the American's bidding till he could find a way out of this mess.

Phelps had thought he could trust the American. It seemed he was foolish to have done so. Everything he had planned so well had disappeared into thin air. The situation he was in was crazy; in fact it was also looking bleak. Jason

Phelps knew he had only one man to blame for all that. The man he called Jarrett. But where was he? There had been no sign of him. Phelps wondered whether the mystery man was in Mexico. As it seemed, Hubbard knew nothing about the man. Phelps was certain about one thing. If Jarrett hadn't stumbled onto his plans, all, this chaos wouldn't have followed. There was also the unfinished business with the Rat. Phelps had found it hard to believe the man was still alive and was in Mexico. Phelps kept thinking. How could I have made such a mistake? Hubbard had told him that one of his spies had spotted the Rat at a hotel. Before their departure the American had asked Abrego to send some of his best men to bring the man to the house. Phelps wondered whether that had been done. Damn you Baker Phelps thought. And damn you Payne wherever you are. The dead man had made a mistake to recruit Baker into his organization. Phelps knew that Rat had been spying for someone who seemed to know him pretty well. He ruled out the possibility that Hubbard could be the one Baker was working for, since the American had shown no enthusiasm whatsoever when he had spoken about the crook. So who could it be then? Who wielded enough power to have done this to him? Phelps admitted to himself quietly that he had made a lot of enemies while building his empire but he just couldn't comprehend who this was. The fugitive was sure about one thing. This enemy had put him out of business for good. Phelps focused his mind on the present situation, but he still kept thinking.

The pilot took the helicopter towards more dense vegetation and that's when Phelps spotted something. It looked like the spot he had told Hubbard about. In fact that was what it was, but it was covered by tall trees and bushes. Phelps nudged Hubbard and pointed at the area. 'That's the forest over there' he said. 'That's it! Tell the pilot to bring us down somewhere near that place I'm showing you'. 'What do you mean?' Hubbard shouted out. He was alert all of a sudden. He had spotted the hidden place too. Phelps repeated what he said again. He tried to make his voice loud enough so that Hubbard could hear it over the droning noise of the helicopter. 'That forest leads to the burial site I was telling you about. You'd better tell your men to get ready. Anything could be waiting for us down there'. Hubbard asked the pilot to take the aircraft near the spot and find a place to land them down. He then turned round to face the men and issued some orders in Spanish. The men responded immediately checking their weapons, equipment and food supplies. Jason Phelps grimaced. He suddenly remembered it would take them at least another day to get to the clearing if they started their journey to the city of Tikal. Phelps just wanted to get this over and done with.

81

CHIMAIJEM I. EZECHUKWU

He wondered for a moment if his plan would work. Someone's got to pay for this mess I got myself into, and I can't think of something better but to start making you and your men start paying first. It's a shame all this is happening Rex. Sometimes things don't happen the way you expect them to. You can't be too careful in this world. He remembered the pilot was flying back to the city to report back to Abrego. The man was coming back for the group in the next few days. Phelps thought about the only flaw in his new idea. He checked the possibility of his plan working. He knew he had come up with something that was worth trying out, so he decided he was going to take this chance and see how things worked out. Phelps recalled Abrego was to make radio contact from time to time when they reached the place. Hubbard's right-hand man was to make sure the spot was significantly marked on a map he had been given. Hubbard had sternly warned his man not to enter the city unless he gave him orders to do so. So what then was on Hubbard's mind? Jason Phelps wondered if he could bribe the Mexicans who were with the American, and if he couldn't, could he get hold of the radio that Hubbard was carrying on him? Phelps spoke Spanish fluently so that would be no problem. He just didn't have a weapon to protect himself to disarm the pilot if things came to the worst. The radio Hubbard carried was his only chance of escape. It was also the only link all the men had with the helicopter and its pilot. To steal the radio from Hubbard seemed like a really good idea. Jason Phelps smiled faintly as he thought about his new plan again. As the pilot kept searching for a place to land near the land mark he had been shown, Phelps wondered if he could escape from Hubbard and his men.

IV

Quentin Baker entered the big garage. He tried to be quiet. It was a dark place. The Rat was suavely dressed in a grey suit. He kept moving till he suddenly stopped in his tracks. Something happened. The lights were switched on.

'Good evening Senor Baker. I hope you had a nice flight from London?' A voice said in a clipped tone. 'I'm glad you could make it'. Rat covered his eyes from the blinding light in the place. 'I made it' he said. 'So what? Let's get down to the business at hand'.

Baker saw the man talking to him in the far corner near the switch. He was standing near a crate. The man wasn't bad looking but he was scruffy in his clothes. His name was Sergeant Miguel. 'I've heard a lot about you Amigo' Miguel said dryly. 'Senor Farrell warned me about you the last time I worked with him on a case. He said you were a devil'. The Rat sighed. 'What else did that fool tell you?' He asked. 'Nothing that would concern you I'm afraid' Miguel said. 'But I'm aware I shouldn't take chances with you Senor. Just what exactly do you want to know?' The Sergeant unbuttoned his jacket and he let the Rat see his holstered pistol. Quentin Baker grinned. He said nothing because he spotted something else. He noticed the trailing wire on the floor which was connected to a phone. The telephone was on a wooden table in the garage.

Rat had packed a bag and had flown into Mexico City from London during the night using an alias. He had also checked into a good hotel. He had enjoyed his flight even though his plane was slightly late leaving Heathrow, and had to refuel at Miami. Before he left London he had already made plans to see the police sergeant. He had worked briefly with the man before. But that had been a long time ago. Rat felt he could use the man's services while he was in town. He knew that Miguel was a dodgy character. Quentin Baker had agreed to meet Miguel here. But he had no idea the garage belonged to Hubbard. The Rat had asked the police man to make inquiries about Jason Phelps. He also wanted him to find the mystery man he called Jarrett. 'You've made your point Sergeant' Baker said. He took his eyes off the phone. 'Now where's Jason Phelps?' 'One of my informants followed your friend, Phelps' Sergeant Miguel said. 'He was seen in the company of an American crook named Rex Hubbard. You've heard of him haven't you? The man said there were three of my country men with them. They were all seen leaving in a helicopter that was from a military base outside town'. 'Where do you think Hubbard was taking Phelps?' the Rat asked curiously. 'I have no idea Senor. My informant said he tried to find out where they were going but the commanding officer in charge of the base wouldn't tell him. What has all this got to do with your business here, if I may ask?' Phelps could have gone anywhere with that man Baker thought But who are we kidding? He must have taken Hubbard with him to find the hidden treasure. 'Nothing' he said finally. 'Where does Jarrett come into all this?' 'I don't know yet'. Miguel said distastefully. 'I couldn't follow him as you had suggested. My colleague, Sergeant Lopez, unfortunately decided to assign me to a homicide job. But he took him, with some others to a place called the Unicorn Hotel. I discovered that one of the two men I saw with this man was his boss. I did not catch this man's name. The elderly fellow with them was probably Professor Titus James. Sergeant Lopez is out somewhere with that lot right now. I just don't know where'.

83

He moved away from the crate. 'One of my men said he had left in a jeep yesterday evening with the others'. 'Not good enough' the Rat said coldly. 'Something tells me you've not been doing your home work very well. And I don't like that'. He suddenly raised his right hand in one fluid motion and as if from nowhere a little throwing knife appeared in it. He threw the knife and in a flash it went hurtling towards the crate. The small object embedded itself there. 'You shouldn't have done that. Besides, I do not think it was necessary'. Miguel said. 'I take it you are then annoyed with me Senor Baker?' He was not put off by Baker's outrageous act at all. 'You bet I am. And you know that', the Rat said gritting his teeth. Sergeant Miguel went to the crate and examined the spot the knife had plunged in. He muttered something under his breath. Miguel proceeded to take the weapon out from where it was embedded. He looked at the knife with an expert eye. He liked what he saw, because the small piece was beautifully made. 'That seems to have made me feel a bit better'. Baker said. Miguel beamed a smile. 'You're very strange, Amigo', he said. 'Maybe Senor Farrell was right. You are the devil in disguise. Anyway, I can't see what I've done wrong. But I can see that this man Jarrett is certainly giving you cause to get annoyed. I wonder why?' You bet he is Miguel, but I'm not telling you why Baker thought I'm going to nail him to the wall and I'm going to make Phelps pay for the agony he's put me through.

As Baker came forward to collect the throwing knife, Miguel whipped out a semi-automatic pistol. 'Not a step further Amigo'. He said still smiling. 'You're full of surprises. Catch your knife'. Miguel threw the throwing knife in midair and Baker caught it. Rat then strapped the weapon back on his right arm. While Baker put on his jacket to hide the small piece, the police sergeant watched with amusement. He was still holding his pistol. 'Now where were we?' the Rat asked eventually. Miguel was about to answer that question when the phone on the wooden table started ringing. He looked at it. And so did Rat. 'I know this is putting it mildly, but Sergeant who's ringing you? Don't give me a reason to believe you've blown the whistle on me'. The phone stopped ringing. Sergeant Miguel laughed. 'You are absolutely correct Senor Baker', he said. 'You see, I arranged for us to meet here tonight because someone very important in this country wants to apprehend you. This man has obviously paid me good money. The ringing phone is only a signal to tell me that he is on his way in'.

Quentin Baker looked at the unwavering pistol held in the police man's hand. The Rat knew he couldn't do anything. He was trapped. 'I'll get you for this Miguel' he said decisively 'I've always known you were a con artist. But I never imagined you would be this good. So go on then, who owns this place and who is paying you to do this job?' Sergeant Miguel chuckled as two Mexicans walked into the garage. Both of them were well dressed. One of the men carried a pistol. He looked like a bodyguard. 'May I have the pleasure of introducing myself Senor Kidman or should I say Quentin Baker?' The other man said. He lit a thin cigar as he spoke. 'My name is Garcia Abrego. I have reason to believe you are the one known as the Rat. My employer owns the garage Senor, and I hired Miguel. Sergeant Miguel as I understand has a reputation in these parts for double-crossing former friends and potential enemies and before I forget my employer cannot be here tonight due to some unforeseen circumstances. He is an American. I'm sure you've heard of him. His name is Senor Rex Hubbard'. Quentin Baker could only feel a cold chill run down his spine.

CHAPTER 13
Part I

The big jeep came to a stop near the clearing. Logan was feeling tense. He wondered if it had anything to do with knowing that Jason Phelps was in the wilderness with his associates, trying to find the secret treasure of Tikal.

So, all those people died because of that. You're going to jail, Phelps, that I'm going to make sure, he thought. This is the end of the road for you, because I'm going to take you down.

Logan took a deep breath and looked at Lopez. The Mexican was taking a good look at the area he had parked his jeep in. There was shrubbery everywhere and not a soul in sight. Lopez had driven the jeep through the night. The men had eaten and slept in the vehicle for most of the journey, but not on rough ground. They wore clothes that would protect them from mosquito bites and other poisonous insects. They all looked tired and worn out. It had taken all most two days to get to the clearing. The journey had been hazardous, but the next bit was even worse.

Logan knew it would take them at least another day to get there. He turned his gaze on his boss. Hawke sat with Professor James in the back seat. The detective didn't say much during the journey. 'So what do we do next?' Logan asked. He had put that question to nobody in particular. 'We walk' Lopez said. He smiled faintly looking at his companions. 'Do you have any objections?' Professor James shrugged and looked at the sun. It was really hot. Hawke shook his head. 'Let's do it' he said at last. 'Hang on a minute, how far do we have to walk? And what do we do about the truck? Hunters or poachers might spot it, are you sure it's safe here?' 'According to the Professor's map we have at least a few miles to walk' Lopez said. 'We will reach the hidden city, and the jeep will come to no harm if it's left here. I don't think there's danger here, and I don't think anybody would attempt to steal it either. Besides, there's no one around this place for a hundred miles'. Hawke nodded his head reluctantly. 'Then we'd better check our gear before we go' he said. Logan got out of the big vehicle and dragged out his backpack and a cutlass with him. 'We had better hurry skinny man' he whispered .We don't have time to lose'. 'I agree' Lopez whispered. He had got out of the vehicle too. The other men followed them. So who said all this would be easy Logan thought. Damn it! Where are you Baker? Why do I have the feeling you changed your plans? Logan shivered, and all of a sudden he felt very tense again.

The next few hours were strenuous. The four men had to slash and cut their way through the wilds of the jungle making camp where they could. The men travelled mostly at dawn till about ten thirty, then again from about four till it got too dark to travel any further and rested during the night. Although the heat of the sun was dehydrating, they kept moving when they could. The men eventually spotted the hidden city on the third day of their long journey. This was while climbing down a hill, and that's when they discovered the trail which had been made by a set of footprints. The men followed the foot marks that were evidently made by another band of men. Logan looked down at the ruins of the hidden city. 'Someone must have beaten us to it boys' he whispered. 'But if my imagination is not running wild I'm sure we've got Phelps and his goons right where we want them'. 'Yeah, you're not joking'. Hawke said dryly. 'Someone's down there all right, and I hope to God it is Jason Phelps and whom you say it is'. Professor James tried to say something but then he heard a gunshot. The noise came from somewhere in the old city. Hawke grabbed the Professor and hid in the bushes. The other men also hid themselves too.

Sergeant Lopez took his revolver out from his holster immediately. 'Whom do you think that gunshot was meant for Amigo?' he asked Logan. 'I have no idea', Logan whispered. 'But there's only one way to find out', There was another gun shot. This time it came from near one of the ruined buildings they could see. The old structure used to be a notable worship place of some sort. 'What do you mean Senor Jarrett?' Logan smiled grimly at the Mexican, and then looked at his boss. 'Oh no, you don't'. Hawke said angrily. 'What are you up to?' 'Nothing' Logan whispered sibilantly. 'But I suggest it's time we got in on the action'. Sergeant Lopez didn't understand what Logan meant. But he followed him down the slope into the Bad Lands.

II

Jason Phelps ran into the old temple. He flung himself in desperation against a wall. Phelps was sweating like a pig; his clothes were covered in dirt. Everything in the place stank, and it looked spooky too. Phelps didn't care. He had finally made a run for it. Although he knew that Hubbard and his men might now be close on his heels what mattered to him most was to evade them somehow and get back to civilization. Phelps couldn't believe his luck. He was free at last but for how long? He had no food or supplies on him, except the rifle he had stolen from one of the Mexicans he had killed that morning near a stream. The stream was close to their camp. What on earth was he going to eat for the next few days and how was he going to survive?

Phelps had led Hubbard and his men away from the burial site. He had pointed them in the wrong direction. His plan was to head back and find the burial site on his own. Phelps realized that Hubbard and his men hardly knew their surroundings in these parts, so he decided to escape from the camp. At sunrise he had lured one of the Mexicans to the stream. He had woken up Hubbard and had told him he wanted a quick bath. The American had agreed. Hubbard told his man to watch him closely. Phelps disarmed the Mexican with a punch and then took the man's gun and killed him with it shooting him twice in the chest. Jason Phelps then fled.

He stood beside the wall wondering what to do next. Phelps knew his initial plans to escape from Hubbard wouldn't have worked if he hadn't weighed his options. So one thing stuck to his mind, he knew he wasn't out of the woods just yet. Phelps thanked his stars because Hubbard had decided not to radio his man for the rest of the trip. Phelps knew he had to hide, but where? Not in this filthy place he thought, it stinks. He tried to look around and he could see that some of the temple's interior decorations were still visible.

He heard something and turned round. At first he thought it was a rat scuttling past him then he realized it wasn't. Phelps could see shadowy figures holding burning torch sticks. They were coming straight at him. The two huge figures were now standing a few feet away from him. Since he couldn't see much in the dark, he was becoming afraid. 'Who are you?' he asked viciously, breathing heavily. The two men said nothing. They wore loin clothes and stared at him as he tried to come forward. Jason Phelps cringed in fear because his worst nightmare had just begun.

III

The Rat walked into the quiet sitting room with his cane. He was weak. He had sunken cheeks and his dark grey suit now looked stained with dust. A Mexican followed closely behind him, the man carried a pistol. It was aimed at Baker. The Mexican was one of Garcia Abrego's henchmen. Abrego was in the sitting room. He was locking up a safe. He eventually hung up the religious picture of the Virgin Mary which hid it. There was another henchman in the room. He was a heavy set bodyguard and he stood in one corner. Abrego nodded at the henchman who had come in with Baker. The henchman bowed his head and left closing the door behind Baker.

'Good morning Senor Baker'. Abrego said. 'I understand you slept well'. Abrego went towards a desk and sat behind it. He looked puzzled as he gazed down at the radio and the map on the chest of drawers. The Rat fumbled for a cigarette and a small lighter in his jacket pocket. He found them and then lit the cigarette which now dangled from the corner of his mouth. 'What is the matter with you Abrego?' he asked almost coughing. 'You've almost starved me to death and left your daft dog over there, to knock me around for information. You know, it would help a great deal if you introduced me to your boss. He's an American isn't he, what did you say his name was again? Hubbard? I hope that's not his desk'. The bodyguard looked at his boss, the expression on his face changed. It was now ugly. The man didn't like Baker's attitude. He went towards him. 'No' Garcia Abrego said in Spanish. He smiled thinly. The bodyguard stopped in his stride. 'Stay where you are Enrique'. Abrego said finally in English. 'The man is only trying to amuse me'. 'You can say that again'. Baker said dryly, looking around. The Rat was annoyed with himself for falling into the hands of the enemy. And he had good reason to be too. He had fallen into a trap set up by the police sergeant. The mysterious men in the garage that night had knocked him out unconscious and had brought him back with them to the house.

Sergeant Miguel had let his fellow Countrymen search him when he was unconscious at the basement, because his sheath wasn't strapped on his arm any more so he couldn't find his throwing knife. While the Rat had been locked up in the small room downstairs, he had craved revenge on Miguel. Rat had wondered where the police man had gone off to, after he had finished his dirty work for Abrego. The police sergeant hadn't come back to the house with the Mexican gangsters. Rat knew he had to catch up with the traitor one day if he escaped death. Only one thing seemed to matter right now, how to escape, fast.

CHIMAIJEM I. EZECHUKWU

The Rat knew he was in deep trouble, but one thing gave him great consolation. And that was the sword he carried with him. It was barely noticed since it was hidden inside the cane he used. The Rat enjoyed using the weapon and was an expert with it. Whenever he used it there was instant death. In the past he had also used the cane as a fighting club instead. He had become proficient with this deadly weapon. The Rat only used his sword stick in extreme cases, and he thought that this was one of them. He had no idea how many more henchmen were in the house. He had only seen the thug in the room, and the one who had escorted him.

The Rat had discovered he was a captive in Rex Hubbard's house. He knew that Farrell wasn't going to like any of this, if he found out. He remembered that Farrell had funded his trip to Mexico. At that moment he wished he had found out what Farrell had been hiding from him before he left England. Thanks to Jason Phelps he was probably not going to find out anything about that at all. The Rat decided to strike at his enemies without warning. He was determined he wasn't going to give up without a fight. He knew this was the second time he had been in here, and he had seen Garcia Abrego cast his eye at the box. So he wondered if there was any money kept in the safe. He had thought about that well and hard in the room where he was held captive. The Rat knew he would need money. The hotel where he had checked in would start asking questions about him. He had been missed for two days now. He had to abandon his things there, but that didn't matter anymore, his escape from Hubbard's house did. He only wondered if he could, since he was still feeling weak. The Mexicans hadn't given him much to eat in the last few days. They had only given him some raisins, bread and water to drink. Abrego had ordered his men to beat him up since he had refused to talk about his business in the country. Rat knew that if Abrego's boss walked in on him he could kiss his chances good bye. He decided it was time to go into action.

Garcia Abrego stood up from where he sat. 'Come now, senor' he said, smiling crookedly. 'I must admit that I'm not enjoying your joke. But I can understand why you are upset. I'm surprised that my employer, Senor Hubbard, has not contacted me yet. He's gone away on a short trip'. He looked at the radio on the desk. Abrego's features were somewhat bewildered again by something in that brief moment. 'In the meantime I'm in charge of everything here and so I can do as I please. And, yes, this is Senor Hubbard's desk. You see, my employer trusts me implicitly'. For a second Baker wondered why the Mexican couldn't keep a straight face. He couldn't find an answer, so he put the small lighter back into his jacket pocket. He finally said, 'So he's gone treasure hunting. Where's Miguel, and where's my goddamned throwing knife?' Garcia Abrego made a gesture to his bodyguard as he came round the desk. The man lunged at Baker. But that's where he made a mistake. Even though Quentin Baker was weak, his reflexes were surprisingly sharp. The Rat gave the bodyguard the shock of his life. As the man came to attack him, he stabbed him hard in the face with the already lit cigarette. The bodyguard yelled in pain and as he groped for balance was stabbed again. Rat finished the job off with his walking stick, hitting the man on the head in a deadly swipe. The bodyguard crashed to the floor and was dead in seconds.

'Enough of this, you fool' Abrego said stunned. He was now standing a few feet from the Rat. He was holding a Lugar. It was pointed at Quentin Baker. 'You're full of surprises Rat'. Abrego said. The Mexican gangster took a good look at the dead figure on the floor and shook his head. 'Look' Baker said breathlessly, 'I'm sorry. But I don't know what you're talking about. Come on man, don't you think it's time I left this place, we could also do business you know'. Abrego wasn't smiling as he walked towards Baker. 'I will have some explaining to do when I see Senor Hubbard'. He said coldly. The Rat suddenly fell over touching something softly on his walking stick. It was a small button that unlocked the sword which was hidden in it. Abrego kept coming and as he was now almost standing over his captive something happened. The Rat struck, in a swift move he plunged his weapon right through Abrego's stomach. The Lugar went off with a bang as he looked at Baker in utter surprise. Blood ran out of his mouth and he slumped to the floor dead.

Baker crawled towards the gun as he heard footsteps. 'Damn you lot'. He panted on the floor. The door swung open. The other henchman came into the room staring at the dead body of the bodyguard. Quentin Baker shot the man twice in the head. The Mexican was dead. 'Bull's eye' the Rat said. He dragged himself up with his cane. Baker went towards the door. He listened for a while and locked the door. 'Where's everybody around here?' he asked. Quentin Baker dragged himself away from the door and went back to Abrego's corpse. He searched the man's pockets but found nothing. He took the dead man's gold watch. The Rat got up and went to the safe. He went to work on it. After a few minutes he opened it. He searched desperately for money but there was none. He found something else, a small bag of precious gem stones. After a quick look in the bag he guessed they would be worth about a hundred grand in England. He grinned and wrapped back the gemstones in the bag and then closed the safe. He knew it was time to go. Before he left, he took a good look at the map and the radio. He also looked around for his throwing knife. He couldn't find it.

CHAPTER 14
Part I

Rex Hubbard looked up into the sky as the two vultures soared into the sky. The American shaded his eyes with his sweaty hand. It was steaming hot. The two birds found a tree and perched on it. Hubbard knew what was going to happen if he left the spot with his men. He suddenly felt pity for the late henchman. He swore silently in Spanish. Hubbard was angry. He knelt on one leg checking the body of the Mexican that had been shot twice in the chest. Hubbard closed the man's eyes as he had got up from the rough ground, where the corpse lay near the stream. He cursed himself for letting Jason Phelps escape. The two Mexicans were beside him; they were holding rifles and were ready to start looking for Phelps at their master's bidding. Hubbard and his men had come running to the spot when they had heard the gun shots from their camp. The American hadn't given his men the word to search the area for Phelps yet. He was really annoyed, he was also thinking. The American felt that everything he had planned and anticipated on this journey had fallen apart.

Hubbard realized that he could get lost with his men in these Bad Lands if they didn't find Phelps. The American knew he had to contact Abrego or the air pilot who had flown them in with the radio. But he wasn't going to do that just yet. Hubbard didn't want to give his men the impression he was apprehensive. The American wished Abrego was around at that moment. He knew the Mexican would know what to do. He had been resourceful to him that way all these years. Hubbard was still annoyed with his man. Abrego seemed to have messed up things a bit. He couldn't stop Lopez from thwarting their plans.

93

CHIMAIJEM I. EZECHUKWU

Hubbard wondered for a moment whether Abrego had taken care of the Rat. He also thought about the Professor and his friends. The American wondered if they could find Jason Phelps. Phelps thinks he's going to get away with this, Hubbard thought. Well, you won't. You're not going to cheat your way out of this when I catch you. And you can count on that.

The American looked at the two men. He said, 'Phelps must have crossed the stream and headed towards the woods over there'. He paused and pointed his finger at the ruins of the old temple. 'Let's go. And don't get lost' Hubbard upholstered his gun. He gazed down at the corpse again and shook his head. Hubbard then wiped his face on a shirt sleeve and headed down the stream with his men.

II

Jason Phelps trembled in the dark corners of the ruined temple. He couldn't believe he was cornered again, but this time by two half naked men. They were carrying burning torch sticks and were standing in his way. Phelps could see that the two strange men were looming over him. They wore shiny medallion chains around their necks. Phelps' cursed his bad luck. A thought crossed his mind. He wondered whether the two men were ordinary villagers and if they weren't, were they head hunters. These people were known to roam the hinterland looking for human beings to sacrifice to their various gods and deities. Phelps also wondered whether they were the guardians of the temple. The guardians defended the hidden city. Phelps was not sure whether these men were the guardians. He tried to make some quick decisions.

As shivers ran down Phelps' spine, the thought of becoming mangled human flesh did not stay well with him. For all he knew these men could be anybody or even cannibals who hadn't eaten for days. Phelps knew one thing for sure. Time was running against him. Rex Hubbard must have sent his men after him to follow his trail. Phelps knew they must have heard the shooting somehow. Phelps raised the rifle he was carrying with him and aimed it directly at the two strange men. 'Who are you?' Phelps asked again. He was nervously trying hard to see in the dark. Phelps was still mad with himself. He had no idea where he was in the ruined temple.

He looked to see if the two big men were armed. They weren't and there seemed to be no sign of anyone else in the place, but he certainly wasn't too sure about that. He could swear that he had heard a faint noise somewhere in the ancient building. He just didn't know where. The two men said nothing for a while. Then suddenly one of them muttered something incoherently. Phelps wondered what it was. He decided to ask a question. 'What did you say?' he asked. He was still keeping a watchful eye on the pair. He was hesitant. Nothing happened for a moment. Then something did. The man on his far left started murmuring and made gestures. Phelps couldn't understand what the man was trying to say but he knew this could be some kind of trick. He was right. It was. As the man on his far left kept babbling, the other man flung down his torch stick and tried to stamp out the flames on the dusty floor. Phelps' tried to find out what the natives were going to do next. The native who had thrown down his burning torch stick suddenly turned round and came charging towards the fugitive. The half-naked man knocked Phelps over using his strong bare hands. Phelps fell down losing his footing. But he held onto the rifle and opened fire wildly in the air as he slumped on the floor. Phelps twisted round with difficulty, despite his fall he set the barrel of the gun on the native and blew him away. The man was flung to one side of the large hallway which Phelps finally discovered he was in.

Phelps picked himself up quickly and nearly fell again. He aimed a shot at the fallen native. Phelps found his target but with great difficulty. He kept shooting at the man till he made sure there were no more bullets in the gun and his victim was dead. The full impact of the bullets resounded everywhere in the place. Phelps cursed his luck again. He knew that someone outside the building would hear the shots. He was out of breath. Phelps dropped the empty weapon on the ground with disgust. The weapon clattered with a thud on the floor. Phelps remembered the other half-naked man was not in sight. Phelps' eyes had by now grown accustomed to the darkness in the place.

The burning torch stick on the floor gave away the fleeting shadow creeping behind him. The other man had hid somewhere during the attack. Phelps wasn't prepared for what happened next. He got swiped on the head and he fell like a log. Phelps tried his best to get up but he couldn't. He was exhausted from the fight he had had with the other half-naked man. And with another blow to the head he went into oblivion. The man left Phelps unconscious body for a moment and examined his dead companion with the remains of his own burning torch stick. The half-naked man shook his head and grunted. He went back to where Phelps' lay. He examined him, lifted him and carried him off on his right shoulder. The man walked towards the big doors that led out of the place and stopped in his tracks. He heard something. It was a faint noise. He listened intently for a moment. Nothing happened for a second and then the powerful flashlight hit him. The half-naked man was forced to shield his eyes with his free hand. He realized there were fumes of smoke everywhere in his pathway. The man wondered what was happening. He

95

seemed unsure for a moment and he was forced to unburden the load he was carrying. The man was dizzy. In moments he was down beside the still figure. He clutched his throat and started coughing roughly. He felt as if his lungs were on fire. He was in a state of anguish. The man suddenly could hear voices but he could not place where they were coming from. They were obviously coming from somewhere inside the ruined building. The man convulsed violently on the floor. He kept coughing. The smoke that had filled the room was choking him to death. He held his throat. The expression on his face bore that of agonizing pain. He still tried to shield his eyes from the light. After a while he slipped into unconsciousness. As he wandered off into oblivion, his thoughts were on what was happening in the ancient temple.

III

Logan and Sergeant Jose Lopez moved towards the ancient temple once known as the domain of the gods. The two men still carried their gear. They were sweating profusely. The gates of the temple were rusty. There was no one in sight. Logan believed that the gun shots could have come from somewhere within the temple walls or nearby. The two men therefore agreed to check it before heading off into the wilderness again to look for their friends. The two men finally reached the gates. The place looked haunted. There were bones and skeletons everywhere. The temple reeked of death.

Phelps and his associates might have even made camp here for all we know. Damn! Where are you Phelps? Logan wished that his boss and the Professor were there with them. He was worried. But he didn't share his feelings with Lopez. 'So what do you suggest now?' Lopez asked tiredly. He wiped his face with a soaked handkerchief. 'There doesn't appear to be a sign of anyone having been here, not even the others'. 'I'm sure they're hiding out somewhere'. Logan whispered in grim fashion. Lopez grinned. 'Forgive me if I say this'. He said calmly. 'I think you were brash with the last speculation you made. I have no intentions whatsoever of leaving our colleagues behind'. Logan grimaced and shrugged his shoulders. 'I'm sorry Lopez' He whispered apologetically. 'I guess it's been a long day. This is all getting to me. 'I guess I feel the same way too' Lopez said. 'But we can't think of that right now. We have to find where those shots came from. I'm not convinced those gunshots came from that brush near the ruins of the temple'. Logan shook his head in disagreement. 'I have the tendency to make mistakes sometimes' he whispered. 'So you could be right. But it won't do us any harm if we check the temple or will it?' There was no time to answer that question because the two men heard the chatter of gun fire within the ruins of the old building.

'Did you hear that senor?' Lopez asked. 'Those were gun shots and they came from the temple. Karumba! What do we do now Amigo?' 'Crikey!' Logan whispered. 'How do I know? Come on. Follow me'. The two men pushed open the rusty gate. They ran up the pathway that led towards the entrance of the ancient temple. As Logan climbed the staircase, he reached for something in one of the bags he was carrying. Lopez tried to figure out what he was doing. He eventually said, 'What are you doing senor Jarrett?' At first Logan said nothing. Then he smiled grimly and whispered in a menacing undertone 'You'll see'. Logan approached the door that led into the ancient temple. He bent down beside it, and reached into the duffel bag he was carrying. Lopez was right beside him, and he was still puzzled. Logan got out a canister and a gas mask from his gear. The object looked very much like a gas bomb. Lopez realized what it was and gasped.

'Knock out gas?' he said. 'Are you sure this is wise Amigo?' The police sergeant suddenly remembered the small object had come with other items Hawke had placed on order before boarding the plane to Mexico. 'You bet I am' Logan whispered. 'Anything you know about these weirdoes might now come in handy. That's if they're inside there. So don't forget to whip out your hand guns'. He slipped on a gas mask and unscrewed the canister. After counting up to five he threw it in. Two full minutes later he moved stealthily into the building holding a semi-automatic pistol he had chosen for himself on this trip. Lopez hastily slipped on his gas mask. He followed Logan into the big hallway. He also carried a torch with him and switched it on. Lopez felt he heard something and waited a second. For a moment he wondered if Lopez was alright. It was extremely dark in the room but the police man followed the beam of light which couldn't make out much because of the fumes of smoke that had filled the place. The two men waited for the smoke to dissipate. Then they tore off their gas masks and went in search of the victims.

Lopez could hear someone coughing. He wondered whether the person was wounded. There were still fumes everywhere. Logan pointed his gun where the coughing was coming from. He found something because his beam of light had spotted a figure. 'It's a pity' Logan whispered suddenly. 'We might not be able to help the poor sods. Damn! Who knows, there could be more bodies lying around this place'. He tried to kneel down carefully to examine the figure on the floor. It was the half-naked man. 'I hope you know what you're doing?' Lopez said nervously. 'That man could still be conscious. He's dressed like the

97

guardians. The temple guards' Professor James told us about. In fact he may just be one'. 'This gent's been knocked out flat' Logan whispered. 'So where does that leave us now?' 'I don't know Sergeant' Logan stammered. 'But that leaves me with only one choice'. 'Which is what senor?' 'Find Jason Phelps or whoever was shot'. Lopez said nothing. Logan rose from where he knelt and made sure the half-naked man was unconscious. He cast a quick glance at the remains of the burning torch stick on the floor and caught sight of the other body. He found Jason Phelps and rolled him over taking a good hard look. Logan looked up at Lopez. 'Jason Phelps is right where we want him. Here'. 'What do we do with him?' Sergeant Lopez asked. Lopez was now holding his pistol. He was unsure about Logan's actions. But he didn't mind as long as all this led to his culprit, Hubbard. Logan said nothing then grunted, he was pointing his pistol at Phelps. He shook the fugitive up from his unconscious state.

'Where am I?' Jason Phelps asked dazedly. Then he realized he was on the floor staring straight up at Logan with the beam of light right in his face. 'You've ruined me Jarrett' he said slowly. 'I'm afraid you brought all that upon yourself when you decided to associate with scum bags like Baker and Farrell. You're going down for a long time. And I'm going to make sure of that, if it's the last thing I do'. Phelps tried to get up slowly. He was forced back down roughly by Logan. The fugitive was dumbfounded when his captor mentioned Farrell's name. Cold shivers ran down his spine. Well I'll be damned, Phelps thought, I wouldn't be surprised if Farrell had anything to do with this. He was onto me right from the start, why didn't I see this coming? Then it came flooding back to him and he remembered something, his encounter with Farrell six years ago.

Phelps had refused to give Farrell a character reference when he needed one from him because Farrell had wanted to do business with three of his best business friends. Phelps didn't like that, but that wasn't the problem. He had found out that Farrell was up to something. It automatically would have connected him with Hubbard's drug schemes and other operations in the United Kingdom. Phelps couldn't let that happen, so denied Farrell a lot of money in the end and great business deals that never took off. Jason Phelps remembered vividly that Farrell had walked away from his office vowing to get back at him someday. He had not forgotten the look on the man's face. Why do I get the feeling that scheming demon was the one who planted Baker as a mole in the organization? But why, is he working for Hubbard too? Damn him.

Logan stepped back a bit and made a gesture to the Sergeant to take charge, Lopez did. He quickly got the handcuffs out from a bag he had slung on his shoulder. "If you do anything even a little bit, dodgy Phelps I won't hesitate to shoot you' he whispered. Lopez handcuffed Phelps. The half-naked man was still unconscious. 'I don't think he's going anywhere that one. We won't need him'. Logan whispered. 'He's still unconscious'. 'Who's your friend Jarrett?' Phelps said slowly'. He's a cop' Logan said crisply. 'His name's Lopez'. 'I am Police Sergeant Jose Lopez' the Mexican said. 'I run things in the Vice Squad in this country, if you want to know that Senor Phelps. I have heard so much about you. I was wondering if you had by any chance come across another desperado here by the name of Rex Hubbard. I understand you are well acquainted?' Jason Phelps said nothing. 'Move, Phelps'. Lopez said. 'We haven't got all day'. He pushed the fugitive roughly and walked him towards the pathway which led out of the temple. 'What do we do now, how do we get hold of the American?' Lopez asked looking at the ruined place. Don't worry about that' Logan whispered. 'We'll come up with something Sergeant. Right now let's get out of here and find the others. We heard gunshots here Phelps!' Logan stammered after a while. 'It seems you had difficulty with your target. I assume that was one of them'. Jason Phelps was just about to say something when they all heard a gunshot. It came from somewhere. They were climbing down the steps of the ancient building. Logan dived to the ground taking the fugitive down with him. He saw Lopez go down too, but the policeman was dead.

'Who's shooting?' Logan asked incredulously. He was still holding down the fugitive. They couldn't hide anywhere for cover. Logan tried to find where the sniper was hidden. All of a sudden it dawned on him again that Hawke wasn't around to help him with this. He remembered that his boss had warned him not to rush into things. He had never listened to that warning. He felt it wasn't necessary. Well, on this occasion it seemed it was, because Lopez was dead. Crikey! He thought frantically. Where are you hiding, you freak?

There was another shot and it hit him in his left arm. Logan shrieked in pain. Phelps took advantage of that by shrugging him off and taking his pistol. The fugitive dragged himself away from his captor trying to find a hiding place. Phelps eventually struggled to get up on his feet, but when he did he was shot in the head. He died instantly. Logan had managed to get to Lopez while he still lay on the ground. He was still in a great deal of pain and losing blood. He took Lopez's gun which was still clamped in his hand. Logan realized that Phelps had taken his own and bolted off; he knew it was the only thing to do. He now pretended he was unconscious.

CHIMAIJEM I. EZECHUKWU

Minutes passed and nothing happened. As he opened his eyes slightly, he suddenly heard the murmur of voices. He could see that three men had shown up and they were all carrying rifles. It appeared they were hiding somewhere near the temple. The leader of the team went to the farthest area where Phelps' corpse lay. He spat on the dead body and said something in Spanish. Logan assumed it was Hubbard. The man directed his gaze where he lay, just beside Lopez's still form. Logan closed his eyes. He suddenly opened them again. He tried to take aim with the gun. He couldn't. He was weak. Rex Hubbard and his men didn't know what hit them. They all fell down. But Logan did not pull the trigger!

The three men had all been shot. Logan passed out a few seconds then regained consciousness when he heard a familiar voice. He knew who the voice belonged to. 'You do look a real mess sonny'. Derek Hawke said angrily. He stood over him. 'Thank God you're here skinny man' Logan whispered. 'I thought I was a goner'. 'I'm tired and fed up of saving you Mac' Hawke complained. 'What happened here? It seems like we've got a lot of explaining to do when we get back to London. Meyers will certainly need answers'. 'Where's the Professor?' Logan asked. He tried to get up and was doing this with difficulty. Hawke pointed towards the hills. 'He's safe where he is' he answered. 'Now are you going to tell me what happened?' 'You'll never change Hawke'. Logan whispered. 'You'll never change'. He smiled thinly.

IV

Logan sat quietly in an armchair at home. He was thinking about the past few weeks. Ruth Ryan was in the sitting room with him. Logan had informed her he was back in town. Ruth had come round to the flat. She was standing up watching him. She said nothing but looked amused. The bland expression on Logan's face didn't give away much. Logan knew he hadn't wrapped up this affair as he would have liked to, but he was happy to know that things had ended the way they did back in the ruins in the hidden city of Tikal in Mexico. Well, you can't have it both ways because nothing's perfect he thought. Logan had told Ruth all about his adventures in Mexico. He realized suddenly that the long arm of justice had somehow prevailed. Jason Phelps had actually caused enough misery and harm to last a life time. Logan felt it was probably his time to die. He found out the newspapers had very little to say about the crook since his escape from England, so probably no one knew he was dead.

Logan was still feeling sore from the wounds he had got in Mexico. But, he was happy to be home in London. He had been in England now for almost two weeks. He had left Mexico with his friends. When they got back to the hotel they had checked into, his boss had suggested they leave the country quietly. Hawke had decided it would be a good idea not to look for the treasure trove anymore. He believed the dead bodies of their enemies would cause problems for them. So they headed back home. The journey back to civilization had been quite difficult. It had practically taken two days again to get out of the wilderness and make it to the clearing. Professor James had guided them well, throughout their sojourn in the wilderness. But he had taken some minor injuries too. Logan wondered whether he was now feeling better. The Professor and his daughter had now flown off somewhere to an island in the Caribbean, to get some peace and quiet.

Logan learnt later it was Meyer's treat, it was simply his way of saying 'Thank you' to the Professor who had put his life at risk. Meyers had even agreed to see to his late friend's funeral arrangements. That is, when the Professor and his daughter came back from their trip.

Logan remembered vividly that Hawke had found a radio on Rex Hubbard. Before they left the site, Hawke had used the radio and had got in touch with someone who was to contact his employer. It's a shame you're dead Phelps, you were quite a formidable criminal Logan still thought. The good news is the gold's still where it should be. Tikal.

It seemed as if Logan was not aware of anything around him, or his girlfriend's watchful gaze. But he was. Logan knew Ruth had grown used to his habits. She was still watching him. Logan felt he still had to find some answers connected with the job. He decided to meet Detective Sergeant Willie Briggs. Logan planned to meet the policeman somewhere in town. He wanted to find out if Briggs could tell him a few more things about Ken Farrell and his associate, the Rat. Logan wondered if Briggs could tell him whether Baker was back in London. Logan was puzzled about that. Quentin Baker hadn't shown up. There was something not right about all that, but Logan didn't know what. When they got back to England, Logan remembered Hawke had warned him to stay away from trouble and keep out of sight. He hadn't seen or heard from his boss since then. He had tried to get hold of Hawke that morning; unfortunately he couldn't because Hawke wasn't at any of his contact addresses. Logan wondered whether Meyers had sent him off on another job, he hoped his friend was all right. Hawke might be busy doing a job for the old man. It's a shame he still doesn't know about his ex-wife's involvement in this affair too.

CHIMAIJEM I. EZECHUKWU

Logan wondered if Meyers knew Baker was a crook. Logan also knew he had to find out what had happened to Baker, because he couldn't understand why the Rat was connected with Hawke's boss. Or why he had simply vanished.

Logan's train of thought was suddenly interrupted by Ruth's voice. 'What's wrong Mac?' She asked. Logan got up from his seat and smiled wryly at the girl. 'I've not been much company, have I Sweets?' The girl nodded her head 'No', she said. 'I'm afraid not. But I think you did everything you could to solve this job. And you tried your best to help all those innocent victims who died. Don't be hard on yourself darling'. 'Didn't try hard' Logan began. 'I'm quite sure that might cost me somehow'. 'What do you mean?' Ruth asked. 'Quentin Baker is still out there somewhere' Logan whispered. 'Ken Farrell was conniving with him to bring down Phelps for some reason. I didn't find out what that was really all about. Anyway, Rat didn't show up in Mexico as I thought he would. I still don't know what happened to him, it appears he knows a lot about my boss'. He paused then continued. 'I asked you here because we're going into town to meet Briggs. I hope that he just might fill me in on something else that could be connected with Farrell's past, or the Rat's dealings with Phelps'. 'Good' Ruth said. 'When do we leave? 'Soon' Logan whispered. 'I'm looking forward to meeting Briggs'. Ruth said. She went towards Logan and kissed him. He responded and held her in his arms. 'So am I' he whispered.

The phone on the desk rang. 'It could be your boss' Ruth said. 'I hope it is' Logan said. He went to the desk and picked up the phone. 'Jarrett' he said. 'I have to give you credit'. Quentin Baker said. 'I underestimated you, Jarrett. But I won't let that happen again. You didn't undertake the assignment. You kept on sticking your nose where it shouldn't be'. 'Where have you been Rat? I always knew you would survive those gun shots somehow. Listen'. Logan whispered 'You might think this is over, but it's not'. He gestured to the girl to switch off the lights in the sitting room. Ruth did just that and stepped back. 'I know all about the tricks you managed to pull off with that creep Farrell'. Logan whispered 'I also know about the part you played in the Lukman affair. You knew about George all along. You were probably the loser in Phelps' private organization. You also knew about Samantha Hastings and her connection with my friend Derek Hawke. I haven't figured out yet, what you were doing at George's place and what your friend's connection is in all this'. 'You have always been quite ingenious Jarrett'. Quentin Baker said. 'But I suppose that is what one should expect from a great detective like you. I've always been fascinated with your deductions. I only wanted you to keep an eye on Payne. I work for Ken Farrell sometimes. I've never been able to figure out why he hated Jason

102

Phelps so much. You could say he was blackmailing the guy. Phelps had done something that Farrell knew about but I don't know what it was. Phelps suspected me of spying on him and managed to convince Payne I was no good for the network they'd created together. They decided to dump me and that's when they set me up at Lukman's house. I lost a leg trying to escape the police in that place. I didn't take much notice of the girl. I was just doing business. Anyway, I'm sure the man's now paid for all that because I'm aware you know that he's dead. Word has it that he was gunned down by a friend in Mexico. I've just come back from there myself'. There was silence for a while. Logan didn't know what to say. Quentin Baker laughed. 'I'm sure I must have surprised you Jarrett' he said. 'Phelps is dead and I'm pleased about that. But I had another brush with death in Mexico. The man responsible for that hasn't paid yet. But he will. Now remember, I know every move you make. I'm sure our paths will cross again'.

The phone went dead. Logan went straight towards the window. The girl followed him. They stood there for a while. There were no pedestrians out in the street. Suddenly Logan spotted someone walking down the road. It was Baker. Logan knew then the crook must have rung him from a pay phone near the flat. Logan still wondered if Hawke was all right. He thought about prowling the streets for some answers. He knew Ruth would understand. The meeting with Briggs would have to wait. Logan believed the war he had waged with crime at that point was not yet over. There were so many unanswered questions hanging in the balance. He sighed. Looking at the girl beside him he whispered, 'we still have a situation here darling'. 'I know Mac' she said simply. 'But you'll take care of it'.

CHAPTER 15
Part 1

Derek Hawke was comfortably sitting on a brown leather couch in his employer's study. The old man's place was beautifully furnished with oak wood. It was also quiet. Hawke's employer was behind a desk. He was in pajamas and wearing a light-blue dressing gown. He logged off the lap top computer on the desk and closed the file he was looking at. The file was Hawke's photo-copied report on Jason Phelps demise and the fantastic affair in Mexico. The lawyer had been crosschecking the information.

The old man got up quietly and went towards the drink's cabinet. He poured some red wine into two glasses then moved towards Hawke and offered him one of them. Derek Hawke took the drink and noticed there was a somewhat puzzled expression on Meyers face. Hawke wondered what was going through the old man's head. Meyers had plenty of time to go through the report he had sent to him via e-mail. So what was it? Hawke had sat there waiting for nearly an hour. The old man had got in touch with him on the phone. It was their first meeting in the flesh since Mexico.

Hawke then wondered if things could have been different if Phelps and Sergeant Lopez had survived the shooting near the lost city. The mysterious men he had shot were obviously Jason Phelps rivals. There just wasn't time to ask questions. But Hawke was now quite sure of one thing. None of those men would ever find the hidden treasure again simply because they were dead. Meyers wanted Jason Phelps alive and returned back to the UK. Unfortunately the American and his men had got to him first before that could happen.

Hawke had noted these facts in his report. And the old man had expressed his annoyance when he had mentioned all this to him before the sojourn back to England. Hawke's employer hadn't said much since then. Hawke had wondered why. Hawke tried to say something but Meyers cut him off politely with a gesture as he made his way back to the desk with his drink. 'Drink up Derek', he said. 'I've got things to tell you and we've got a lot to discuss'. Hawke simply nodded his head. The old man went back to the desk with his drink and opened a drawer. He got out the cigarette case and the cigarette holder. He slid a cigarette into the holder and lit up. Then he asked, 'what about your friend Logan, Derek? I'm assuming he's now well rested from his journey since he sustained some injuries during this caper'. 'I haven't seen him in a while, but I presume he is well rested by now'. Hawke said. 'He should be okay to handle a job anyway, if that's what you mean?' The old man shook his head slightly. Hawke couldn't tell whether this cynical action was a negative response. 'I'm not quite sure about that yet' he said.

Hawke sipped his drink while thinking. He knew his boss was puzzled about something. He just couldn't put a finger on what it was and why. The old man then said, 'I've gone through this report simply because of Phelps death, it still intrigues me. Are you sure he's dead?' Derek Hawke said nothing. He simply nodded. He got up from the couch and looked at his watch. Then he asked, 'Are you satisfied with the report Sir?' 'I wouldn't say I'm not'. Meyers replied. 'But I cannot hide my thoughts of you losing Lopez as well. He was a good man. I'll have to contact the Mexicans about that'. 'How did they take his death?' Hawke asked. 'Need you ask?' Meyers said bitterly. 'The man was a fine operative. The Mexican Police believe that his death is a great loss and I tend to agree. I still can't believe Jason Phelps is dead as well. He's been known to cheat death before so I wouldn't be surprised if he became the new Christ and rose from the dead. This brings me to another matter I wanted to discuss with you. Have you by any chance been in touch with Professor James or his daughter?

Hawke suspected something was wrong when Meyers asked that question. The detective winced. As far as he knew they were still holidaying somewhere in the Caribbean. Had something happened? He just knew it seemed odd and out of character for the old man to ask him this. 'No Sir' Hawke said, 'Is there a problem Sir?' Meyers sipped the remains of his drink. He looked at the empty glass with interest then put it on the desk. 'I suppose you could say that'. He opened a desk drawer and took something out of it. It was a document of some sort. Hawke couldn't fathom what the old man was trying to do with it. 'I think

105

CHIMAIJEM I. EZECHUKWU

you should know there is a problem'. Meyers said. 'The Professor and his daughter are cutting their holiday short. There's word from another source of mine in the Mexican Police that there might be an attempt to abduct both of them. That's why I've asked them back so that I can keep an eye on them'. The detective was surprised by this. He asked, 'What exactly happened?' 'We haven't finished with this case yet Derek', Meyers said. 'I've been told the Professor may be kidnapped by Colombians who are working in the Caribbean'. 'Why?' Hawke asked. 'It doesn't add up'. 'I think I owe you and Logan an explanation Derek'. Meyers sighed. He unrolled a map on his desk. It was a copy of the same map the Professor had shown him with the others in Mexico. 'You see, nobody knows for sure where the treasure is hidden on the map the Professor showed you lot. According to Mexican myth there was gold buried there during the Mayan Period. The problem is nobody knows where'. 'Is there something you're not telling me Sir?' Hawke asked. He tried to control his temper. 'I'm sorry Derek'. Meyers said apologetically. 'Why bring me into the big picture all of a sudden?' Hawke asked. 'Well, it appears from my observation Derek that you haven't been completely fooled by the chain of events going on in this case'. The old man said. He kept his eye on the map and was still smoking his cigarette with the cigarette holder. 'Will you come here for a moment?' 'What the bloody hell is going on?' Hawke said. 'I thought you trusted me'.

He reluctantly moved towards the desk. Adrian Meyers took his gaze off from the map for a minute and looked at the detective. 'Oh, I do trust you completely Derek' he said. 'I just wasn't sure whether you or Logan could handle the pressures of knowing that there were different elements involved with this case. You see, for a long time now a high-ranking Policeman here in London has been working with me to help the Mexican Police. He is also a spy working for someone. He has prevented me from solving this case from the very beginning. He has tried to stop me from smashing a smuggling ring Phelps was connected with. The racket was put together by the American and Phelps was a partner in it. The American, I presume, is dead because he was probably amongst those you shot near Tikal'.

The question on Derek Hawke's mind spoke volumes. What was his employer covering up? 'Why choose the Professor's brains if you knew this all along?' The old man sighed again. 'I was giving the Professor and my dead friend Paul the benefit of the doubt, as they say. I knew they were still willing to believe that the treasure was buried out there. Hawke asked, 'Who do you suspect? 'Commander Ken Farrell in the British Police' Meyers said. 'I had to be certain if I could trust someone with this case Derek, because my plans to help the Mexican Police weren't working out. It appears Farrell was probably responsible for that. I now know that he knows that Phelps is dead. A few nights ago a small party was thrown for some European colleagues at the Home Office, which I couldn't attend. But some people did. Apparently, Farrell was one of them. Somebody overheard Farrell tell someone at the party that Phelps was dead. Farrell was talking to a Colombian called Dominic Samosa. My source said Farrell seemed threatened by this man, but he didn't say why'.

The old man paused. He eventually said, 'Derek, the Colombians are involved with this case somehow. But I just don't know how. Farrell has been hiding information from me since this began. I need enough evidence to prove that in order to convict him'. Hawke hesitated a bit when he heard the name Farrell. He remembered Logan had mentioned something about this man. He finally asked, 'What are you going to do Sir?' Meyers slapped his forehead gently. He ignored the question. He said, 'I almost forgot to tell you about that idiot Kidman'. The detective was amazed. Great! What next? He thought. 'Farrell had recommended this guy as a personal assistant'. Meyers said. 'It just occurred to me that he was sent to keep an eye on me. I'm almost certain now that Farrell thought I had something that might put him away. I only wish I had seen it coming. Kidman cleared his desk this morning from the office and left. He didn't leave any notice whatsoever. I'm sure he isn't what he claims to be'.

These unforeseen developments had placed the job that had been undertaken, in a serious quandary. There was no telling who else was involved with this job. Hawke was at a loss for words for once. He knew he was being offered a proposition to solve this problem once and for all. He only wondered if Logan would agree to participate in this madness. During the conversation Meyers face had grown pale. He tried to cheer himself up by putting on a weak smile. Meyers said, 'If you and your friend decide to undertake the task at hand. I want results. I want to know what Dominic Samosa is doing in London. I'd also like you to take interest in Farrell's operations. Infiltrate his set up and bring him down Hawke'. Derek Hawke shook his head in disbelief.

'When exactly are you expecting the Professor and his daughter back?' he asked. 'In a couple of days I should presume'. Meyers said. 'I'll take care of that. I'll also take care of the little mess you had with your friend at 'Crows' so that the police won't trouble you'. He made a gesture at the telephone on the desk. 'In the meantime I think you should call Logan'. 'I certainly will - do I have a choice? - I don't think so' Hawke thought glumly to himself as he picked up the phone. From the look of things his work was cut out for him. It was going to be one hell of a long night.

II

'Are you kidding skinny man?' Logan asked incredulously. He was still in the flat with Ruth. Hawke was sitting in a chair in Logan's sitting room. Logan was on his way out when Hawke caught him on the phone. Hawke had asked Logan to wait for him at the flat. When Hawke eventually arrived at the apartment, an hour later he explained the situation. He presented the new matter in its full light. Logan introduced Ruth to him. Hawke acknowledged the girl's presence with a nod. Then he said, 'It's not a joke, Mac. Since you haven't bothered telling me more about Farrell, I was wondering when you would get round to that. I want you to find out what he and his friends are really up too. In fact I want you to get to the bottom of what this business is really all about'. 'Easy enough for you to say' Logan whispered. 'I knew something wasn't right about this case in the first place'. He got up from where he sat and moved towards the window. He turned round almost immediately and gazed at his boss. 'We've been on a wild goose chase right from the start'.

Logan wasn't in the least surprised when he learnt that the Colombians were involved in this case. There was obviously more to all this than met the eye. He wondered whether his boss had found out about his late wife. He reckoned it wouldn't be a bad idea if Hawke now knew about her involvement in all this. But maybe that could still wait. That's because there was something else. Quentin Baker was still at large. Logan thought about that for a while. He concluded that Baker probably had a secret agenda of his own. The Rat had conned Hawke's employer and was presumably still in touch with Farrell. Logan knew he had to find out what was really at the bottom of all this. It seemed the business of the day would therefore have to start with reacquainting himself with Police Commander Ken Farrell- the Rat's dodgy associate. Logan folded his arms quickly and swore under his breath. 'What do you intend to do?' he asked. The detective got up from his chair. His eyes leveled with Logan's steely gaze. 'I'm not going to wait around for you to come up with a solution sonny, that's for sure' he said sighing. 'I'm going to work things from my end. But you're going to keep me posted as usual. Meyers planned to meet Farrell somewhere. He's rescheduled that meeting. They're meeting in the city

tomorrow evening at nine o'clock, in a small restaurant. It's called 'Roses' and its near Aldgate. I think it would be a good idea to follow this lead'.

'What about the Columbian called Samosa?' Logan asked grimly. 'I'm going to make a few phone calls once I get home'. Hawke said. 'If I come up with anything, I'll let you know'. 'Has it crossed your mind all this might be connected with drug smuggling?' Logan asked again. 'There's obviously something going on with the Colombians. I bet they're immersed in something evil all right'. 'The thought has crossed my mind'. Hawke said. 'However I fail to see the connection with this matter'. 'There are other cronies lurking around and they are all linked with Meyer's case' Logan whispered. 'You do have a point' Hawke said. 'Fortunately, we know Phelps and those rivals of his are dead. But there seems to be another threat in town'. 'I'm concerned about the Professor and his daughter'. Logan whispered. Derek Hawke looked at Ruth. Then he said, 'I shouldn't be worrying about that if I were you. Just get back to work Mac. We don't have much time. I'll be going in a minute. It seems you two have some business to finish off'. Logan glanced at Ruth. 'You can relax skinny man'. He whispered. 'Ruth's okay. Her loyalty to me is not in question or in doubt'. Hawke simply said, 'Do whatever you have to do to get the job done my friend. But remember one thing. Stay out of sight'. After his boss left the apartment Logan whispered, 'That went well'. Ruth Ryan smiled warmly and nodded. 'You can say that again' she said. 'Your boss is a sensitive fellow. He needs to loosen up a bit. Why haven't you told him about the ex-wife?' 'At some point I will'. Logan whispered. 'I'm getting worried about you darling. Your boss seemed unsure about something. What are you going to do about that?' 'At the moment nothing I'm afraid'. Logan whispered. 'But I'm going to go in search of some answers. I'm going to look up Willie on my own. You're going to go home now like a good girl. I'll stay in touch. Nick Slater will probably find Baker'. The girl nodded her head and got up gracefully from the couch. She went to the phone on the desk. 'I'll call a cab' 'Do that' Logan whispered. He took a few steps and looked at himself in the mirror then whispered, 'I've got work to do'.

III

Sergeant Willie Briggs locked up the office and was now making his way to his car. He was going home. His car was parked across the street. As Briggs climbed into the car, he froze as the chill of cold blue steel touched his neck.

He knew immediately someone was in the car holding a gun at him. It was probably the mystery man he called Jarrett. The man had phoned him up at the office and had suggested a meeting that night. 'How's your case coming on

Willie?' Logan asked. Briggs heaved a huge sigh of relief and wiped the beads of sweat on his forehead. 'I think I'm getting somewhere with it Mister Jarrett' Said Briggs. 'You nearly scared the wits out of me! What can I do for you?' 'Relax Briggs'. Logan whispered. 'Tell me more about Ken Farrell'. He lowered the gun and put it back in his shoulder holster. Briggs tried to turn in his seat to take a glimpse at the dark figure sitting in the car with him. He stopped fidgeting and gave up when that was a bit difficult to do. He looked at the mirror in front of him and could see a profile in the darkness. It was huddled in the back seat.

'I don't understand what you mean' Briggs said. 'I thought you said you weren't sure whether Farrell had anything to do with your case'. 'It's a long story but I'll spare you the details' Logan whispered. 'Something came up and it's got Farrell's name written all over it. He's been working for an American crook called Hubbard. Hubbard was shot dead a couple of weeks ago in Mexico. I was there when it happened. I was in pursuit of Jason Phelps'. 'I've told you all I know'. Briggs said. 'Think Willie'. Logan whispered. 'It's important. Farrell might be adept at covering his tracks. But have you ever thought that he might be using the resources he's gained access to, in the Vice Squad to do this?' 'That assumption could be quite true'. Briggs said. 'I told you the guy's a dirty cop. But what has that got to do with the crook that got shot?' 'Plenty - I'm afraid'. Logan whispered. 'That's why I need you to do some research for me on your database'.

'What exactly do you want?' 'Learn what you can about Farrell's operations. The names of the smuggling networks he's brought down and the drug busts that were made in the past year under his command. It could crack this case wide open. Send what you've got on the e-mail account at my address'.

Briggs nodded his head. 'It seems you've got this case pretty wrapped up Mr. Jarrett. What makes you unsure?' 'A few people linked with this investigation believe that Farrell might be secretly running Hubbard's criminal operations for him here in London. It's also assumed at this time that some Colombians are interested in Farrell's deals. It doesn't look good Willie'. 'What's the connection with Phelps?' Briggs asked. 'I'm not quite sure' Logan whispered. 'But it appears he was a business partner of sorts' he hesitated a bit then added, 'Jason Phelps is dead too. He gave up the ghost in the same shoot out. Keep this under wraps' Briggs. The media know nothing of this'. Briggs wiped more beads of sweat from his forehead. 'I didn't see that one coming'. He said. 'How's your boss handling all this?' 'He'll live'. Logan muttered. 'He still doesn't know about his ex-wife, does he?' Briggs asked. Logan said nothing. He grimaced in the dark. When Briggs realized, the mystery man wasn't saying anything. He said, 'I think I made a major discovery tonight. It's connected with the case you're working on'. 'What is it?' Logan asked. 'Forensics found something interesting. The corpse in the car wasn't Tom George. It belonged to his stooge. Lenny Miller' Briggs said quietly. 'So where is George?' Logan asked. 'Nobody knows'. Briggs said. 'But the boys in my squad are now looking into it'. For a moment Logan was lost in thought. He eventually said, 'Keep in touch Willie, So long!' 'I still believe this case of yours is strongly connected with mine' Briggs said. He looked at the windscreen. He could see the backseat door of the car was open. Logan had quietly let himself out and had gone.

IV

The following evening Logan entered the restaurant called 'Roses'. He was smartly dressed in a black overcoat and a dark suit. It was a quarter to nine o'clock. Logan had gone home the other night thinking about the latest twist in Briggs' case. The whole affair was bizarre. There was no denying the fact whether there was a connection between the two cases. Logan only wished his boss knew about the link. He decided to keep this a secret too. His boss had not contacted him yet. He decided to focus on the job at hand. He was nervous and he knew why. He didn't know what to expect in this upper class establishment. But he reckoned this was a good sign.

Earlier on that day, he had checked his e-mail account. Briggs had not sent the information yet. Logan knew it was going to take some time. He had also done a background check on the posh restaurant with his lap top. Logan sat at a table near a window where he could take in everything at a glance. The lights in the diner were bright as shining stars. Soft classical music was being played. A few couples were eating and drinking. They were all dressed to kill. The women had their best jewelry on. Logan wondered whether the two men had turned up at the restaurant. A waiter approached and Logan ordered an ice-cold lemonade drink. He decided to wait. The waiter brought the drink. It was in a tall glass. Logan savored the drink. He liked it. After what seemed like a while, he saw the two men he was expecting. They made their way to a table. He recognized Meyers from pictures in the tabloids and instinctively knew the other fellow was Farrell.

The man was tall and wasn't bad looking, but he had shifty eyes and looked dangerous. Both men were smartly dressed in expensive suits. The two men sat down. They declined to have drinks and they took no notice of the

CHIMAIJEM I. EZECHUKWU

dining couples or the single individual in the restaurant. Even though the two men talked quietly Logan could overhear their conversation. He was sitting across from their table. 'The last time we spoke on the phone you mentioned Phelps' Farrell said. 'Have you found anything more?' 'No. I haven't' Meyers said. 'But I can't quite seem to put my finger on what this whole business is really all about Commander'. Ken Farrell looked around and then noticed Logan at the table across them. He turned his gaze back at Meyers. 'What have our Mexican friends come up with then, I take it you've got some news?' he asked. 'Yes. I do'. Meyers said. 'But I'm still thinking about it'. 'What do you mean?' Farrell said. 'The Mexicans' Meyers said. 'Believe some Colombian crooks are involved with this. In fact they have established that they are here planning something in London'. 'What do our friends want us to do?' Farrell asked. 'They still want us to find the connection'. Meyers said. 'They believe the American's got men running an operation here in London. And Jason Phelps as you know is still under suspicion of running part of that operation'. 'Phelps is a fugitive'. Farrell said. 'And according to my sources he's fled the country'. 'My contacts have confirmed that as well'. Meyers said dryly. 'So since we don't have enough to prove Phelps interest in this case, we should still find a connection'.

'Any ideas?' Farrell asked. Meyers took out his cigarette case and lighter from his pocket. He adjusted the holder with a cigarette and lit it. Then he said, 'Kidman'. Farrell was a bit surprised. The expression on his placid features showed this. He asked, 'What about him?' 'He's probably involved with this mess Commander'. Meyers said. 'He had disappeared for weeks only to make a brief appearance at my office yesterday. But he's vanished again. I've been wondering if you knew what he's been up to.' Farrell didn't answer that question. His cell phone started ringing. He made a gesture of pardon and dipped his hand into his jacket pocket. He clicked his phone on. He said, 'Hello?' he then waited for the person on the other end to respond. After a few minutes he broke off contact with his caller.

'I'm sorry' he eventually said. He put away the phone. 'That was an associate of mine. He wants to see me urgently. He's got some vital information for me'. 'Do you have to leave now?' Meyers asked. 'I'm afraid so' Farrell said. 'But in order to answer your question, Kidman's not been in touch with me. I haven't the foggiest idea where he is or what he's been up to. It never occurred to me, that he could be involved with this business'. 'I'm sure he is'. Meyers said. 'But you might have to find that out for yourself. He's a dodgy fellow Farrell. I wish I hadn't taken him under my wing'. Farrell got up from the table. 'That was probably an oversight on my part Sir'. His mood changed slightly. He

112

looked around him and made another mental note of Logan again. Logan gazed at the man too. The old man got up from the table. He said, 'that will be all for now then Commander. Please keep me informed'. 'I definitely will Sir'. Farrell said. 'And you can count on that'. The two men left the room. Logan finished his drink and cautiously followed suit. Who had called Ken Farrell? Logan thought. He went in pursuit of the policeman.

V

Ken Farrell escorted Adrian Meyers to his car. Then the policeman climbed into his own sleek car and drove off. Logan flagged down a taxi cab and trailed Farrell's car. Things are definitely heating up! Logan thought. He was sure Farrell had taken interest in him at the restaurant. Farrell had probably filed him away somewhere in his memory. Logan reckoned the police man was aware he was being watched all along. Ken Farrell was obviously a professional and seemed like one who didn't like taking any chances at all. Logan had a strange feeling Farrell was almost certain Meyers was onto him somehow. Logan wondered momentarily if other things would unfold in this case.

The taxi cab driver kept tailing Farrell's car. He did this at a snail's pace. Farrell made a couple of bends and had now turned into a Lane. Logan knew instinctively he was in familiar territory. He immediately ordered the cab driver to drive past the Lane. Farrell parked his vehicle in the Lane. He climbed out of his car and made for the bungalow. The lights in the house were on and as he had expected but he was unaware he had been followed. Farrell had plenty to think about. He knew Meyers had shown tact during their conversation at the restaurant. He kept wondering whether the old man was onto something. Farrell suspected he possibly could be. He thought about other things.

An associate was now in town. This man had arrived from Mexico City. He was a Mexican cop. Farrell knew this man was crafty but a reliable source. The policeman had phoned Farrell because he had brought back some news concerning the two Colombian henchmen who were in town. As Farrell quietly unlocked the door to the house, he wondered what Sergeant Miguel had found out. The man had made his way in a taxicab from Heathrow Airport and was now waiting in the house. Farrell had told him where to find a spare key on the grounds of the bungalow. He had also promised him a share in the proceeds he was going to make from Hubbard's UK network.

Farrell entered the sitting room. The Mexican was in there. He was on a settee. Sergeant Miguel was helping himself to a drink while admiring the colorful portrait in the apartment. It was a framed picture of Farrell. In the

113

photograph he was immaculately dressed in the ceremonial regalia of the police force. On one of the leather settees in the room was a brief case. Farrell guessed it was the Mexican's. Farrell made his presence known by coughing. Sergeant Miguel went for his pistol when he saw Farrell. He then relaxed. 'Nice place you have here' he said. 'I agree' Farrell said sternly. 'Exactly what time did you get here?' Sergeant Miguel looked at the wall clock in the room. He said, 'Ten o'clock. Is there a problem?' 'I believe the old man is onto something' Farrell said. 'I'm almost certain someone was watching me tonight'. 'This person you saw at the restaurant could probably be an associate of Rat's'. Sergeant Miguel said.

He set down the glass he held on a small table that was in the middle of the room. 'Very much so' Farrell said. 'But I doubt that. Quentin Baker operates alone. He has come back from Mexico and gone into hiding. Apparently he's become a problem. I think it's time I took care of him'. 'You do have a way with words amigo' The Mexican said. Farrell ignored this remark and said, 'The man I saw sitting across me at the table tonight didn't come across as a pushover. Anyway, what have you got?' 'The two henchmen you seek have been identified accordingly. Their dossiers are in my briefcase'. Sergeant Miguel said. 'Emmanuel Gonzalez and Cristian Delgado work for a Columbian drug lord named Hosea Cortez. Cortez is a wealthy man and he's had a well-documented rivalry with the American. Cortez also lives in Mexico. Gonzalez and Delgado are professional hit men but are unknown in the UK. They were sent here to find out about Hubbard's operations. As I understand, he has instructed his boys to take control of Hubbard's organization in London. These men have sworn to let nothing stand in the way'. He paused then continued. 'Cortez is also setting up a small network here in the UK. His goons have already hired some men to start running things. You definitely will have your hands tied with that sort of competition on your turf'. Farrell went to the curtained window and peeked through it. He was making sure nobody was within an earshot of this conversation. It appeared nobody was, so he turned round and faced Miguel. He said, 'That problem will also be taken care of'. He went to the drink cabinet and made himself a whiskey. Outside the house, a shadowy figure lurked in the dark. Logan was hiding a few feet from the window. He had his back to the wall.

The taxicab driver had dropped him off in a nearby street. Logan had walked into the quiet lane where Farrell's house was situated. Logan had seen the lights in the house. He had placed a small listening device on the window. It was a micro-transmitter. Logan now checked his earpiece and the mini recorder in his coat pocket. He could hear every word of Farrell's conversation. He was also taping it. In the sitting room Miguel only looked with fascination at his host. Farrell asked, 'Do these two men have anything to do with a business man called Dominic Samosa?' 'How would I Know? Miguel asked. 'My informants didn't come up with anything like that. Who is he?' 'He's another Columbian visiting the UK. However, I know him. We go a long way back. I did business with him but that was a long time ago. I'll probably have to pay the man now'. 'I hope you remember our deal Senor. Otherwise, I will have to come clean with your British Police'. Farrell sipped his drink then said, 'I hope that's not a threat Miguel. I can assure you, if it is you will regret it'.

The Mexican gulped the remains of his own drink then said, 'You have the trump card Senor'. Logan had heard enough of the conversation. He felt it was time to go. He stopped to think for a moment. Quentin Baker was up to something again he thought. Perhaps the Colombians have hired him to do their dirty work for them. The plot in this whole affair keeps thickening. Logan didn't know what to expect anymore. Baker was probably not in Farrell's employ anymore. But he was apparently somewhere near, and up to his old tricks again. Logan only wondered where?

CHAPTER 16
Part I

'.....I did business with him but that was a long time ago. I'll probably have to pay the man now'. Hawke listened to the end of the recording on the mini tape. He was sitting across the table with Logan at Charlie's Tavern. Logan had asked his boss to meet him at Charlie's the following morning. He wanted him to listen to the tape. So after breakfast there, they discussed the case. 'I admit I'm impressed Mac' Hawke said. 'But unfortunately this tape won't be enough to convict Farrell or any of his associates. I would suggest you keep it safe. It could be useful. Anyway, I've got some news for you'. 'Has this got anything to do with Samosa?' Logan asked. Hawke nodded. 'Yes' he said. 'Dominic Samosa is an accountant. He's also a shrewd businessman. He speaks English and three other languages fluently. These are Spanish, French and German. Samosa's had a privileged education and he doesn't have a criminal record. That notwithstanding, it seems he's been involved with some dodgy deals. These deals have had nothing to do with the current problem. My contact tells me the Colombian has come into town to collect some money owed to him by someone. I haven't been told who it is yet. ' 'Is there a catch to all this Hawke?' Logan asked. 'What do you think Mac?' Hawke asked. He answered his own question. 'I came to the conclusion that Samosa might just be in town when Farrell was planning something big'. Logan unveiled his plan to reel Farrell in. Hawke didn't like the idea but grudgingly had to accept it could be pulled off. 'Be careful Mac' Hawke said finally. 'Remember Kidman may be up to something as well. Which brings us to one question? Whom is he actually working for and whom do we now consider as the real culprit in all this? This case has been a wild one right from the start. So do what you do best. Find the truth'.

The next day Logan received Briggs reports on Farrell via e-mail. These reports stated volumes about the man's previous drug busts. There was also information on his current operation. It had a lot to do with two Colombians visiting the UK. It seemed Farrell had his hands full with these tourists. While going through these reports, Logan discovered Briggs had left a long list of contact numbers and names. Briggs had also put down Farrell's office number too. Logan eventually dialed the number. 'Who's this?' Farrell asked. He was in his office writing up a report for his superiors. 'My name's Jarrett'. Logan answered harshly. 'What can I do for you Mr. Jarrett?' Farrell asked. He remembered he had heard that name before. 'I've got a solution to your current problem'. Logan whispered. 'What are you talking about?' Farrell asked. 'What is your interest in this man, if I may ask?' Farrell asked again. 'He owes me money Commander' Logan whispered. 'But the fact is I've got something which might be of interest to you'. 'What might that be?' Farrell asked. He was becoming somewhat nervous. Logan played the tape for him on the phone. Farrell was surprised when he listened to the tape. After a few minutes Logan said, 'Can you now see why we should meet Commander Farrell'. 'Where do I meet you?' Farrell asked. 'There's a back alley near Charlie's Tavern'. Logan whispered. 'It's situated in Wood Green. Come there tonight. Eleven o'clock prompt. And don't bring anyone'. Logan dropped the receiver on the cradle of the phone. He had given Ken Farrell something to think about. Ken Farrell's mind raced with questions as he got off the phone. What was Quentin Baker up to? Farrell kept thinking. He needed answers. He wondered whether this was some trick. It could be. He was going to play along with this madness simply because of one reason. The man he called Jarrett had something in his possession; a tape. Farrell wondered whether his place was still bugged. He scrambled up the phone and dialed his number at home. He called Sergeant Miguel. 'Hello' Sergeant Miguel said picking up the phone. 'We have a problem'. Farrell said quietly.

'What is it Senor?' 'Well' Farrell said. 'You've probably heard of a bloke called Jarrett?' 'Yes'. Miguel said. 'Rat remarked about this man when I met him in Mexico'. 'He eavesdropped on our conversation last night. In fact he taped it. He claims Baker put him up to this. I believe he's up to something. I'm not taking any chances. He's asked me to meet him somewhere tonight and he's told me not to bring anyone'. 'Are you out of your mind?' Sergeant Miguel asked. 'No! But that's why I need you to go over every inch of the house. Search the bloody place for bugs damn it!' He dropped the phone and stood up from his desk. Farrell paced the floor for a while. He then went back to his desk and banged his fist on it. 'I'll kill you, Baker!' He scooped up the phone and called one of his informants. He found out from this informant where the meeting point was situated.

That night Farrell parked his vehicle across the street and walked cautiously towards the alley. He decided not to carry a gun on him. On his way to the meeting point Sergeant Miguel phoned and confirmed his fears. The policeman couldn't find any listening devices in the house. Farrell reached the dark alley and saw Logan. Logan held a pistol in one hand and a pencil flashlight in the other. Farrell became nervous. He decided to play it by ear. When Farrell was near enough to see Logan's face, he recognized him. 'You're the bloke I saw last night at the restaurant' he said angrily. 'Where's Rat?' 'I was hoping you could tell me that Commander'. Logan whispered. 'What exactly do you want? Farrell asked. 'Why do I get the feeling you are blackmailing me?' Logan shrugged his shoulders. 'I can't help but feel in a way that might be true'. He rasped. 'Rat seems to have vanished for some reason. I understand he works for you occasionally'. 'He does' Farrell answered cautiously. 'But I haven't seen him. I'm not quite sure you know what you're dealing with here Mr. Jarrett'. 'Oh I do'. Logan whispered. 'Where's the tape recording of the conversation I had with my colleague last night?' 'I've still got it'. Logan said. 'But it won't be in my possession that long if you don't cooperate with me'. 'What do you mean?' 'I want you to find Quentin Baker' Logan whispered. 'I need my money Commander. Otherwise, I'm going to give that tape to the cops. I know you won't like that'. 'How much does Baker owe you?' 'That's none of your business'. Logan whispered. 'It could be if we came to some kind of arrangement' Farrell said. 'You see, if I help you find Rat, you could help me get rid of him. I'm willing to pay you good money for that and employ you in my organization'. 'I'm listening, Commander'. Logan whispered. 'How much are you willing to part with?' Farrell smiled evilly in the dark. He said, 'Lots more than you can imagine Mister Jarrett. If you agree to kill Rat'

II

Meanwhile, in a pub near Heathrow Airport Rat was sitting at a table with Dominic Samosa. 'You come highly recommended by someone I represent Mr. Baker. But your reputation still precedes you?' Dominic Samosa asked. The Rat laughed. 'I'm only a freelance agent and there are no strings attached in my line of work'. 'I hope so my friend, for your sake. My business partner wants no complications whatsoever'. 'I thought you said your associate wanted to have a chat with me'. 'Yes' Samosa said. 'But he requested that I should meet you here first'.

'When am I going to meet him?' Dominic Samosa said nothing. The Rat wondered if his host was thinking about that question. It seemed the man was absorbed in thought for a while. 'What's all this about?' Quentin Baker asked. 'You haven't given me any clues yet'. 'My associate wants you to find the list for him'. For a moment the Rat looked stunned. 'Have I hit a nerve?' Samosa asked. 'If my information is correct, before your unfortunate accident, you were assigned to undertake the same task by Jason Phelps'. 'What exactly do you want and what's this business all about?' The Rat said angrily. He stubbed the remains of the cigarette he was enjoying in an ashtray. 'As you know, Jason Phelps is dead'. Samosa said. 'My associate and I believe he failed in his quest to get hold of the list. It's probably hidden away in Paul Lukman's home. We want you to find it and bring it to us'. 'Well, since you know so much what's in it for me and what is Farrell's interest in all this?' 'You'll be paid handsomely Rat'. Samosa said. 'We know you studied the layout of the Lukman home thoroughly. Farrell must not know anything about this operation. I have some business to sort out with him but it has nothing to do with this' 'Out of curiosity' The Rat asked. 'What is all that about?' Again Dominic Samosa wouldn't say anything. Quentin Baker sighed 'I give up' he said. 'You need not worry about that'. Samosa finally said. 'My associate simply wants to know whether you are going to undertake this assignment.' 'I'll try my hand at this job'. Rat said. Samosa smiled thinly. He had contacted the crook and had one thing in mind when he called him on the phone. He wanted Baker to come and work for him. The Rat agreed to do so under such short notice. 'There's something else' Samosa said dryly. 'Farrell is upset that some of my Country men are on his turf trying to take over. He suspects you have a hand in that, and is looking for you. He's planning to take them down with the help of a Mexican policeman named Miguel. It amuses me to know Farrell is threatened in his own territory'. The expression on the Rat's face changed at the mention of Sergeant Miguel. He recalled the run in with the man in Mexico. The Rat craved revenge. He shuddered at the thought of Farrell working with the Mexican. He was going to contact a few people to find out where he could get hold of Miguel. 'I guess you could consider the Commander a softie'. He said tersely. 'I've had nothing to do with his recent misfortunes with these people. Did you say Miguel was helping him with this matter?' Samosa nodded his head. 'Yes' He said. 'Do you know him?' 'Let's just say I've met him'. Rat said dryly. 'I didn't like him to be

119

quite honest'. Samosa pretended he didn't hear that last bit. He finished his whiskey and stubbed the thin cigar in the same ashtray the Rat was using. He got up from his chair. 'Goodbye Mr. Baker'. He said. 'I will contact you soon'. Dominic Samosa left the place. 'You better had'. Rat muttered. I'm going to enjoy taking up that job of yours'.

III

Emmanuel Gonzalez looked up from the desk. His partner Cristian Delgado walked into the suite they had at the Hilton Hotel in Park Lane. He asked, 'Where have you been Cristian?' Gonzalez's partner shrugged his shoulders and grinned. He was looking smart, but was casually dressed in a T shirt and plain trousers. 'I went downstairs'. He said. 'And I've been chatting with a beautiful lady in the bar. She's nobody you should worry your head over my friend'. Delgado said. 'Did you phone the boss?' 'No, he phoned us'. Gonzalez said simply. 'We've got trouble heading our way. It appears that Sergeant Miguel is in London, and he's been tipping off someone here about us. Guess who? Ken Farrell. The boss wants us to do something about it'. Delgado nodded. He sat down on the sofa. 'Have you got an address for the Sergeant?' Gonzalez smirked and said, 'Miguel's using Farrell's house. You have to kill him there and make sure nothing is traced back. The boss was very specific with his instructions. He also wants you to implicate Farrell in that mess'. 'Rest assured, my friend' Delgado said. 'You can be sure that will be done. I'll have a shower and change into something else. How did the boss get hold of this information?' 'Samosa told him'. Gonzalez said. 'Remember he's got informants in London. The boss has agreed to give him twenty kilos of heroin for his trouble. He wants it to be a generous gift because he believes the man's services will be of use again'. Cristian Delgado got up from where he sat. He went to the window. It was a warm day. Delgado saw the beautiful view and the swimming pool on the hotel floor below theirs. There were only a few people in or around it. A young man sitting near the pool wore colorful swimming trunks. And, a woman was wearing a very small designer bikini which made her stand out from the other people there.

'I'm going to shower'. He said. 'I'll carry out the job tonight if that's possible. But, I'll need more information to work with'. He headed for his bedroom. Gonzalez sighed and decided to check his pistol. It was holstered under the expensive suit he was wearing. When Delgado came out he was undressed, but wrapped in a big towel. 'You better get it right Delgado'. Gonzalez said, 'Senor Cortez wants no mistakes here. Remember he still wants us to keep an eye on the new syndicate in London'. The contract killer said nothing from the bathroom.

CHAPTER 17
Part I

A taxi dropped off Cristian Delgado on a lonely back street that night. The time was eleven o'clock. Cristian Delgado was smartly dressed in a dark suit. His partner Gonzalez had made contact with an informant that afternoon. He had clarified a few things with this man. So Delgado now knew that Farrell was not going to be in the house at that time, because he was attending a Police social function in the city with a few colleagues. He also knew that Sergeant Miguel had not left the house since he had come into London. The contract killer had been given a lay out of the big house. He had also been given information of Sergeant Miguel's activities in there. The informants had been keeping an eye on Farrell's residence. They were also watching from a distance with a camera with a long lens fitted to it. On this night they were called off, so that the assassin could carry out his job.

Cristian Delgado was now more than eager to carry out the job. Before he left the hotel that night, he decided he would take the back alley. He had his reasons. He wanted the element of surprise on his side when he took care of his victim. Delgado knew Sergeant Miguel was no fool. So even though he had access to all that information he was still taking precautions. There were no lights in the house. That seemed a little bit strange. Delgado remembered the informant had pointed out that the lights were always switched off in the early hours of the morning. So why weren't the lights on at all or had Miguel gone to bed? Delgado couldn't come up with a logical answer. He grew suspicious all of a sudden. But concluded it would not be a problem.

Delgado reached the back door of the house. He produced a small flashlight and a slim sharp object. The object allowed him to get into the kitchen which was empty. Delgado put it away and lifted his revolver from his holster. He moved stealthily into the tiled hall way. The assassin decided to go up the staircase and check the rooms. He suddenly dropped that thought and searched the sitting room instead. Delgado made his way into the sitting room and he noticed a dimmed glimmer of light coming from somewhere. He moved towards it and discovered he was standing near a desk. On the desk was a reading lamp. The glimmer of light came from there. Delgado suspected immediately that someone could be in the house. He almost fell over something as he stepped forward. Delgado took a look with his torch. It looked like someone's corpse. He cautiously bent over to examine it. He rolled it over and recognized the man on the floor.

It was Sergeant Miguel. He was dead! Delgado nearly jumped out of his skin when the next thing happened. The sitting room light was suddenly switched on. In that instant something was thrown in the air with lighting speed towards him. It was a specially designed throwing knife. Delgado couldn't react in time. And that cost him his life. The knife stuck in his throat. The contract killer died instantly.

The Rat made sure he was dead. He didn't know who the guy was. He didn't care. The crook took the knife away and wiped it on the dead man's expensive suit. The Rat had killed Sergeant Miguel as he had promised. He had incidentally finished off the job by making sure there were no witnesses. Quentin Baker switched off the desk lamp. He then turned off the light in the sitting room. He walked out of the house with his walking stick. As he did, he smiled in the dark. He knew Farrell might have a heart attack if he found the dead bodies in the house.

II

Logan looked through the window of his apartment. He saw it had begun drizzling outside. He stood thinking about his meeting with Ken Farrell. Logan needed to put Farrell and Baker behind bars. The Rat was probably aware of Farrell's current plans to take down the Columbian syndicate in London. And he probably knew far too much about Farrell and his activities. Perhaps that was why Farrell wanted to get rid of him. All these hoodlums will be brought to Justice, Logan thought. His body was still aching from the beating he had taken previously and his head was hurting too. His phone suddenly rang. He went towards the desk and picked up the phone. 'Jarrett', he said. 'We've got a problem Mac'. The voice on the other end was frantic. It was Hawke. 'What is

123

it this time?' Logan sighed. 'Two men were found dead in Farrell's house tonight. One of them was Sergeant Miguel. The other man was a Columbian tourist by the name of Cristian Delgado. Word has it on the grapevine that Delgado was a contract killer. He was visiting the UK with an associate. Emmanuel Gonzalez, Another contract killer'. 'What was Miguel doing here and how do you know all this, Hawke?' Logan asked. 'Briggs phoned me up. He told me'. Hawke said. 'I understand Farrell's still in shock. He was nowhere near the house when this happened. He was attending a Police social function in the city. It's the season for such events and Briggs was there. Anyway, Farrell's been called in for questioning. Nothing serious I should imagine. But he might be put under surveillance. He won't be sleeping at his place tonight. He's made other plans'. 'I don't quite see the connection yet'. Logan rasped. 'Do you think Farrell had something to do with it?' 'Sergeant Miguel was one of Farrell's informants Mac'. Hawke said. 'I don't think Farrell did this. Everyone saw him at the party. He could have easily got rid of the Mexican policeman if he wanted to, using one of his goons to do the job. We mustn't forget the other victim was a professional killer. He was in the house too. Something's not right here'.

'Have you spoken to the old man?' 'No'. Hawke replied. 'But I will. He must have heard about it anyway. It's all over the news'. 'What caused the deaths of the two men?' 'Briggs thinks it was a knife'. 'Delgado?' Logan asked 'Both deaths were probably caused by the same weapon'. 'It doesn't add up' Logan whispered. 'What do you intend to do?' 'I'm going to keep my ear to the ground on this one sonny' Hawke said. 'What's happening on your end?' 'Farrell's hired me'. Logan rasped. 'He wants me to kill someone'. 'What!' Hawke asked 'When?' 'Calm down Hawke. He hasn't set a date yet. Besides, I've got to find the man first. He seems to have vanished. I convinced Farrell I mean business. But I've got this feeling that he's onto me somehow'. 'I don't like the sound of that'. Hawke said. 'But be careful Mac. I'll contact you later'. The phone went dead. Logan put it down and went back to the window. It was still drizzling outside. He kept thinking. He remembered he had promised to release the tape in his possession to Ken Farrell once he killed the Rat. But what had this new sequence to do with the Colombian called Dominic Samosa? Logan turned round and looked at the phone on the desk. It was time to call Ruth. He was going to tell her to set up a meeting with Nick Slater.

124

III

Ruth phoned Nick Slater the next day at a café called 'Noel's'. It was near Bounds Green tube station. Ruth had chosen the spot. It had a nice beer garden and it was near a beautiful playground for children. The informant didn't like the idea of meeting the girl's boyfriend. But he had no choice in the matter since he hadn't been paid for his services yet. He also wanted to share some information he had acquired but for a price.

The time was almost seven o'clock and he was now sitting at a table with the others. Nick Slater felt uncomfortable. He despised the fact that the girl was trying to use him again. 'So what exactly do you want me to do Mr. Jarrett?' he asked nervously. 'Find the Rat and keep an eye on him'. Logan rasped. Nick looked at Ruth. 'What's in it for me this time'? He asked. Ruth dipped a hand in her leather handbag and brought up a wad of notes. 'You couldn't resist the temptation of asking about that could you?' She asked. She handed over a wad of notes. Nick Slater took the money and counted it. It was fifty pounds. 'Now where were we?' he asked looking at Logan. Logan brought him up to speed with the current occurrence. 'I want you to deal with this' he concluded. 'Farrell has something up his sleeve. Quentin Baker could probably be a part of all this'. 'If I recall, you were gathering more information on Rat' Ruth said. Nick sighed. 'Yeas' said. 'I still am. But something's not right, I'm afraid'. 'What is it?' The girl said. 'Well'. Nick began sourly. 'I couldn't get hold of his medical records. My contact at the hospital believes it disappeared into thin air as if it never existed'. 'What could have caused that?' Ruth asked. She was surprised. 'That's something I'd also like to know'. Logan rasped. 'I believe it might have something to do with your caper Mr. Jarrett'. Nick said. Logan whispered, 'Find Baker'. 'I hope I get paid for this'. Nick said. 'You will' Logan whispered. 'You get paid more if you produce snapshots'. 'That's comforting to know' Nick said sarcastically. He got up from his seat. 'You'll get your results' 'fast if I may add' Logan stammered. 'I never thought I'd say this Nick but good luck' Ruth said. 'You're going to need it'. Nick looked at the girl. He said, 'Won't we all. I've got your address and I know your number pretty lady. You'll be hearing from me'. He winked at Ruth and left the café. 'What do we do now Mac?' The girl asked. 'Nothing' Logan said. 'We wait Sweets. At least until Nick Slater turns up with something concrete again'. He was thinking again. Logan wondered if the Rat had become someone's target.

IV

Ken Farrell was quietly eating supper alone in the dining section of the Hutton Hotel. The small posh hotel was in Ilford in Essex. There were two elderly married couples eating in there as well. The place was well equipped with various facilities. It also had its own café, restaurant and bar.

Farrell had packed a bag with a few clothes. He had decided to stay there for a while till things cooled down. As Farrell ate his meal, he thought about the recent events which had shockingly taken place in his home. Sergeant Miguel was dead. Farrell had also discovered the body of another dead man in his house. The police had identified this person as Cristian Delgado. Farrell knew Delgado and his partner had been posing as tourists. The two men had been staying at the famous Hilton Hotel in Park Lane. Farrell was aware Delgado's partner Gonzalez had checked out of the Hilton now. The police were still looking for him. Farrell knew Baker was involved with this mess. He remembered the crook had complained bitterly about Miguel. The Rat had probably eliminated the victims in his house with a specially designed throwing knife. It was his calling card.

Farrell suddenly remembered Internal Affairs had kept asking him questions that were linked with the murders. Some of Farrell's colleagues were sympathetic with his situation but the rest amongst them were doing everything possible to discredit him. They were trying to lay the blame on him. His superiors had suspended him until they came up with something concrete. Farrell wanted to see the mystery man he called Jarrett. But he concluded that would have to wait. He was anxious to get hold of the tape the man had in his possession. He also wanted to take care of another thing; The Colombian drugs ring in the UK. Since the media had caught wind of all this, the news of the mysterious deaths had been circulated by major television and radio stations in town.

Farrell finished his meal and got up from his table. A young waiter came towards him carrying a tray. In it was a cell phone. 'There's a man on the line for you sir'. The waiter said. 'Did he say his name?' Farrell asked. The waiter shook his head. 'He only said he was a blast from your past', he said. The waiter set down the tray on the table. He bowed and made his leave. Farrell picked up the phone. He asked, 'Who's this?' 'Baker, you fool' the Rat said. 'How did you find me?' Farrell asked. He decided to sit down again. 'You've forgotten I've got my own connections'. The Rat said. 'Besides, the incident that's occurred at your place seems to be all over the news'. 'What do you want,

Baker?' Farrell asked nervously. 'You've kept yourself busy'. 'What do you mean?' 'Well'. Farrell started. 'There's no denying the fact that you definitely had something to do with all this'. 'I'm not going to admit that' the Rat said. 'Dominic Samosa has some business to settle with you. He knows a lot about your new operation so if I were you I'd watch out'. 'What's your point?' Farrell asked. 'You might need me, that's my point' the Rat said simply. 'You double-crossing Rat!' Farrell said angrily. 'Where have you been hiding? I'm sure you've sold me out'. 'I think you're becoming paranoid' the Rat said. 'Say what you want but I will have the last laugh'. 'We do have to meet, Farrell' Quentin Baker said seriously. 'In fact I'd like us to do that tomorrow night at your place. I'm sure the police would have concluded their business at the scene of the crime by then'. 'Are you crazy or what?' Farrell asked. 'I'm sure you must be out of your mind. I won't have anything to do with you again'. 'You don't have a choice Commander'. Quentin Baker said. 'I've got a business proposition to make. I'll be expecting you there by ten sharp'. The cell phone went dead. He put it on the table. He saw that one of the elderly couples was staring at him. But he didn't take any notice of them. Farrell decided to think for a while, he was worried. The conversation he had with Baker didn't reveal much. Quentin Baker wasn't telling him something? Farrell knew he had to stay one step ahead of the scoundrel. He tried to figure out what Baker was really up to now.

But the Rat's message was clear. Dominic Samosa was going to come looking for him if he didn't pay his debt or comply with the man's needs. The thought of that sent shivers down Farrell's spine. He wondered what to do next. He had hid the information he had received from Sergeant Miguel in a safe on his premises. He decided to get hold of the dossiers before anybody else did.

Farrell believed it would therefore be a good idea to dash down to his house. He wanted to pick up the dossiers on the two Colombians and dash back to the hotel. On the way he would phone Jarrett. He wanted the mystery man to find Baker's hideout. Most importantly he wanted him to kill him there.

Farrell quickly got up from his chair. He ignored the stares thrown at him by the same couple and headed towards his hotel room. He changed into something warm since it had become a very chilly evening. He wore an overcoat over a turtleneck sweater and clean trousers. Farrell made his way towards the reception desk at his hotel. He politely told the desk clerk he was going out for a while. He left and headed towards the parking lot.

Farrell was climbing into his vehicle when something happened. Two gun shots rang out from somewhere in the dark. The first shot shattered the windscreen of the car, and the second one hit him right between the eyes. Ken

Farrell was thrown off balance by the power of the slug. He dropped dead in his own pool of blood. Seconds later someone slid out of a car parked in the same car park. It was a man carrying a rifle. The man briefly examined Farrell's body. He had to make sure that Ken Farrell was dead. He then climbed back into his car and drove off. His name was Emmanuel Gonzalez.

CHAPTER 18
Part I

Logan climbed into the car parked across the street, it was a red mini. Nick Slater made sure Logan had strapped himself in his seat then drove the car onto the road. After a while Logan asked, 'So what have you got for me?' Nick Slater turned round slightly and directed his gaze towards the camera with a long lens at the back seat then looked at the man beside him. He said, 'I think I struck gold Mr. Jarrett'. 'What do you mean?' 'I kept an eye on the Rat just like you asked' Nick Slater said. 'I saw him tonight. I caught the whole thing on the camera too'. 'Good' Logan whispered. 'Take me where you saw him'. Nick Slater kept driving and eventually steered the car into the lonely lane where Farrell's big house could be seen through the drizzle of rain.

Slater parked his car a few yards away from the house. 'I'm sure I saw him here about an hour ago'. 'The police might still be guarding that place' Nick said 'But I would give anything to know what Rat was doing near the house, especially after what happened in there, a few nights ago'. Nick had kept a close watch on the Farrell house. He had a hunch the Rat would probably go there. His hunch had paid off. After confirming his findings he phoned Logan. He asked to meet him somewhere near Farrell's place. 'The cops were nowhere near the place' Nick Slater said, 'I did see Rat' Nothing happened for a while. Then suddenly something caught his attention. A black car zoomed past them and parked a short distance from their car. Someone came out of Farrell's house. At first Nick couldn't make out who it was. But it looked like a man dressed in a dark trench coat, carrying a suitcase. 'Grab that camera of yours' Logan said. Nick Slater grabbed the camera from the back seat and started taking photographs of the mysterious fellow. The man crossed the road to where the black car was parked. He climbed into it and it was driven off. Logan could not see who was driving the car.

'What do we do?' Nick asked curiously. He put the camera on his lap. 'Follow that car' Said Logan. Nick Slater drove off and as he picked up speed gradually, he made sure the occupants in the black car did not spot his vehicle. As he got closer, he could see that the car was a BMW. The man in the trench coat was Dominic Samosa.

II

Emmanuel Gonzalez parked his car on a street in South London. He hurriedly got out of the car and took with him a black suitcase. Gonzalez crossed the street and unlocked the door of the house. He went in. The place was a secret hideout. It was owned by a contact working for his boss. It was actually a bed and breakfast accommodation. Some corrupt Columbian politicians stayed there when they were on holidays in England.

Gonzalez switched the light of the small hallway on and climbed the staircase. He opened the door of the small bedroom and went in. He put the suitcase on the bed and opened it. Gonzalez gently caressed the high-powered rifle he had used that night then put it away in a wardrobe in the room. The suitcase went under the bed. The assassin knew he still had work to do. Although he had avenged his partner, he now had to make contact with his boss through Samosa. Gonzalez wanted to tell Hosea Cortez that Ken Farrell was dead. But there had been a slight complication. The British police force was now looking for him. They had probably discovered that he was Delgado's associate.

Gonzalez had quietly checked out of the Hilton Hotel at Park Lane that morning. He had decided to lay low and stay here for a while. Gonzalez knew he had to abandon the assignment which he was asked to accomplish with his late partner which was to make sure that the new drugs' ring formed was run smoothly in the UK. Now unless a miracle happened this would not be. Gonzalez looked out of the window. The phone on the wall started ringing. At first the assassin was hesitant to pick it up. Then he eventually did. Gonzalez wondered who was on the other end of the line. He hadn't gotten in touch with anyone yet, so who knew where he was staying and how?

'Who's this?' The person on the phone said, 'You need not worry to say my name aloud, my friend. Even though I understand this line is a secure one'. Gonzalez recognized the voice. He knew whom it belonged to. It was Dominic

Samosa. Gonzalez believed his boss had probably heard something about his recent feat. Cortez may have decided to act upon what he had been told. It almost seemed possible that Samosa had been hired now to bring him in or kill him. Gonzalez wondered what the task was and how much was the man paid to carry it out. 'What do you want? Gonzalez asked cautiously. 'Senor Cortez is concerned about you, amigo'. 'Is there any particular reason for that?' Gonzalez asked. 'I should assume you know why'. The man said. 'He is aware of the present predicament you find yourself in. So he has decided to trade you off for a while till things settle down'. 'How did all this come about?' 'I've been paid to help you. I will encourage you to render your services when it is needed. You only have to pack your bag if you have one with you and wait'. Gonzalez couldn't believe his ears when he heard this, but he decided to carry on with the conversation. 'What are you talking about?' Gonzalez asked. 'I can only tell you what I know' Samosa said. 'My job at this point in time is to ensure that you've got this information'. 'What else do you know?' Gonzalez asked anxiously. It seemed Cortez had made other plans'. 'You'll be in this country for a little while longer as I understand'. Samosa began. 'I don't think you should worry'. 'A hit went down tonight'. Gonzalez said. 'You need not say more amigo' Samosa said. 'A reliable source relayed that to me. Senor Cortez has made sure you will travel back safely to Mexico after you render your services to me'.

Suddenly there was a knock on the door. Gonzalez quietly whipped his gun out. He told Samosa. 'Take a look outside from the window'. Samosa then said. 'There's a black car parked on the street. It's waiting for you'. Gonzalez took a peek from the window. He could see a black vehicle parked in the street. He could also see the make of the car. It was a BMW.

'There's a black car parked outside all right'. He said. 'Then you are in business as my new employee'. Samosa said. The phone went dead. Gonzalez placed the receiver back on the cradle. He sighed. He wondered what lay ahead now.

III

Adrian Meyers sat behind his desk in his office. 'You were supposed to keep Farrell alive. What happened?' he asked. 'I've no idea' Hawke shrugged his shoulders. 'My source simply stated that the poor chap was shot dead in a car park that belonged to a good hotel restaurant in town. According to the police report he was only going out for a short while in his car'. 'This happened while the police were investigating the deaths of the two men found on his premises?' Meyers enquired. Hawke nodded his head. 'And according to that

131

same report internal affairs were investigating Farrell and his most recent pursuits. What did they find?' 'Nothing I'm afraid'. Hawke said. 'They were still investigating the man when this happened'. 'I'm disappointed Derek' Meyers said. 'Where does this investigation take us from here?' 'I don't know Sir'. Hawke said. 'But I know that all hope is not lost yet'. 'What do you mean?' 'Logan has a taped conversation with Farrell on it. I've listened to the tape. It may not serve as evidence in a court of law. But it shows that Farrell was really up to no good'. 'When can I listen to this tape?' Meyers asked. 'And where's Logan?' 'The last time I checked, he was trying to infiltrate Farrell's nest. That's come crashing down now. So he might be looking at another angle. And only the good Lord knows what that might be. I'll try to contact him, Sir'. 'This is now urgent Derek. I need that tape. It could give us answers to this whole mystery' the old man said. 'You listened to the tape. What did you think?' 'What if I told you the dead policeman called Miguel could have had some strange dealings with Ken Farrell. On the tape Samosa's name came up'. 'Interesting' Meyers quipped. 'But I wonder why?' 'I'd like to know as well' the detective said. He got up from his chair. 'I'm trying to dig up something dirty on Samosa. I haven't found anything yet. He's managed to keep every single business deal he's done in the UK clean or so it seems. I'll find that loophole'. 'What about Kidman?' 'Logan was following a lead in that direction too. But the trail's gone cold'. 'Well' Meyers said. 'I'm going to write up a report on the latest incident. I'm also going to phone my contacts in Mexico. I'd have to ask them to stall closing this case from their end till we straighten things out from here. Meantime, I've got something else to tell you'. 'What is it Sir? Hawke asked. 'Professor James and his daughter are back in London. They came back a few days ago' Meyers said dryly. He looked at his watch. 'And they will be here any minute. I understand they're discussing a date for my friend's burial. I think you should wait'. 'What about the rumored attempt to kidnap them?' The detective asked. 'Was that just a fluke?' 'I don't think it was Derek'. Meyers said puzzled. 'The Colombians were trying to pull a fast one. My contact's information was accurate'. 'Do you really want me to stick around Sir?' 'You might as well run along after you see them come into the office'. Meyers said. 'But, I will be discussing the funeral arrangements with them. I'll fill you in on the details later on. And, that's only because I want you to attend the funeral service with me'. 'I'll think about it, Sir'. Hawke said. 'I don't like funerals'. 'Who does? Meyers said smiling wryly. 'Besides, you don't have a choice. You're coming anyway. Just treat it as business as usual'.

SNAKE AMONGST SHADOWS

There was a knock on the door. A lady walked in. It was the old man's new secretary. She said, 'The Professor is here Sir'. Meyers nodded at her. The detective sat down again. Professor James and his daughter stepped into the room. 'Good Afternoon Professor' the old man said. 'I hope you had a pleasant trip back to London'. He extended his hand. The Professor shook it. Meyers made a gesture for the couple to sit down. They did. Hawke got up and shook the Professor's hand. Moments later he made his way to the door. He said, 'I think I'll be making my way Sir. I'll talk to you soon, Professor. It was a pleasure meeting you'. Adrian Meyers nodded his head. As Hawke left the building he knew he had to find Logan.

IV

Ruth Ryan was at home looking at the Rat's snapshot. Her informant had phoned her about the job done the previous night. He was there with Logan. 'What do you think?' Nick finally asked. He looked at the girl. Ruth got up from where she sat and looked at Logan. He said nothing. 'What are you going to do?' She asked. 'I don't know yet' Logan whispered. 'But I'd like to find out how all this is linked with Tom George'. Nick Slater got up from his seat and made for the door. 'Nick' Ruth said. 'Where are you going?' 'I thought we had finished talking'. Nick said. 'Besides, I really have to go. I've got some private business to attend to. I'll be back to collect what belongs to me'. 'We haven't finished this conversation yet' said Ruth. She looked at Logan again. 'Someone else was driving the black car'. Logan rasped. 'I wonder who? It was quite dark'.

Nick Slater hesitated a bit then made his way to the door again. 'I'll come back if you do request my services' he said. 'What do I do next Mr. Jarrett?' 'Nothing' Logan whispered. 'I'll take things up from here. But if I were you, I'll keep in touch'. Nick nodded his head. He shut the door behind him and left the flat. Logan suddenly switched on his smart phone. It was ringing. 'Hello' he said'. 'I've got some information for you Mac' Hank Bell said. 'Come and see me. The same place'. 'What's all this about Hank?' 'George'. Bell said. The phone line went dead. Only a handful of people had Logan's mobile phone number. The big man was one of them.

Logan decided to ring Hawke. He did. 'I presume something's up'. Hawke said. 'Where are you?' 'Never mind that' Logan whispered. 'I've got some news for you'. 'What's that?' Hawke asked sarcastically. 'Tom George is involved in this caper after all. But I'm yet to find out how' 'I thought he was dead?' 'He's not' Logan rasped. 'That's why I want to find him'. 'Professor James and his daughter are back in town'. Hawke said. 'When did they come back?' Logan asked. 'A few days ago; I saw both of them today at the old man's office. They're now making funeral arrangements to bury Paul Lukman'. 'Why don't you tag along with them?' 'Perish the thought Mac'. Hawke said. 'The old man thinks that would be a good idea too. But I disagree. Anyway, he wants to listen to your tape. He believes it might be useful'. 'I told you it would' Logan whispered. 'You're never patient' 'Enough of that'. Hawke said. 'When do I get the tape?' 'Don't worry' Logan whispered. 'I'll have it sent to your door step'. 'That's okay. As long as nobody gets hold of it before I do'. 'Kidman's in London' Logan said slowly. 'And I'm almost sure he's part of this little charade now. He's probably been paid to do a new job'. 'What makes you so sure about everything you've told me so far?' 'I've come across some photos which suggest that. He's been hanging around Farrell's place'. 'You're ahead of me then'. Hawke said sourly. 'I've found nothing more on Dominic Samosa or even the Colombians'. 'You will'. Logan whispered. 'I wish you knew how I feel' Hawke moaned. 'We might need to meet up soon to discuss strategy. In the meantime keep me posted'. The line went dead. Logan put away the phone and looked at Ruth. 'I need a favor from you, Sweets' he whispered. 'What is it darling?' 'Go over to my apartment this evening. Pick up the tape. It's in the compartment built in the bedroom. Use your spare keys'. Logan whispered. 'Seal it and deliver it by hand. I'll give you Hawke's number and his address. Guard the tape with your life'. 'What are you going to do Mac?' 'I've got some catching up to do with an old friend'. Logan whispered 'I'm going to meet Hank Bell'.

CHAPTER 19
Part I

Logan went into the Fair Blues restaurant. It was midnight and the place was empty as usual. He spotted the big man at the table and approached him. Logan knew his friend always had his ear to the ground and would know when there was danger ahead. Logan still couldn't get one thought out of his head. That Tom George was presumably alive and was hiding out somewhere. What had Hank Bell found out about the crook and how was it connected with this whole mystery?

'Is the seat taken?' Logan asked. Bell sniggered. He shook his head. 'Sit down, Mac' he said. Logan took a seat at the table. 'What's the matter Hank?' Logan asked. 'Still, investigating that mugging linked with George?' 'Yeah' Logan whispered. 'Why?' 'Well' Bell began. 'It looks as if it's quite a case. Word has it that George was closely associated with some Columbian drugs gang, new in this town'. 'Tell me more', Logan whispered. 'This Colombian gang clashed with a London drug cartel a couple of weeks ago. And, the police have been trying to take both gangs down ever since'. Bell said. 'George was linked with this new outfit until he got snuffed out. Now, a man by the name of Samosa is running things temporarily for them. He's a ruthless business man. He's also worked for George in the past as a courier. But this was some years ago. His orders come straight from Mexico. From a crime lord he's close to, called Cortez. Cortez has contracted Samosa to do his dirty work for his men. That's one of the reasons why I phoned you Mac'. 'So you don't know who these people are?' Logan asked. 'I haven't the faintest idea', Bell said. 'But there's something else'. 'What is it?' Logan asked. 'My source told me George was also seen with a young woman a couple of times. It's been assumed he was

135

sharing vital information with her'. 'It doesn't make sense' Logan rasped. 'One can always assume they were working together. Why?' Amazing! Logan thought. So Willie Briggs was right all along. Logan then told the big man about his adventures in Mexico and what he had learnt about the elusive criminal named Tom George.

Logan suddenly heard something and almost got up from his seat. He'd heard Footsteps. He swung his head round and looked towards the door. He saw Hawke and swore. Hank asked, 'Do you know this fellow?' Logan nodded his head 'He's my boss' he whispered. 'Is there something you're not telling me, sonny?' Hawke asked, 'You're starting to give me the creeps'. Logan whispered. 'Where did you spring from?' 'Your girlfriend delivered the tape' Hawke said 'and she told me where to find you'. He walked into the room and took a good look at the big man. 'Who have I the pleasure of meeting, friend or foe?' Hank sniggered. 'What do you think mate?' Hawke ignored the question and turned his attention to Logan 'Samantha Hastings used to be my wife', he said. 'So what aren't you telling me Mac?' Logan hesitated a bit. 'Why didn't you tell me you were once married to her?' he finally whispered. 'It was a long time ago Mac' Hawke said. 'What has she got to do with this anyway?' 'It appears she's been in on all this, right from the word go. Now, I think you should sit down because although you got divorced a long while ago, I've got some bad news for you. Eddie Payne wanted Samantha dead. She was mugged by Joe and his boys. It killed her. I was informed by Briggs, he knew you would be upset so he's been trying to hide it from you ever since'. Derek Hawke looked stunned by this news. He regained his composure immediately and shot a look at the big man. 'How do you know this Mac?' 'Take a chair. Derek, I've got something else to tell you', Logan whispered. 'Hank Bell is my friend. When he hears something dodgy, he tells me. This seems like one of those times', the detective pulled a chair up and sat down. He still looked shocked.

'Spill the beans Mac' he said. 'And I need a drink', the big man got up from where he sat at the table and went behind the scanty bar. He made a drink and brought it back in a tray. It was a whisky. 'The drink's on me mate', he said. Hawke nodded. 'You can stay Hank'. Logan whispered. The big man went back to his chair. Logan told Hawke all he had learnt about the dead girl. He only wished he had done this earlier. His boss listened to everything he had to say. 'So you see'. Logan whispered. 'Your ex-wife's involvement not only complicates issues, it's opened up a whole can of worms which already leaves a bad taste in my mouth'. 'But why tell me now? You could have let me in on all this weeks ago'. Hawke said. 'I'm sorry' Logan whispered. 'I didn't want to hurt you or jeopardize everything until I was quite sure of all the facts'. 'I'm assuming Sergeant Briggs was in on this too', Hawke said. 'I knew something wasn't right. You've been hiding things from me, Mac. What else is there?'

'There's nothing else, and I've told you everything I know. Briggs knew about your ex-wife. He's been working on a similar homicide case that's why. I just didn't want him to tell you'. Hawke drowned the whisky and got up from his chair and said, 'I loved her Mac. But my marriage to her didn't last. To think it would come to this' 'Why did you leave her?' 'I found out she was a corporate spy. I didn't like that. She was also cheating on me at the time', 'so what happens now?' Logan asked. 'I don't know yet but I think you should investigate the leads you've got', 'I will', Logan whispered. 'I know someone who could point you in the right direction', Bell said. 'He was Lenny Miller's best mate. His name's Desmond Morris. He's a tough nut. If he's shoved around a bit, he might know something. I'll set up a meeting with this guy. Leave it to me', 'I don't really want to drag you into any of this old friend', Logan whispered. 'You're not' Bell said simply. The detective got up from his seat. 'I think I'll better leave you two to it then', he said. 'I need some answers damn it! I don't care anymore what you do to get them', Hawke headed towards the door then looked back at Logan. 'Thanks for shielding me from all this, sonny. But let's get to work. I'll mourn later. The old man really thinks he'll be able to get to the bottom of this business with that tape of yours. We must bring these cohorts to justice!'

After Derek Hawke left the restaurant Logan had one puzzling question on his mind. Were the new drug's gangs involved with the lost treasure of Tikal? 'Set up that meeting Hank', Logan rasped. 'You can count on that'. Bell said. 'How do you think your boss is taking his ex-wife's death?' 'I don't know' Logan whispered. 'But he'll survive. There's a great possibility he might not focus on the job from now on. But he's got to. It's a shame the ex-wife got involved in something she couldn't handle. And that makes me wonder about something?' 'What's that?' Bell asked. 'Where the hell is Tom George?'

II

Hank Bell phoned Des Morris that night. The meeting was to be at the man's place the following evening. Bell knew Morris was a thug for hire. The man ran a racket on the docks. Hank Bell knew this because he had worked for him there. Morris was swarthy and tough faced. He lived exuberantly upstairs in a flat near Soho Square. He was smartly dressed in a powder blue suit. A cigarette dangled in his mouth and he had a glass of red wine in his hand. He was behind an oak desk. Morris quickly looked at his wristwatch. It was nearly nine o'clock. 'Make this quick Jarrett. So what's all this about?' he said gruffly. 'Bell didn't actually say', Logan sat comfortably on a couch. He was wearing a dark windcheater. He was also carrying his duffle bag on him. 'I'm interested in Miller's offer' Logan whispered. 'What is that, if I may ask?' Morris asked. He was slightly baffled. 'He was recruiting people for a new Colombian syndicate in London', Logan began. 'He approached me because I run a small close protection service. I was wondering if you knew anything about this deal, since he's your close friend'.

The thug left the glass of unfinished wine on the desk and stubbed the remains of his cigarette in an ashtray. 'It seems Miller ran into a bit of trouble. He's dead', he said. 'The word is that he was running his mouth off about that job. He was sliced with a knife. It's quite unfortunate since nobody was supposed to know he was doing a job in the first place'. Morris suddenly went for his revolver. It was strapped in a shoulder holster. He wasn't quick enough. Logan beat him to it. He pulled out his own pistol with lightning speed. Logan held his Beretta with ease. He stood up and pointed the gun directly at the thug. Logan was quick to spot the bulge of the revolver hidden beneath the thug's jacket. 'One move and you've had it' he whispered with deadly calm. 'Throw down your gun and kick it towards me' he continued. The thug hesitated for a second, but finally unstrapped his gun holster and did this. Logan could see the weapon in it was a revolver. He picked up the gun and emptied the bullets and put them in his pocket. He went towards the thug. 'You made a big mistake Morris' he rasped. 'I don't know what your game is Jarrett' Morris said. 'I thought you said you wanted to discuss business?' 'This has a lot to do with business all right' Logan whispered. He put down the empty revolver on the desk and turned round swiftly. In the blink of an eye he smashed his fist in the thug's jaw. It sent the man reeling to the floor. 'Where is Tom George?' he asked. 'I don't know what you're talking about'. The thug groaned in pain while on the floor. Logan grabbed him by the collar and picked him up. He punched the thug again and he fell over. 'I don't think you're telling me the truth punk'. Logan whispered. Blood dripped from the thug's mouth. He was cut open. Logan made for the door. 'Sorry things didn't work out with you Morris' he whispered. 'I'll get you for this! 'Morris yelled from where he lay on the floor. Logan closed the door behind him. He stood near the door in the dark hallway.

Morris crawled slowly to his desk and staggered up to his feet. He was dripping blood all over the place. He phoned someone. 'I need to see you. It's urgent' the thug said. 'Someone knows about the new syndicate. I had a visitor at my place tonight. He was trouble. His name's Jarrett'. The person on the other end responded to this. After a few minutes' Morris said, 'Then it's settled. I'll come round tonight'. He dropped the phone and swore. He then dug his hand into his pocket and wiped his split lip. 'You won't get away with this, Jarrett' he muttered. 'I'm going to make sure of that'.

Logan put away his gun. Then dug his hand into his bag and came up with a sharp object and a tranquillizer dart gun. Logan turned his attention on the front door. He opened it with the sharp object. It took a second. The thug was startled when Logan walked back into the sitting room with the weapon in his hand. The thug moved nervously away from the desk 'What is this?' he asked. Logan pointed the tranquillizer dart gun straight at the man's face. 'Start talking Morris' Logan whispered. 'And don't waste my time. You'll regret it if you did. Whom were you talking to?' 'Why do you want to know?' Morris asked. 'It's business' Logan whispered. 'Now tell me everything you know'.

Desmond Morris talked. He did that for quite a while too. When Logan felt he had picked up enough information from the man, he shot him with the tranquillizer dart gun. Logan made sure the dart hit the right spot. The thug suddenly grabbed his left arm and fell to the floor. He slipped into unconsciousness. Logan quickly dropped the weapon into his bag. He put a listening device in his ear and placed a micro transmitter in the man's shirt pocket. Logan phoned Bell on his mobile phone. 'I might have everything I need', he whispered. 'I'm going after Tom George and the rest of the ungodly'.

III

Dominic Samosa was in a big sitting room with Gonzalez. It was beautifully decorated with Chinese antiques and mahogany furniture. The contract killer had to admit that the room was exquisite. Gonzalez wondered if this was some ruse to get rid of him permanently. He had arrived at the house in the black chauffeured car. The place was in Shepherd's Bush, West London. Surprisingly Samosa had welcomed him. But so far nothing had happened. 'Does Cortez want me dead?' Gonzalez asked. 'My friend wants you alive and well'. Dominic said. 'But he wants you to work for me. Senor Cortez thinks you'll be useful right here while things cool down a bit. So I'd be careful about what I'd do if I were you. Right now, we seem to have a little problem'.

The chauffeur who drove Gonzalez back to the posh place stepped into the living room. He was now immaculately dressed in a dark brown suit. He was a tall, sturdy fellow with a goatee beard. He smiled wryly as he asked, 'I hope you're not arguing gentlemen'. Gonzalez's jaw dropped. He looked at Samosa

139

then at the newcomer. 'Who is this?' he asked. 'I don't remember you telling me your driver was in on the deal'. 'I didn't', Samosa said simply. 'However, allow me to introduce you to Mr. Tom George'.

Tom George bowed then said, 'Ignore the deception Gonzalez. It couldn't be helped. I face the same predicament you do. The police are probably looking all over for me now. I did a little disappearing trick. It was for a good reason too'. George said. 'Someone wants me dead. A man called Rat. I know for a fact he killed your partner Cristian Delgado'. 'Mr. George is going to work with us' Samosa said. 'I've worked with him before. I trust his judgment'. Gonzalez frowned. 'I don't have a problem with that' he said. 'But tell me why?' Tom George sat comfortably on one of the sofas. He looked at Gonzalez for a good minute then said, 'I'm the kingpin around here Mr. Gonzalez. Ken Farrell almost ran your boys out of town. He didn't like the competition. That's why he hired Baker to kill me. I'd like you to keep an eye on the man. He's dangerous. Anyway, Cortez wants this entire operation running smoothly and I'm going to make sure that's achieved'. 'What's in it for me?' Gonzalez asked. George grinned. He said nothing. He looked at Samosa. The Colombian said simply, 'A heavy pay check'. 'Did you say there was a little problem?' Gonzalez asked. Samosa nodded. 'An informant phoned this evening' he said. 'He's been invited here. He's run into some sort of trouble. I guess he wants to tell us all about it'. Suddenly the doorbell rang. The man at the door had a walking stick. It was the Rat.

IV

Des Morris got up slowly from the floor on unsteady feet. He was still a bit groggy. The thug looked at his watch. It was smashed to bits. This was probably during his fall on the floor. There seemed no other explanation for it. Morris looked at the wall clock in the sitting room. It was now 10.30pm. He was late for his meeting at Shepherd's Bush. Morris searched his pockets frantically for a minute. He relaxed when he found his car keys. The thug left the flat in a hurry. He dashed down the stairs towards his car. He climbed into it, driving off towards the meeting place. In the trunk of the car lay a dark figure. It was Logan.

Meanwhile Baker walked into the sitting-room. Dominic Samosa had opened the door for him. Samosa looked at Baker curiously. 'What exactly is this?' he asked. 'I thought we had an agreement'. 'I'd like to know more about the operation' Baker said. 'I'd also wondered if I could meet your associate at such short notice.' 'How did you find me?' Samosa asked. 'I've got my sources' the Rat said. Samosa muttered something under his breath. He didn't like this conversation. 'What were you doing at Farrell's tonight?' Rat asked. 'That's none of your concern'. Samosa said. 'The assignment is, and I will talk about that, when I deem it fit. Ken Farrell is dead. I have it on very good authority he was shot down like a dog'. The Rat shrugged. He didn't like that answer. He had turned up at Farrell's place as planned. He had wanted to discuss his newest venture with him. The Rat was aware that someone had been on Farrell's premises. But he didn't get a good look at the person. 'Who shot him?' he eventually asked. 'You're about to find out'. Gonzalez said.

The assassin was pointing his pistol at the Rat. And so was Tom George. Quentin Baker asked, 'What is he talking about?' 'You killed the man's associate at Farrell's place'. Samosa said. 'His name was Cristian Delgado. What do you have to say about that?' The Rat shrugged again. 'The poor sod stood in my way' he said. 'I was nosing around looking for someone else'. 'Do you have any names?' Samosa asked. 'Sergeant Miguel' the Rat said. 'A Mexican cop, I had a score to settle with'. 'I killed Farrell, if you didn't know'. Gonzalez sneered interrupting the conversation. 'You're next on the death list Rat!' He aimed his pistol at the Rat's head. Samosa looked at Gonzalez. He said, 'If I'm not mistaken, this isn't part of the plan'. The Rat realized he had fallen into a trap. He wasn't really surprised. But he was slightly taken aback when he saw that Gonzalez was prepared to shoot him right there in cold blood. Then Baker wondered why the man hadn't shot him dead yet. He believed it had to do with the job he had accepted to undertake. He turned his attention back to Samosa. 'Do we still have a deal?' he asked. 'Yes'. Samosa smiled thinly. 'But there's been a new development'. The Rat sighed. 'And what could that be?' he asked. There was a knock on the door. 'That must be Morris' Samosa said. He took a peek at the window. It was. 'Put down the gun and keep an eye on him. I'll get the door 'he warned Gonzalez. 'It's a pleasure to meet you at last Mr. Baker. My name is George' Tom George suddenly said. 'I've heard so much about you. In fact I've been looking forward to this moment'. 'You don't know the half of it'. The Rat said dryly. 'So have I'.

CHAPTER 20
Part I

Des Morris parked his Mercedes-Benz car in the street. He hurriedly climbed out, and headed towards the beautiful house situated in the exclusive area of Shepherd's Bush. Morris was nervous. He had good reason to be too and didn't want any complications. There were lights on in the house. The thug knocked on the solid oak door and was let in.

Meanwhile Logan opened the trunk of the car. He climbed out. He had hid in Morris' car, for the best part of an hour. It had taken that long to get to the house. Logan slapped something under the bonnet of the car. It was a small tracking device. In his head a clock kept ticking. He knew he had to think fast. He wished he knew the layout of the house. It was quite an old building.

There were no pedestrians walking the street. Logan moved quickly like a cat. He approached the building and broke into it. He pick-locked the door, and went into the basement with his pencil torch. He looked around and could see it was used as a storage room. But it was cold, dark and damp. Logan unlocked the door that led into the main building. He climbed the stairs like a fleeting shadow. His eyes were ice cold. He whipped out his pistol and switched off his torch. Then adjusted the earpiece in his right ear and listened for static. The frequency range was loud and clear. Logan could hear voices in the house quite clearly.

He kept moving through the endless corridor lit by an old-fashioned electric bulb. Logan could still hear the voices as he made his way in the house. They're probably in the sitting room he thought. But where is it? He decided to hide somewhere. He looked for a hiding place and found an empty bedroom.

He slipped into it and kept listening to the voices in the house. He froze when he found out Baker was in the house too.

In the sitting room Gonzalez asked, 'What do we do with Rat?' He lowered his pistol and looked at Samosa. 'I'm going to let George decide that' he said. The Rat shrugged. 'What are you talking about?' he said. 'I won't hesitate to kill you, Rat' George said smiling evilly. 'But that would obviously defeat the aim of having you here. You tried to kill me! '. He suddenly nodded his head to the assassin.

Gonzalez lunged at Rat and knocked him out cold. 'Rat won't be of any use to us if you kill him'. Samosa said. 'No. He won't' George said smiling. 'But I don't intend to do that'. The Rat was on the floor. His body was limp. Gonzalez looked at Samosa. He asked, 'now what?' 'It's somewhat complicated my friend' Samosa said. 'But we will now see if it's possible to get hold of the information we need'. 'We'll have the list'. George said. 'After I deal with this'. In a split second he shot Des Morris twice in the head. The man slumped dead. George went through the man's pockets and found the micro transmitter. He smashed the device to bits with his shoe. 'He's better to us dead than alive'. George said. 'I'm afraid we'll have to clean this mess up. This intruder called Jarrett is near here somewhere. That was some kind of listening device on Morris'. 'I thought Morris was on your payroll'. Samosa said. 'As you can see, he's not anymore'. George said. 'Both of you owe me an explanation'. Gonzalez said. 'Morris was just a mere stooge' George said. 'I can't afford to let anyone else upset this operation at this stage. Someone else almost did. It was his best mate and he's dead too'.

'What information are you guys talking about?' Gonzalez asked. He was surprised by the sudden action. 'We want Rat to steal this information from Paul Lukman's house. Jason Phelps tried to steal it. He failed. Samosa and I have now invested in this little venture'. 'What do we do with him then?' Gonzalez asked. He pointed at the Rat. 'I'm afraid he'll have to be locked up in one of the rooms'. George said. 'Samosa and I are going to pay Mrs. Lukman a visit. She probably might not want to cash in on this deal since she knows nothing of it. Quentin Baker's a clever thief and that's why we've hired him to do this job. He also knows the layout of the Lukman residence. I'll get rid of Morris. We'll be using his car. I'll dump it somewhere afterwards. There's a beer in the fridge. Grab it and wait'. Gonzalez looked at Samosa and sighed. He knew he was in for a long night.

II

Dominic Samosa and Tom George left the house in Morris's car. They found the car parked on the street. Gonzalez helped the two men dump the corpse in the car's trunk. The dead man was wrapped in a black plastic sheet. As Gonzalez walked back to the house, he remembered he had to confine the Rat. Gonzalez entered the sitting room and found himself looking into Logan's Beretta. Quentin Baker was still unconscious. 'Who are you?' Gonzalez asked. He was stammering. Gonzalez was surprised to see Logan in the room. 'Never mind that', Logan whispered. 'You've got work to do'. Gonzalez was scared. 'What are you going to do?' he asked again. Logan ignored him. Then he said, 'Shut the door. Drop your gun on the floor and step forward. Don't try anything funny. You're going to carry Rat'.

Logan had found the sitting room. He had left his hiding place and had eavesdropped on the rest of the conversation. He knew the listening device he had placed on the dead thug was found and destroyed. Gonzalez did as he was told. He closed the door gently. Then unbuttoned his jacket and took his revolver out. He dropped the gun on the floor and stepped away from it.

Logan said, 'We're going somewhere'. 'Where is this?' Gonzalez asked nervously. 'Shut up', Logan whispered. 'You'll know soon enough'. He nodded at the limp figure on the floor. Gonzalez picked up the Rat's stick. Then he hoisted him up on his shoulder. Gonzalez led the way. They went through the long winding hallway and then stopped at an oak door. The door led into the bedroom Logan had hid in. He instructed the man to open the door, and Gonzalez switched the light on. He stepped into the bedroom. 'Leave the light on'. Logan whispered. 'You might need it'. 'What are you going to do?' Gonzalez asked. 'That's none of your business' Logan rasped. 'But I guess you deserve an answer to your first question. Call me Jarrett'

Gonzalez dropped the Rat on the huge bed. He took a good look at Logan. 'So you're Jarrett?' he asked eventually. 'You're the rattlesnake'. Logan shrugged his shoulders. 'You could say that if that makes you feel better' he whispered. 'But your bosses appear to be the ones hiding amongst the shadows'.

Logan closed the door behind him. He locked it with the bunch of keys he had found dangling in the keyhole. He saw no reason to stay in the house anymore. So he left the same way he came in. Logan picked up a signal from his ear piece. It sounded like a vehicle's indicator light He dipped his hand into his bag and clicked on the special electronic compass on his smart phone. The sound of the signal grew stronger. Logan could see the car was headed

144

somewhere towards North London. He phoned Scotland Yard afterwards and left an anonymous message with the desk clerk. Logan asked the policeman there to make sure the two crooks in the house were apprehended. Then he switched off his smart phone. He knew the two men were safely locked up at the house at Shepherd's Bush. But in the back of his mind, he feared worse could still happen. His steely eyes picked out a car now parked in the street. It was a dark blue Astra. He went towards it. There was no one within sight. Logan broke into the car. He climbed into the vehicle and hotwired it. He eventually drove off. It took him approximately twenty seconds to do this.

Logan knew Hawke would skin him alive if he found out about this, but he recalled his boss had instructed him to do whatever it took to bring down these men. Logan's ear piece was still picking up strong signals. While driving the car through corner streets and alleys, he wondered whether he should call his boss on the phone. After a moment's hesitation he did. 'How are you holding up?' he asked. 'I'm okay', Hawke said. 'I'm at home doing some research for the old man'. 'Well, I'm in a stolen vehicle. It's a dark blue Astra. The registration number is FC 71 UF D. I'm driving it, and going towards North London'. Logan whispered. 'Tell me you're not joking Mac'. Hawke said. 'I'm not', Logan whispered. 'I'm onto something and I think you should know about it'. Logan told his boss what he had learnt from Morris. 'If what you say is true' Hawke said afterwards. 'It means the old man might know something we don't. This list is a mystery to me. Are you sure the Professor's daughter is not part of this charade?' 'Don't know', Logan whispered. 'If the Professor's daughter is involved then she could be doing this to pick up some cash or get rid of this information'. 'Okay'. Hawke said. 'I'll stay on top of this one. I'm off to see Meyers at the Lukman residence. The Professor is staying there with his daughter. I need this case solved. I'll take care of the mess you've made'. 'I'm touched'. Logan whispered. After a while he asked, 'What kind of research are you doing for the old man?' Hawke sighed. He said one word. 'Samosa' 'Interesting', Logan whispered. 'Found something more on him?' Hawke chose his words carefully. He said, 'Yes. It seems Samosa lent money to someone. Guess who?' 'Cut to the chase Derek', Logan snapped. His voice cut like a razor. 'Ken Farrell', Hawke said dryly. 'And it figures too. I should have known. The man's been in business with the Colombian for a few years'. 'Then there's a great possibility Farrell's been working for Samosa too'. Logan whispered. 'Yes, there is', Hawke said seriously. 'But that doesn't explain what's been happening. We have to tread carefully. The old man is still working on that tape of yours. He still wants answers. We haven't found any. I just hope this little

145

discovery of yours breaks the camel's back and provides us with the last straw'. 'So do I', Logan said slowly. 'I'm going to contact Briggs' He made a turn and went into another bend. 'How would that help right now?' Hawke asked. 'It won't', Logan whispered. 'But Willie deserves to know anyway. He saved my life remember? Besides, he's been investigating a murder case and it's linked with this caper'. 'Be careful Mac' Hawke said. 'Briggs won't be able to explain to the police you're the missing man. Anyway, keep me informed. Good luck'. Derek Hawke bid farewell and dropped the phone. Logan switched off his smart phone. He steered the car round another bend in the road and took a short cut.

Logan eventually drove into North London. He pulled up the stolen car into a street in Seven Sisters. The car he was tailing had stopped somewhere nearby. Logan climbed out of the stolen vehicle, and for a moment checked his bearings with the electronic compass. He also checked his pistol. Afterwards he went in search of Morris' car. Logan found the car parked in an alley. He wondered where the two men had gone. They had disappeared. Logan could feel a cold chill run down his spine. Suddenly another vehicle drove into the alley. Headlights flashed. He recognized the car. He knew who was behind the wheel. It was Sergeant Willie Briggs. Briggs' car screeched to a halt in front of him. He climbed out. He was holding a pistol and pointing it at Logan. 'What are you doing here?' Logan asked. 'I'll ask the questions Mr. Jarrett'. Willie Briggs said. 'I hope you haven't got yourself into trouble again?' 'What do you think?' Logan asked. He looked at the Mercedes Benz car for a second then continued. 'I've got some explaining to do Willie'.

III

Emmanuel Gonzalez frantically looked for a way to escape from the bedroom. He could not find any, so he went to where Baker lay on the bed. Gonzalez shook him up, and the Rat stirred. Baker opened his eyes slowly.

'You've got some nerve', The Rat said. He tried to get up. 'You're not in the position to talk right now', Gonzalez said. He was furious. 'What do you want?' The Rat asked. He ignored what the man had said. Gonzalez punched him in the mouth. 'I can handle it'. Gonzalez said eventually. 'I don't think so'. The Rat said. He wiped his bleeding nose with his hand. 'Why do you care?' Gonzalez asked. The Rat laughed. 'Let's just say I'm tempted to make you an offer' he said. 'But before I do that, how did we end up here?' Gonzalez hesitated a bit then said, 'Someone called Jarrett walked in here when Samosa and George left the house. He held me at gun point and forced me to bring you into this room'. 'Then we do need to get out of here', The Rat said. 'I bet the police are looking for me right now. You might want to stay here my friend, but I don't. Your bosses will eventually get rid of us. Jarrett wants to see me behind bars. I'd like to think you could ensure that doesn't happen. In return for your services you'll work for me. I can also get you a new identity. That's my offer'.

The Rat scrambled out of the bed and grabbed hold of his walking stick. He went straight to the door. Gonzalez thought for a moment. The man had made a good point. He had also made a good offer. Gonzalez didn't want the police authorities to get hold of him. He wanted to escape from this place. 'What then do we do?' he asked. 'I think you should leave that to me' The Rat said.

IV

Sergeant Willie Briggs lowered his gun as he approached Logan. He was cautious. 'You definitely have some explaining to do Mr. Jarrett'. He said. Logan whispered, 'I'll explain everything to you in a minute Willie'. He reached the car, and opened the trunk. He was holding a torch. Des Morris' body was stashed in an awkward position. Briggs came forward with his own flashlight. He saw the corpse. 'Who is that?' he asked. Logan said slowly, 'Morris'. Logan closed the trunk afterwards. Briggs asked, 'What's this business about?' Logan turned round to look at Briggs. He said slowly, 'Tom George decided to abandon his man here. He's with Dominic Samosa. The man is a Colombian'. 'I'm almost sure I saw two men walking out of this alley a few moments ago'. Briggs said. 'One of them stopped a taxicab. It was near a huddle of houses on the other side of the road. They were in a hurry. For the hundredth time what is all this about?' Logan stepped away from the car. 'Those men were probably George and Samosa'. He whispered. 'Morris was a hatchet man. George killed him and dumped him off right here. Who tipped you off?' 'I was following a lead from a reliable source', Briggs said. 'Morris was the focus of this enquiry. It's a shame he's dead. He was connected with my investigation in more ways than one. I'm certain of that now. I found out he was associated with the gang that mugged the Hastings girl'. 'Well'. Logan whispered. 'I guess I've been reluctant to tell you everything I know. It's time I came clean with you'.

Logan told Briggs about his investigation. He concluded by saying, 'I wish you hadn't found out this way. I'm really sorry'. 'How do we find George and his associate?' Briggs asked. He was blown away with astonishment. 'We don't. I do' Logan whispered. 'But I'd like to contact my boss, first. You could find out if your boys apprehended the crooks at the house in Shepherd's Bush'. 'I'll do that right away' Briggs said. He dialed a number on his mobile phone. Logan tried to get hold of Hawke with his own smart phone. He couldn't get through to him. Hawke's phone was switched off. Logan felt that was strange. He turned his attention back to Briggs. The police man had finished making his phone call to the desk clerk on duty at Scotland Yard.

Briggs looked a bit confused. 'What is it?' Logan asked. 'I spoke to the office', Briggs said. 'They sent three police detectives to investigate the place. It seems they've escaped'. 'I feared that would happen', Logan whispered. 'I believe Baker's now pitched his tent with this unscrupulous contract killer. He's that resourceful'. 'What about Hawke?' Briggs asked. Logan shook his head. 'His phone's switched off', he said. 'But I've got a very good idea where he'll be. I'm going there'. 'Where is he if you don't mind me asking?' Briggs asked. 'He'll be at Lukman's place', Logan said slowly. 'I'm going there now. But I want you to bring in the Calvary'. 'Would that be necessary?' Briggs asked. 'Think so', Logan whispered grimly. 'I've got a bad feeling Derek's in trouble over there' 'What gives you that idea?' 'Hawke didn't answer his phone. That's a little bit unusual. Besides, George and Samosa might have headed there, in that taxi'. 'Very well, then'. Briggs said. 'I'll put out the word that Baker and his new associate have made a dash for it. My contacts might just search them out'. 'I wouldn't have it any other way. So long', Logan whispered. He walked away into the night. Sergeant Willie Briggs decided to phone a contact.

V

An hour later, Logan waited patiently in the blue Astra. He had parked the vehicle near a block of flats on Camden High Road. His cold bitter eyes looked through a spyglass. He dropped the spyglass in his lap, and now checked his Beretta. Logan was satisfied with the check made on the weapon. He looked at his wristwatch. From the street light in the area, he could see the time was now a quarter past one o'clock in the morning. He picked up the spyglass again and focused his attention on the house across the street. It belonged to the late Paul Lukman. Logan watched as a black cab drove into the street. Two men climbed out of it. The bearded one paid the fare and the cabbie thanked both men and drove off. Logan climbed out of the car, and melted into the darkness. He followed the two men.

They were saying something to each other. 'We meet the girl', George said. 'If she doesn't co-operate, then I think we should waste her'. Samosa nodded his head. The two men headed towards the house. Moments later George knocked on the door. Someone came out. It was the Professor's

148

daughter. She tried to shut the door, but thought better of it when she saw the pistol George held. It was pointed at her. 'Wouldn't do that Mrs. Lukman', Tom George said grinning. He walked in and Dominic Samosa followed him. The Colombian could see the lady was quite pretty. 'What can I do for you?' The girl said. 'I'm busy right now. I've got visitors'. 'They can wait. I've come to discuss business with you'. George said. 'This is my associate. His name's Dominic Samosa'. 'I simply don't have the time for this'. The girl said unhappily. Tom George grinned. He liked the cozy place. It was exquisitely decorated. He had always known Paul Lukman had a unique sense of style. As George walked into the house; he looked at the three men in the sitting room with disdain.

'Who is this, Tabby?' Professor James asked. 'Who are these men?' Dominic Samosa quickly took his pistol out. He aimed it at the Professor. The girl didn't answer the question straight away so George continued his banter. He said, 'This is your father, the famous archaeologist Professor Titus James, I presume. . And these gentlemen with him are obviously his associates'.

Derek Hawke didn't move a muscle on his seat. He was in the house with his boss. But he had not spoken to him yet about his findings on the case. Derek Hawke looked at his boss. The old man was sitting comfortably on the long leather couch next to him. Meyers seemed a bit shaken by all this. Hawke wished the element of surprise was on their side. He knew it wasn't. He was worried.

'Who are you?' Professor James asked again. 'My name is of no consequence right now'. George said. 'But I used to work for your late son-in-law. I'm surprised your daughter didn't tell you Professor. Anyway, I've come to discuss business with her'.

'His name is Tom George, Dad'. The girl said eventually. 'He was Paul's business associate', she had found her voice. The girl was shaking like a leaf. 'He's also a prominent figure in London's underworld. He's wanted by the police authorities right now', Adrian Meyers said coldly. He stood up abruptly. Dominic Samosa moved towards him. But George shook his head. 'I'd like to listen to him' he said. 'What's your name old man?' 'Adrian Meyers' the old man said. 'You're the hotshot lawyer, aren't you?' George said. 'I remember Lukman mentioned your name once'. 'You're here to snatch that list from under our noses?' Meyers said. 'That won't happen I'm afraid'. 'Why's that old man?' George asked. He was surprised. 'The information you seek is safely kept somewhere. I saw to it. And that was a week ago'. Hawke was stunned. He couldn't believe his ears. So Mac was right after all. This caper had nothing to do with the treasure trove of Tikal.

What was going to happen now? 'I've known for quite some time you might try to pull a fast one George', Meyers said. 'Paul Lukman was a close friend of mine. He told me all about you. He also told me about your rackets. Unfortunately you can't have that information. I asked my banker to lock it up in a safe'.

George withdrew his cell phone, from his breast pocket and made a gesture for silence. It was ringing. He then said, 'Who is this?' After a few minutes he dismissed the caller and turned it off. Tom George turned his attention back to Samosa. Then he said, 'Bad news. The police were at the house. Rat's escaped and Gonzalez is nowhere to be found. I'm changing some of our plans. We'll be taking the old man with us. The girl is of no use to us now. So she dies tonight'. George pulled the trigger of his gun and the girl crumpled to the floor in a pool of blood. Professor James stood up from his armchair in shock. He went to his daughter's fallen body. So did Hawke. The detective checked the girl's pulse. She wasn't dead. Professor James didn't know this nor did the hoods.

'What do we do?' Samosa asked. He was annoyed. 'So far things haven't worked out the way you planned.', 'Since the old man holds what we need, he's coming with us', Tom George said. 'Call it kidnapping if you want to. He's our ticket out of here so get his car keys!' Adrian Meyers reluctantly handed over his car keys to the Colombian. 'It seems we've got a hero here' Samosa said. The detective was still beside the fallen girl. George shrugged his shoulders. 'It's your call' he said. Dominic Samosa came forward with the barrel of his gun. He knocked out Hawke with a swift blow to the head. The detective was unconscious in seconds. 'Leave him there'. George said. 'Let's go'.

The two crooks left the house with Adrian Meyers. As they approached the street, something happened. They were cut down by a hail of bullets. The crooks fell on the ground like logs. Dominic Samosa was dead on the spot, instantly. Tom George was in unimaginable pain. He was alive. But he couldn't move. He was bleeding and sweating profusely.

Adrian Meyers went down on the ground as well. But he got back up when the gunfire had stopped. He heard footsteps and looked around. Someone was standing a few feet away from him. Meyers couldn't see who it was. But it was a man. The mysterious figure vanished when a siren blared and a police car drove into the street.

150

Meanwhile, in the house Professor James was huddled in a corner holding his daughter's head in his arms. The girl was still losing blood. Hawke regained consciousness. He got up from where he lay and said, 'your daughter's not dead, Sir'. Moments later four policemen arrived at the house. One of them was Sergeant Willie Briggs. He took control of the situation and called an ambulance.

CHAPTER 21
Part I

The paramedics arrived and tended to the wounded at the Lukman residence. Professor James eventually left with them to help his daughter get more medical attention at Saint Bartholomew's hospital in London.

Sergeant Willie Briggs and his men then combed the street looking for the shooter at the scene of the crime. It was a fruitless search. Briggs suspected Logan was the shooter. But he couldn't prove it because he wasn't absolutely sure if the mystery man did it. Briggs assigned one of his men to monitor Tom George's progress in the hospital. He wanted his colleague to get information from the crook if that was possible. He also phoned the police Medical Examiner. He wanted him to pick up Dominic Samosa's corpse and examine it. While his other colleagues watched over Samosa's corpse, Briggs decided to head back to the house. He hoped to get a statement from the old man.

Inside the house Briggs questioned Meyers. When he finished that, he asked Hawke to escort Meyers back home to his door. 'I really think it would be a good idea if you did', he urged. So Derek Hawke agreed to drive his boss home. He decided to get hold of his car later on. As Hawke swerved his master's black Bentley out on the driveway, Meyers said, 'I could swear it was your man Derek. Where is he?' Meyers was talking about his near death experience in the street. He was still feeling nervous. Hawke shrugged his shoulders. He said, 'Haven't the faintest idea Sir'. 'I thought you had this guy on a leash?' Meyers asked. 'I do', Hawke said. 'There's obviously a good reason for his actions. I tried to contact him but his phone is switched off'. 'We might not have a case anymore'. The old man said angrily 'Since your friend decided to gun down a man in cold blood. There's a slim chance George won't testify, even if he's granted a short sentence'. 'So what's the plan now Sir? Hawke asked. 'I'm not so sure', Meyers said. 'But I can tell you one thing Derek, the police authorities will have a field day with this mess. I understand they're looking for Kidman. Everything now points in his direction. I keep wondering why'. 'What happens to the Professor and his daughter?' Hawke asked frankly. The old man sighed. Then he said, 'The Professor will take some time off to ensure his daughter gets adequate attendance. Tabby's out of danger now, and is being closely watched by the best doctors I know at Saint Bartholomew's Hospital. Paul's funeral will be held once Tabby's in the clear and strong enough'. 'Logan knows about the list Sir'. Hawke said. 'I had my reasons for keeping quiet about that'. Meyers said sighing again. 'I don't want you to take me home yet. I'd like you to take me to the office. I want to show you something'. Derek Hawke nodded his head and glanced at his wrist watch. It was now five minutes past two. He steered the car into a new street and headed for Meyers' office in Central London.

Hawke hoped he knew what he was doing. He couldn't help but think that his boss was up to his old tricks again. Hawke cursed under his breath and thought about Logan. Hawke wondered if Logan had come up with some more answers. He wasn't surprised when he learnt that his friend had gunned down the crooks at the Lukman residence. Hawke remembered he had asked him to do whatever it took to get to the bottom of this whole mystery. There obviously was a reason for his action. Hawke wished he could find him. He also hoped secretly that he would stay out of sight.

Hawke kept thinking - What was his boss up to and where was Logan? What exactly was his boss hiding from him now? The old man refused to say anything more. He was thinking about something else. Hawke eventually reached their destination. He parked the car in the parking lot. The two men got out of the vehicle and headed towards Meyers office. The old man was still contemplating. He had now come to grips with what had happened. He had no choice but to accept it.

It was quite evident that people were still tucked up in their beds. But uncertainty lurked in the air as the two men approached the building. There were no security guards around. That was odd. Hawke became apprehensive and so did his boss. The old man said abruptly, 'something's not quite right here Derek. Keep your eyes open'. Hawke nodded his head. The two men went through the glass doors of the tall building and climbed the stairs. Meyers' office was located on the first floor. They went through the lobby and there was still no one in sight.

The old man unlocked the door that led into his office. 'Don't get too comfortable', he said. 'Remember, we might have unwanted visitors in the building. I'm definitely going to make a serious complaint about the security arrangements. Hawke sat down in an armchair. His eyes took in everything in the spacious room. 'Tell me about the list' he said. Adrian Meyers sat behind his desk. He looked at Hawke shrewdly then said, 'you really want me to tell you how I got hold of that information don't you?' Hawke nodded his head. 'That's because from all indications' he said. 'You've been leading me on Sir'. The old man shook his head. 'You've got it wrong there, Derek' he said.

He got up from his chair and opened a safe on the wall. He withdrew something and passed it over to Hawke. It was a black memory stick. 'I made two copies. This is actually one of them', Meyers said. 'The real thing is now in safe hands. I gave it to Scotland Yard about a week ago'. Derek Hawke ran his eye over the memory stick. He said, 'How did you get hold of that?' He gave it back to the old man. Adrian Meyers put it down on his desk. 'Two days before I reassigned you to the case, the Professor's daughter gave me permission to search my friend's house. I found the memory stick there'. Meyers began. 'It was hidden in his study. Surprisingly, Paul maintained a database of shady contacts on it. These contacts were actually unsuspected crooks. I decided to make copies and keep them'. 'What was Lukman up to?' Hawke asked puzzled. The old man was about to answer that question. But before he could, the door swung open. Logan stood in the doorway. He was holding his tranquillizer dart gun.

II

The silence in the room cut like a very sharp knife. The two men were surprised. Logan came in quietly closing the door behind him. He aimed the weapon at Meyers and shot him in the neck. The old man slumped in his chair. He was knocked out immediately by the weapon's swift effect. He was unconscious in seconds. 'What in the world are you doing here, sonny?' Hawke asked. 'I couldn't help but listen to your conversation outside', Logan whispered. 'Your boss is covering up for his late friend'. 'What are you talking about? Hawke asked. 'There's a lot more to all this than I thought skinny man', Logan whispered. 'Paul Lukman worked for some very bad business men. They've had their sights set on Rex Hubbard's UK drug operation for quite some time. And that's why they asked Lukman to infiltrate Jason Phelps organization. When he couldn't, they got rid of him. These criminals hired those young punks at 'Crows' to commit those atrocious acts in town. They paid those boys to take out the competition in town too. I found out that these business men have been a threat to the Colombians' new operation here. I equally discovered that the police have been looking into their activities and have come up with nothing'. Logan picked up the memory stick on the desk and looked at it. 'I know what you're thinking. But I'm not crazy' he whispered. 'Paul Lukman knew he was fiddling with death. Jason Phelps tried to get him to reveal who these men were. But Lukman wouldn't tell him. That's why Phelps sent his team to steal this. He wanted the information too'. Hawke shook his head. 'I don't believe this', he said. 'Well, since you now have all the answers why the havoc?' 'Someone had to rattle the cage', Logan whispered. 'You killed a man tonight', Hawke complained. 'Briggs believes you had something to do with that. He's not sure because he doesn't have any evidence yet. I'd keep a low profile if I were you. Stay out of sight'. 'I can't at the moment', Logan whispered. 'I've got to wrap this up'. Derek Hawke looked at the unconscious figure behind the desk. 'Don't tell me you're going to kill him as well' he quipped. Logan shook his head. 'We've got a problem' he murmured. 'Hank phoned me. He's learnt that Kidman will pay the old man a visit. That means trouble. Kidman wants this information. He thought Eddie Payne had it. That's why Jason Phelps tried to get rid of him. I had to follow both of you here'. 'Am I missing something, sonny?' Logan grimaced then murmured, 'Kidman's really a thief. He goes by many names but his real name is Quentin Baker. He's also called the Rat'.

'So all these crooks have been after the same thing' Hawke said angrily. 'Why didn't you tell me about Baker?' Logan shrugged his shoulders. 'I've crossed paths with him before. But that was a long time ago. I couldn't tell you about his involvement because I wasn't sure about his part in all this', he whispered. 'So what happens now?' Hawke asked. 'We hide your boss', Logan rasped. 'I've got a funny feeling the ungodly might strike soon'. Hawke sighed. He took the small dart embedded in his boss's neck, and hoisted him up on his shoulder. He unlocked the door that led into a quiet inner room. He laid the old man on a big bed in there. When he came out of the room he muttered, 'You knocked him out flat with that friend of yours. When do you think he'll regain consciousness?' Logan smiled grimly. He whispered, 'He'll be unconscious for a little while'. 'That gives us time to do something then', Hawke concluded. He pressed some numbers on his mobile phone and phoned someone. After he made his phone call Logan asked, 'what was that all about?'

CHIMAIJEM I. EZECHUKWU

'I've just asked JB to come over. Remember him from the Dorchester?' Logan nodded his head. Hawke continued. 'He's still not happy with you. I want him to keep an eye on the old man. At least till things cool off. I don't want Meyers to think I didn't come up with a game plan to counter all this. I don't want him hurt'.

Logan said nothing. He went towards the window. He looked through it. 'The men on that list represent the biggest scum in town' he whispered. 'The Police have been trying to bring them down for years. They haven't caught them yet'. 'So who's Baker really working for?' Hawke asked. 'I don't know yet'. Logan said. 'That's not good enough' Hawke said. 'Never mind that' Logan snapped. 'Look'. Hawke stepped forward and looked through the window. He could see a red mini car pull over in the street. Someone climbed out of it. It was Nick Slater. 'Do you know that man?' he said eventually. 'I do. He's Ruth's informant' Logan whispered. 'But I didn't expect him to turn up here. His name's Nick Slater', this was disturbing. Suddenly Quentin Baker walked into the office. Beside him was Emmanuel Gonzalez. They were both holding their guns. The Rat's pistol was aimed at Logan.

III

The atmosphere in the old man's office was rather tense. Emmanuel Gonzalez took a step forward and frisked Logan. He grabbed his weapons and put them on the desk. He then searched Hawke and removed his gun too. Gonzalez gave Baker the memory stick from the desk and stepped back. The Rat examined it. He pulled up a chair. 'Nice' he said grinning. 'I thought Eddie Payne knew something about this memory stick. It appears he didn't. Anyway, thanks to you Jarrett I've finally got it'. 'You didn't give me anything concrete to work on, when you set that task' Logan whispered. 'I didn't have to' the Rat said 'I knew you were going to follow it through'. 'How does Nick Slater fit into all this?' Logan asked. 'He doesn't. But amongst many other things, he's a free agent', The Rat said. 'He'll be here shortly. Slater's been spying for me. He said the old man worked late. I thought he would be here. That's why we came in from the back entrance of the building. You must have noticed that we've also taken care of the security detail here. Unfortunately, it seems the snitch didn't do his homework well'. 'You've got some explaining to do Baker' Logan rasped. 'So have you Jarrett', the Rat said. 'But what are you doing in Meyer's office?' Hawke decided to speak up. 'Jarrett is an associate of mine. And as you can see, the old man is not here. But, he's instructed us to work from his office'.

156

SNAKE AMONGST SHADOWS

'We meet at last Mr. Hawke', The Rat said dryly. 'I should assume then that both of you are working on a case. What do you know about this?' He was referring to the memory stick he now held. 'I don't know what you're talking about' Hawke said. The Rat got up from his chair and looked at Logan. He said, 'It appears your friend is not joking Jarrett. But I'll take care of that'. He fired a shot at Hawke. Derek Hawke fell on the floor like a sack of potatoes. His jacket was bloody. He was hit in the left arm. Logan tried to help him up but couldn't, because Gonzalez had his pistol aimed at him. The contract killer was ready to make a clean hit.

Nick Slater entered the office. As he closed the door behind him, Quentin Baker shot him in the heart. He slumped dead on the floor. Everything happened in a blur. 'What was that for?' Logan asked. 'Thought you would never ask' the Rat said smiling. 'I had assumed you knew. I have no use for the man anymore. You'll probably be blamed for his death. Mr. Gonzalez will explain things better since I won't be around to enjoy the fun'. Quentin Baker cleaned his pistol with a hanky. He then gave it to Gonzalez. The new henchman accepted it with a gloved hand. 'Three minutes', the Rat said. 'I'll be waiting in Slater's car. Make it quick'. Logan knew exactly what the assassin was going to do next. He was going to finish off Hawke. The murder weapon would be found and the police will believe he did it. After all he was already a suspect in a killing. Logan realized he had to bluff his way out of this one. He had to escape. 'You've confirmed my suspicion's Rat' he whispered. 'You're not making any sense Jarrett' Baker said. 'Who hired you to steal the list?' Logan asked. 'They obviously instructed you to bump off Tom George'. 'Kill him!' the Rat yelled. 'Kill both of them. I'll be waiting'. He limped out of the office with his cane. Gonzalez nodded his head. 'My new associate thinks you're a real thorn in the flesh Mr. Jarrett' he said after a while. 'I can see he's managed to convince you about that', Logan whispered. 'Well', Gonzalez continued 'as you know, all good and bad rivalries must come to an end'. He was about to put a bullet in Hawke when something happened.

Adrian Meyers stumbled out of the room. He was holding a pistol. He looked pale, but that didn't stop him from shooting Gonzalez right in the head. The assassin fell on the floor, and was dead in moments. 'I'll phone the police', Meyers said. 'You'd better get out of here Logan. If I were you, I'd go after that rogue called Kidman. I'll take care of Derek'. 'I've got to know something before I go', Logan whispered 'whose side are you on?' 'Justice prevails in this whole affair', Meyers said. 'So I guess I'm on your side now'. Logan picked up his weapons and put them into his duffle bag. Then he looked at his boss. 'See you around skinny man', he whispered. Derek Hawke nodded his head. Before Logan left the room, he looked through the window. Quentin Baker had climbed into the red mini, and was now driving off.

IV

In the early hours of that same morning Logan used his contacts and found the red mini parked somewhere near Holloway Road. After Baker dumped the car there, it seemed he had done a vanishing act. He was nowhere to be found. The trail had gone cold since then. The next evening Logan phoned his boss from his girlfriend's place. Ruth Ryan was in the sitting room with him when he was making the call. She was sitting comfortably on her favorite couch. 'I'm sure Baker will turn up somewhere if he's still in the UK' Hawke said on his phone. 'My boss has spoken to the police. I'll contact him later so that he alerts the airport authorities'. He was at home resting his arm. It was now in a sling. 'The Rat slipped through my fingers' Logan whispered 'I'm sorry about that'. 'Never mind that', Hawke said. 'You foiled his plans, and apparently stopped the Colombians from setting up shop here. You also stopped a major drug smuggling operation going on in the UK. I couldn't be more pleased if all this chaos was over Mac', 'as you can see, it isn't. You better get some rest Derek', Logan whispered decisively. 'I'm at Ruth's and I'm expecting Briggs'. 'Have you gone nuts?' Hawke asked. 'You should be keeping a low profile'. 'Willie's all right' Logan whispered 'he might be a nerd but he's always come through for me. I want to fill him in'.

'What are you talking about? Briggs can sometimes be unpredictable. I hate to think what he might do if he finds out about your true identity. Besides, you're still a suspect in his current investigation. Stay out of sight!' 'You know what your problem is Derek, you worry too much' Logan whispered. 'I'll take my chances with the man'. 'You won't! Not if I have anything to do with it.' Hawke retorted. 'Get back to your flat and stay there. This case is temporarily closed till we find a new lead'. 'What does that mean?' Logan asked quietly. 'Stay out of trouble sonny'. Logan pretended he didn't hear that, and then asked, 'Are you going to attend Lukman's funeral service with that arm of yours in a sling? Your boss might let you off the hook you know. He'll probably give you time to mourn properly as well'. 'Forget about that' Hawke said bitterly. 'Something else has cropped up. My boss thinks the criminal masterminds behind this mayhem might be on that list'. 'Who are they?' Logan asked. 'Meyers wouldn't say. He wasn't very sure' Hawke said. 'But one thing's certain he could be right. Someone's gone to great length to see that information retrieved'. 'What's next then?' Logan asked. 'I won't be able to do anything until I'm healed and rested. Meyers might then ask me to carry on with the investigation'. Logan scowled.

'That screws up things doesn't it?' he asked. 'I totally agree with you!' Hawke said 'but from what we've found out so far it seems you've managed to uncover a shadowy gang operating under the radar. No one knows about them. It appears they've hired the Rat's services. I've got some serious thinking to do. I'll call you soon. So stay in touch'.

The two men ended their phone conversation on that note and Logan turned round to face Ruth. 'Nick's part in this still amazes me, but it looks as if this case is still drooling with loose ends?' Ruth asked. 'It is, Sweets'. Logan whispered. Suddenly there was a knock on the door. Ruth got up and opened it. Willie Briggs stood in the doorway. He came in with a puzzled look on his face. 'I should assume you had nothing to do with the shooting last night at the Lukman place. I expected to find you there' he said. Logan smiled grimly. He shook his head. 'I'm not going to admit I had anything to do with that incident' he whispered. He dug his hand into his shirt pocket and brought up a photograph. The snapshot was that of the Rat. 'Something came up. Sit down, Willie. I think we've got a lot to talk about'. 'What do you mean?' Briggs asked. He was still puzzled. 'I'd like you to help me catch the Rat' Logan said slowly. 'What are you talking about Mr. Jarrett?' Briggs asked. Willie Briggs was astonished when Logan told him all about the mysterious gang and its connection with the Rat. He knew trouble was around the corner again.

He sensed that Logan was not telling him something. But as always he agreed to help him. Briggs knew one thing for sure. Logan wanted to find this new criminal syndicate. It seemed the gang was the newest piece in a puzzle the mystery man wanted very much to solve. But despite all that Willie Briggs wasn't convinced the man he called Jarrett hadn't anything to do with the shooting the other night. He voiced his thoughts before he left the flat. 'What do you think, Sweets?' Logan asked afterwards. 'Willie's playing along' Ruth said. 'So you'd better find out who's really behind this Mac'. 'I intend to do that', Logan whispered. 'I guess Hawke was right. There's nothing much to do right now so I'm going home'. 'Can I come home with you, Mac? Ruth asked. Logan shook his head. 'I'd like you to stay here Sweets. I'll call you', he whispered. He kissed Ruth and left.

CHAPTER 22
Part I

The taxi driver screeched to a stop in an alley and Logan climbed out of his car. It was almost midnight. As Logan made his way towards his flat, he murmured to himself. He was lost in thought but he was aware of his bearings. Logan couldn't help but wonder what could happen next. Everything up to this point had been intriguing and bizarre. Logan turned into a street when he saw a car parked awkwardly on the road and heard raised voices. Logan kept walking, and wondered who parked the vehicle and who owned the voices. Suddenly he heard a muffled cry for help and stopped abruptly. At first he couldn't see a thing. Then his sharp eye caught the figures in the dark arguing. Two burly men were shouting at another man, and then started to beat him up. The two men hadn't seen him yet. Logan wondered if this had anything to do with the current problem. He couldn't understand why this was happening. He watched the figures for a full minute before springing into action.

In a split second he stepped behind, one of the thugs pulling him away from the man being mugged and hit him very hard on the back of the head. The thug who was unaware of what had just happened to him sagged to the ground in a heap not making a sound. Immediately this happened, the other thug saw the new enemy and dropped the victim. He came straight at Logan and punched him in the jaw. Logan ended up on the ground but managed to twist away from the kick that followed. He got off the ground and lashed out with a powerful roundhouse kick that finally put the villain to sleep.

160

Logan stared breathlessly at the two unconscious men on the ground, then at the helpless blighter trying to crawl out of sight. In a few strides he reached him and tried to help him up. 'Who are you, pal?' Logan asked in a strident voice. Try as much as he could to say something, the guy was badly hurt. His eyes had swollen and his face was cut. Blood dribbled from his mouth and he breathed with difficulty. Logan could see he wasn't going to make it and knew that getting a Doctor would be a waste of time. The man could only say but a few words, audible enough for Logan to hear before he lolled his head and died. He mumbled, 'B-Burke. Farrell hadn't a clue he was being used. The Rat did. Find him or else, nobody will believe you'. Logan was stunned. What could this mean? He thought. He knew he had to find out fast.

II

'You don't expect anyone to believe all that nonsense do you? Derek Hawke asked sarcastically. He was in Logan's spacious kitchen and was pacing the floor. 'I wasn't expecting anybody to, least of all you' Logan whispered. 'But a man died last night and it's connected with this caper'. 'You're a real nuisance sonny' Hawke said 'How do you expect anyone to believe you were at the scene of that crime. Come off it. You don't have proof. Moreover, you made a run for it. You can't even identify who did this guy in. Ignore it for now Mac. It all seems weird'. Logan said nothing. He stood near the window and gazed out into the deep blue sky. Although it was a sunny afternoon, it was getting chilly.

He didn't sleep much that night. He kept thinking of the two unconscious thugs he had fought and the dead man he had left on the street. Logan didn't want to hang around the crime scene. It was risky. That was why he left. He called his boss on the phone the next morning. Hawke came to see him that afternoon. Ruth had paid him a visit that morning. She was also in the kitchen. The girl was listening to the conversation, while enjoying a tall glass of lemonade.

'You think I'm crazy, don't you? Logan whispered. He picked up a newspaper off the dining table that Ruth had brought. Logan unrolled it, when he got to the second page he ran his eyes over a small article which read:

UNKNOWN YOUNG MAN FOUND BEATEN TO DEATH.

The incident hadn't made front page headlines, but the story about the man's death still conveyed an impression. 'Look, the participants in this mess got away after you left', Hawke said. 'How do you explain that?' Logan didn't reply. 'I believe you Mac' Hawke sighed. 'But nobody out there will. Not even Briggs if he gets to find out about this. I wouldn't let my feelings get the better of me if I were you. I'm warning you, stay put'. 'What about Quentin Baker?' Logan asked. He folded his arms. 'The police authorities are still looking for him. But they haven't come up with anything yet and from the look of things right now, I don't think they will. Anyway, don't worry I've asked some contacts to help. I'm yet to receive feedback'. 'What do you think Meyers will make of this?' 'I phoned him this morning and I told him about your exploits', Hawke said dryly. 'He believes that there's a connection and he wants me to look into it while you lay low for a while. My boss is still looking for a way to get that crook George convicted regardless of his medical condition'. 'So in the meantime what do you want me to do? Logan asked. 'Didn't you hear a word of what I said just now?' Hawke asked 'I'll take care of this. I'm warning you Mac. Stay out of sight'. He was almost through the door when he turned round and said, 'You can't seem to outrun the shadows of your past, can you Mac. Scary isn't it?' Logan sighed. 'The Rat's a deadly foe', he whispered. Hawke shook his head. He waved at Ruth as he left. Logan bolted the door. Ruth smiled as she got up from where she sat at the kitchen table. 'What are you going to do now Mac?' She asked with genuine concern. Logan said nothing. His bitter eyes suddenly took a faraway look. He was sad. The adventure wasn't over yet and somehow he had a feeling that crime would strike again if he prowled the streets looking for answers. Who was Burke and where was Baker? Who was he really working for? And what was Hawke's employer up too now? Logan wanted to find out. However, he decided to obey his boss.

Ruth knew all about her man's predicament. She had learned to bear it like a cross. Ruth wasn't worried about Logan. She only cared about him. 'Honestly darling', he began slowly, his expression now a bit nervous. 'I think we both know the answer to that question'. Ruth Ryan nodded and smiled. 'I know Mac' she said. 'Let's wait'.

The End

So What Now?

Logan will be prowling the streets again soon.

Watch out and BEWARE!

&

Stay SAFE!

About The Author

CHIMAIJEM IFEANYI EZECHUKWU was born in Clapton London on May 12th 1966*. He spent several years in England before moving back to Nigeria with his parents.

He attended the famous Ekulu Primary School and then went on to the College of the Immaculate Conception (CIC) in Enugu State. He also attended the prestigious Institute of Journalism and Continuing Education.

CHIMAIJEM returned to the UK in 1997 to continue his studies. He studied Communications with Law, at the London Metropolitan University, Where he attained a BA Honors in the Discipline. He is a qualified Paralegal and is currently a professional Assistant Teacher.

CHIMAIJEM has always been interested in writing. In fact, he started at a very early age. He was always encouraged by his late father. His influences in this area include his fellow African writers Cyprian Ekwensi, Chinua Achebe, Ngugi Wa Thiong'o, Wole Soyinka and more recently Chimamanda Ngozi Adichie, whom he has great respect for.

This is Chimaijem's first book and it is a crime fiction thriller, definitely a different genre from the writings of the afore-mentioned African writers. After getting inspired by such greats as Leslie Charteris* - the creator of 'The Saint' etc... and in honor of escapist writers, Chima decided to put pen to paper and this is the result of that endeavor and promises more to come.

*also born 12th May – 1907!

www.bispublications.com